A TRACKER'S TALE

BOOK 1 OF THE TRACKERS SERIES

KAREN AVIZUR

A Tracker's Tale
Book 1 of The Tracker's Series

ACKNOWLEDGMENTS

There are so many people over the years that have helped bring this book to fruition that I couldn't possibly name them all, but here's a brief sample. At the top of the list is Russell Firestone; my editor, my mentor, and my friend. Thank you for sticking by me when I was doubting myself, for the tough love and the regular love, for all the things I learned from you about writing over these years, for putting up with me and my endless story changes and tweaks, especially to the first novel in this series, and for a dozen other reasons. Trackers would not exist without you.

Thank you to my family, who supported my writing and encouraged my love of reading, even when you occasionally couldn't tell if the person I was rambling on about was a real person or a character in a book. Many thanks to my best friend and the coolest person I know, former physicist and current VFX artist Mark Hennessy-Barrett, for his consults. If something blows up in this book it is with his help, and if there is any science involved you can bet he educated me on the subject (and the science doesn't exist, he probably brainstormed it with me). If someone is punched, kicked, or otherwise bodily maimed, my other best friend and Brazilian jiu-jitsu fanatic Yvonne Henkel was likely consulted. Many thanks to her for Katherine's awesome martial arts moves.

In addition, so much credit belongs to tons of other friends for their support and for consulting on all of the endless extraordinary, ridiculous, and sometimes criminally suspicious questions. This goes out to, but is in no way limited to, Jennifer Anker, James Bartel, German Emilio Beard, Brian Byrns, Missy Coffman, Sabrina Cooper, Brian Downes, Aimee Dweck, Daniel Eighmy, Derek Houck, Zubi Mohammed, Jennifer Prohaska, Danielle Rothman, and Xanadu Scheuers.

A special thank you goes out to three readers: my first real fans in my earliest writing days. A young boy named Zachary Taylor who listened to my Young Adult fiction as bedtime stories; Paromita De, who read through hundreds of chapters of fan fiction that I wrote online; and James Messina, who as well as being my best friend for many years, was a fellow writer and was one of the first people to make me believe I could one day be an author.

Also thank you to Jessica Frere of the Investigative Publicity and Public Affairs Unit in the Office of Public Affairs of the FBI for the many questions she answered. She helped me portray the most accurate version that I could of a nonexistent division of the FBI. The cubicles and paperwork are real. The vampires and werewolves? I'll leave that to the readers' imaginations.

CHAPTER 1

"ARE WEREWOLVES ALLOWED IN THE courthouse?"
It took Katherine Colebrook a moment to
realize the young woman in the elevator had spoken to her,
pulling her from her thoughts. It then took her another
moment to find her voice. "Why wouldn't they be?"

"I've just heard indoors they can get...you know...."

Katherine's light green eyes stared at the woman until it
was clear she wasn't going to continue. "...Bored?"

The woman let out a small laugh. "Right. Bored." Her
tone signified the end of the conversation, or so Katherine
thought, as the elevator stopped at the third floor.

Two middle-aged men entered, wearing tailored suits
and full-grain leather shoes that gave them the instant
classification of lawyer. One pressed the button for the
fourth floor, continuing some small talk about a case they
were working on. Katherine pursed her lips. The elevator.
For one flight of stairs. No wonder America had health
problems.

"Are you going to the sixth floor for that werewolf
case?" The young woman spoke up again, her voice a bit

hushed, sidling a few inches closer. "I saw your FBI badge. Are you here for that werewolf in the news?"

Katherine glanced briefly to the woman before fixing her gaze on the elevator doors again. "Yeah, actually."

"Wow, seriously?" she whispered. "I don't even know any werewolves."

Really? Katherine wished she could say the word out loud, drenching it in sarcasm. The doors opened, letting the lawyers out, and mercifully skipped the fifth floor, going straight on to their destination.

"So are you here to make sure the werewolf doesn't attack anyone or something?" the young woman asked.

"Off the record," Katherine spoke as the elevator doors opened, "I'm here to help him put the psychopath that attacked him and his friends in prison." She looked to the reporter, whose face went slack and then smug. "I don't talk to reporters like you."

"Like me?"

Katherine turned and left the elevator without another word.

———— ⊰✦⊱ ————

Katherine raised her right hand.

"You do solemnly state, under penalty of perjury, that the testimony you may give in the case now pending before this court shall be the truth, the whole truth, and nothing but the truth?" the clerk asked.

"I do."

"Please take a seat."

Katherine sat in the solid oak chair in the witness stand, angling herself toward the jury and folding her hands in her lap. Since she usually went with loose-fitting and comfortable business casual clothes for her day-to-day work at the FBI (with black running shoes, for various job-related reasons), dressing for court wasn't a difficult process. Actually, the only significant difference here in her appearance was that her brown hair was down rather than in a ponytail. For her first court testimony many years ago, she'd been told it made her look older and more confident, and stuck with it as a strategy.

Jury testimony, to Katherine, was a necessary evil of her job. Court cases were important as all hell, but people were fickle and imperfect and expected cases tied up in neat little bows, like on television. Worse still, since she was a psychic, Katherine knew who was guilty and it stayed that way whether or not they were prosecuted. There were few things worse than watching a guilty suspect get off scot-free. And there was only a certain amount of her ability she could use in court. It was like any eyewitness testimony; they couldn't take her word as fact. And people had a tendency to believe some eyewitness testimony over others depending on the witness and how honest it seemed they were being, which was obviously inherently flawed.

Nicholas Hubbard, twenty-five in appearance and thirty-five in age, was a werewolf in the San Diego pack. He had brown hair in a ragged, though handsome, haircut and wore a suit that, though it had clearly been tailored, Katherine knew he found highly uncomfortable. Sitting in a chair at the table for the prosecution, Nicholas stared at his hands folded tightly in his lap. Katherine knew he wasn't looking at Arnold Pastoret mostly because if he did, he'd have the urge to rip his throat out for killing his friends. Not that he would actually lose control like that, but it would show on his face, and that was something the prosecution didn't want to show the jury.

Pastoret didn't seem to be trying to do anything. He sat quietly at his table next to his lawyer, a man in his fifties with a full head of gray hair named Dennis Austin, a lawyer that Katherine had only seen in passing once or twice. Pastoret didn't attempt to speak to anyone, wasn't trying to blend in with his surroundings, wasn't trying to examine the facial expressions of the jurors. He didn't look bored, he didn't look concerned. He just looked like a guy. That's probably what was so scary. He was just a guy. Short of psychic abilities, a passerby would never know the 38-year-old had a past conviction for arson, and two for assault, both of which were hate crimes.

Nicholas's lawyer was the federal prosecutor, a woman in her forties named Jacqueline Harkins. Katherine had worked with the former U.S. Attorney for San Diego, but since Jacqueline had recently been appointed, they'd never worked together before. The woman seemed extremely competent so far, though. She wore a sharp business suit, her black hair held back in a tight bun, and she gave a tight smile as she approached Katherine. "What is your full name and where do you currently work?"

"My name is Katherine Colebrook and I work as an FBI agent in the Trackers division. I work with cases involving parasapiens," she recited, directing her answer to the jurors. Katherine had gone over the simpler sentences in her mind many times, though she hadn't wanted to memorize the more detailed, or emotional, parts of her testimony. The last thing she wanted was to seem robotic on a case like this. The jury needed to feel every bit of it.

"How long have you been working as a tracker?" Harkins asked.

"Over the past two decades I have worked on hundreds of cases, almost all of them involving parasapiens," Katherine said.

"In what other capacity do you work for the FBI?"

"I also work on most of these cases in my capacity as a psychic."

"Which means?"

"I can sense the feelings of others, do minor spells, and I occasionally have visions of events happening or that happened elsewhere."

And there was the bottom dropping out from under her as far as likeability from the jury was concerned. Katherine didn't react, but she knew just about every one of them probably immediately thought the equivalent of, 'Crap, I wonder if she knows I cheated on my taxes.' Or worse. No amount of assurances that she had a healthy respect for privacy would dissuade people from the feeling of unease most of them had when finding out she was psychic.

That was Katherine's main hurdle as a witness, getting the jury back on her side after dropping the psychic bombshell and having the awkwardness that inevitably came with it. A big job, but she'd done it before. The best way, she'd found, was to bring the jury back to the reason they were here. After some more preliminary questions that probably bored the jury out of thinking about Katherine's abilities, the prosecutor started to cover the main facts of the case.

"I direct your attention to May 24th 2017, at approximately 11PM. Where were you at that time?" Harkins asked her.

"I was at Otay Valley Regional Park, just outside San Diego."

"Was anyone with you at the time?"

"Yes, my partner at the time, Special Agent John Sweeney," Katherine replied.

"Why were you there?" Harkins asked.

"To interview Nicholas Hubbard about the deaths of two of his fellow pack members and the fact that he'd bitten Arnold Pastoret, resulting in him being turned genetically into a werewolf."

Katherine didn't look over to Pastoret, but knew inside he was fuming. He hated werewolves. Despised them. And now that he was one? If he didn't get locked up, Katherine wasn't sure what he would do. The only reason he hadn't tried for the silver nitrate IV drip cure was it had been too late. The procedure was illegal, since there was a good chance of the person dying from silver poisoning if it wasn't administered quickly enough. So the police wouldn't let Pastoret take off from the scene of a crime, and obviously wouldn't have arranged for the treatment.

What had happened that night hadn't exactly gone according to his plan.

"Were you able to meet with Mr. Hubbard upon your arrival at the scene?"

"Yes."

"Can you describe his appearance?"

Katherine forced herself to speak in a normal tone, if a bit softer than normal, though this topic seemed to call for whispers. "He was covered in blood," she told the jury. "It was matted in the hair on his head and sporadically on his arms and legs, though not on his clothes."

"As ascertained by forensics, whose blood was it?" Harkins asked, her voice taking on a gentler tone.

"His two pack mates, and Pastoret."

"What firearm and bullets did the suspect use?"

"The firearm was an IMI Desert Eagle," Katherine spoke. "And the bullets were Hornady silver jacketed hollow point bullets."

"Why do people buy silver jacketed bullets?" Harkins asked.

"Objection," Pastoret asked. "Calls for speculation."

"Statistics show 100% of those surveyed buy silver bullets at least partially, and usually entirely, for only one purpose, your honor," Harkins told the judge.

The judge motioned. "Proceed."

Harkins repeated the question to Katherine. "Silver is fatal to werewolves," Katherine said. "Werewolves heal at an extremely fast rate, so they are difficult to kill even with a firearm if you aren't packing silver."

"I'd like to draw the court's attention to this map of Los Angeles National Forest," Harkins spoke, pointing to the display board propped up on an easel to her left. "Ms. Colebrook, does the National Park Service take pains to isolate werewolf territories from campgrounds?"

"Yes, absolutely," Katherine answered.

"Can you describe what that procedure entails?"

Katherine motioned to the map. "There are several widely used campgrounds in Los Angeles National Forest, all of which are clearly marked on maps made available to all hikers. Werewolf territories are marked in red as no-go areas for sapiens, or other parasapiens, for that matter. The maps are accurate to the yard, a procedure that is easy to do since werewolf territories are strict and consistent. And there are minimum half-mile gaps between any territory and any area sapiens are permitted to use."

"And how many times in the past five years have one or more sapiens accidentally wandered into werewolf territory?" Harkins asked.

"Never," Katherine said, shaking her head.

"Objection, speculation."

"Never, as far as we know," Katherine promptly clarified.

During their preparation for the trial, Katherine had suggested to Harkins that she ask, "*Did Pastoret strike you as a moron, Ms. Colebrook?*" But Harkins said it probably wouldn't go over well. Katherine was still tempted to tag it onto the end of one of her answers, though. *Accidentally wandered into wolf territory my ass.*

Katherine's testimony continued, covering her friendship with Nicholas, whom she'd known through her work as a tracker for almost three years, giving her opinion of him as a character witness. Then finally, the questioning was wrapped up and she was dismissed.

It was going to be another week before what Katherine was sure was going to be a painfully irritating cross-examination.

CHAPTER 2

KATHERINE EXITED THE COURTHOUSE TO head toward the parking garage adjacent to the large building, turning her cell phone ringer back on. Her eyes narrowed and her eyebrows furrowed when she saw a missed call and a message from a friend who probably wouldn't be calling for social reasons. She pulled up the message, listening. "*Katherine, it's Dolly. Please call me when you get this. It's pretty important.*"

Katherine stopped at the end of the long staircase she was descending, looking around and finding a nearby bench to sit down on. She put her purse down beside her and dialed Dolly's number.

"Rady Children's Hospital," a voice answered.

"Hi, can I have the psychiatry department please?"

"One moment."

There was a pause and Katherine listened to hold music for a few moments.

"Psychiatry department, this is Dolly Hanford speaking."

"Dolly, hi, it's Katherine. Is everything okay?" she asked.

"Katherine, hello. Thank you so much for calling back. I'm all right. I just have sort of a…situation."

Dolly Hanford was a woman that worked at the mental ward of a hospital just outside San Diego. She had started working there decades ago, and was excellent at her job. If anyone could convince a patient to take their meds, it was the woman who looked like everyone's favorite grandmother. And was just as stubborn.

"What exactly does this situation entail?" Katherine asked.

"Well, there's a fifteen-year-old girl that was checked in here by police. Rebecca Wilson. I'm not exactly sure what kind of trouble she's in. My main concern here is that I think she's psychic, in one way or another."

"How so?"

"She's just been talking about things that I haven't been voicing aloud, during our sessions," Dolly told her. "Things she couldn't know. But also…I think she had a vision."

Katherine's eyes widened. "What happened?"

"She just started screaming and clutching her head like she was in pain. We had to give the poor thing an injection of Haldol to calm her down. And then she started talking about someone coming to kidnap her."

Katherine glanced at her watch and pushed herself to her feet. "All right. You're lucky; I'm actually back in town for the day for FBI business. I can be there in about half an hour."

Dolly let out a soft sigh. "Thank you. It could just be stress from whatever she went through, and I don't mean to overreact, but–"

"I'd rather be there and you end up not needing me, than the reverse," Katherine told her.

"Thank you. I appreciate it."

"I'll see you soon, Dolly." Katherine hung up the phone, standing and grabbing her purse, making for the lot she'd parked in as she dialed the San Diego field office. After a joke about, "Just when I think I'm out, they pull me back in," to one of the SACs Katherine had gotten to know over the years, she explained the situation. She would get in contact with Jackson later to coordinate the case in San Diego, but letting them know she was coming back to their neck of the woods was first on the list. Then of course, once she got back home, the last step would be the mountains of paperwork for doing her job two hours away, or what the FBI considered an excursion of gigantic proportions.

The next call Katherine made was to the first number on her speed dial.

"You're back in San Diego for one day and you're already in trouble?" Alexandra answered.

Katherine narrowed her eyes at her daughter's teasing tone and she smiled drily as she headed down the sidewalk. "Why so cynical?"

"Why else would you be calling unless something happened?"

"Well, a friend needs help," she said. "And she's in San Diego. I don't know how long it'll take, but you know how these things go, so I might not get back to LA today. Just wanted to tell you not to wait up."

"Got it. I wanted to head down to the library," Alexandra said. "Is that cool?"

"Sure thing," Katherine replied. "As long as you have your cell."

"And my pepper spray. And my knife. And my other knife."

Katherine chuckled. "Right."

"We're still on for the shooting range this weekend, right?"

"Of course," Katherine replied. "I did a little research online. Found a great one nearby. We can check it out this weekend."

"Awesome," Alexandra said with an audible smile.

Katherine entered the parking garage, taking out her car keys. "I'll talk to you later. Stay safe."

"Always," Alexandra replied.

CHAPTER 3

DOLLY LED KATHERINE SLOWLY DOWN the hallway of the mental ward at Rady Children's Hospital. The décor was sparing, mostly simple pale yellow walls and solid doors with electronic locks. Katherine had been to this particular ward many times, mostly for psychic children who needed help or for victims of psychic vampires. She always left her gun in a lockbox with security, but kept her badge on her belt since it was regulation for her to keep it on her person whenever possible. Katherine kept her psychic feelers mostly to herself as they walked, not because she was uncomfortable at the idea of being around the mentally ill, but the minds and feelings of some of the hospital residents were confusing, almost overwhelming.

Dolly clasped her hands in front of her as she walked, her forehead creasing with worry lines. "Rebecca was found alone in a restaurant, sitting in the corner and rocking back and forth," she began. "They assumed she'd experienced a trauma, but her demeanor might be normal for her when she gets stressed. She's autistic. She's high functioning, but the police said she wouldn't or couldn't answer their questions last night. They brought her to us and we got her settled in and calmed down. She's fine now. But the police said they can't find her brother Ronald, who seems to be her only family. And from what they told me, he isn't the most well behaved of young men."

"Are you concerned he could come looking for her?" Katherine asked. "You think that's who her vision was about?"

"I'm really not sure. But she seems to have a lot of love for her brother, and I didn't get the sense that he would hurt her." Dolly slid her key card down the slot on the wall next to the door in front of them, and it slid open with a swish. "Rebecca?" Dolly spoke, walking into the hospital's common room.

Katherine followed her, looking around the sparsely populated area. There was a middle-aged man reading in a large loveseat to their right and an older woman sitting almost directly in front of the wall, organizing cards in some complex manner. The teenage girl that Dolly headed toward was sitting quietly at a table by herself, working on a puzzle. Or rather, finishing it. Rebecca's smooth, light brown hair was pulled back into a tight ponytail, nary a hair out of place, revealing delicate facial features. Her lips were pursed in concentration and she was continuously moving, fidgeting, as she purposefully picked up piece after piece and interlocked them.

"She started that puzzle ten minutes ago, by the way," Dolly told Katherine.

Katherine's smile widened as she stared at the girl focusing on her project.

Strong walls around the girl's mind, like a fortress, but there are many doors in them, and they're open, allowing anyone free range inside. She's accepting of new people, though her mind is a strange place for those who are unfamiliar with it. Dizzying with information, the walls inside the fortress separate the rooms, the knowledge, the math, the science, the history. Her family. Her friends. The nonsensical social norms, colloquialisms, frustrating people, tiring people, puzzling people. Puzzles are fun. They are straightforward and always form a solid image at the end. People are harder than puzzles. Even though they are called puzzling.

Her mind stays to itself, but feels the impression of another, and slightly stretches her feelers toward it. Kind person. Strong person. There to help her. Not interesting. The puzzle is interesting. And the stranger can learn things like she can, with her mind, saving the trouble of speaking words and the complexity of conversations.

"You…did the right thing by calling me," Katherine murmured. She shook her head. "This girl is amazing."

"So she is psychic?" Dolly asked.

"Very. Her abilities rank close to mine," Katherine told her. "And she has extremely good control over them for her age."

Dolly's eyebrows rose. "Wow."

"Rebecca, my name is Katherine," she spoke.

Rebecca turned slightly from the puzzle. "My name is Rebecca Wilson. It's nice to meet you," she said. She enunciated her words carefully, her head tilting to the side and down a bit, as if she were giving a slight bow, before turning back to her project.

Katherine sat in the chair next to the girl, waiting patiently as she completed the puzzle. She also opened her mind a bit to the teenager, allowing her insight into who she was and why she was there. Dolly pulled up a chair also, her eyes skimming over the other patients in the room. Once Rebecca had finished her task, she sat back, smiling at her accomplishment. "Rebecca, I'd like to talk to you about your brother Ronald," Katherine spoke.

"Ronald takes care of me," Rebecca said, nodding again, turning toward Katherine, though her gaze floated around elsewhere. "He's a good brother."

"I gathered that from you," Katherine said. She continued to reach out and collect information from the young woman. "You love him a lot."

"I do. He does a lot for me," Rebecca told her. "He helped me take a test so I didn't have to go to school anymore. It's called getting a GED. And he gets me computer equipment that I can use to explore. I like hacking. It's a lot of fun. And I help people."

"He does seem to take very good care of you. But Dolly told me that you were in a restaurant alone when the police found you," Katherine said. Rebecca didn't say anything, though Katherine felt her memories go back to that night, the feelings and smells and sights of the restaurant. Katherine hesitated before deciding to take another approach. "Rebecca, you can tell I'm psychic, like you," she said. "I know what other people are feeling and I see things that are happening somewhere else. And I have visions. Dolly told me she thinks you had a vision earlier."

Rebecca's eyes narrowed, sitting back in her chair, and one leg started bouncing. "I'm not supposed to talk about my abilities," she said. "Ronald said so."

"If you prefer, we can find him and talk to him first," Katherine told her. "Do you know where he is?"

"No. But I live at 344 West Allenby Street, apartment

23, San Diego, CA, 11023," Rebecca said. "You should bring me there. Ronald will come home and we play poker every night. He'll come home to play poker with me."

"I spoke to the police. They said they went over to the apartment and he wasn't there," Katherine said. This prompted Rebecca's lips to twist in annoyance. "Do you know his phone number?"

"Yes. It's 917-555-1225," Rebecca answered.

Katherine took out her cell phone and dialed the number, standing up and walking a few feet away as it rang.

"Hello?"

Katherine hesitated at the voice, which was a bit older than the man she had been expecting to answer. "Hi, is Ronald there?"

There was a pause. "May I ask who's calling?"

Katherine's first instinct was to consider the situation suspicious, so she held back on identifying herself as law enforcement for the moment. "Katherine. I'm with his sister and she gave me his number. She's worried about him."

The man paused again. "Please hold on for a moment." Katherine's eyebrows furrowed at a stain on the carpet, trying to listen for any sounds on the line in the background. "Hello?"

"Yeah, hello?" Katherine answered.

"Can I have your first and last name please?"

Katherine suddenly heard a burst of static and a coarse voice and her heart sunk as she realized who was holding Ronald's phone. "This is Special Agent Katherine Colebrook, FBI," she muttered.

"Damn. Well, this is Officer Kart with the SDPD. I'm sorry to say Ronald was killed last night."

"You found this phone–?" she began.

"No!" Rebecca barked, startling Katherine and Dolly. She started to rock back and forth quickly, bringing her fists up to her face. "No, I don't like it. I don't like it!"

Katherine's heart sunk as she realized Rebecca had sensed what she was learning from the officer. "I'll call you back," Katherine spoke. She didn't wait for a reply before hanging up her phone and rushing back over to Rebecca, whose face was contorted in despair.

Dolly got to her feet, eyes wide. "What's going on?" she asked.

"Ronald's phone was picked up by a cop," Katherine told her, holding her gaze. Dolly let out a sharp breath of comprehension, stunned.

"I don't want Ronald to be dead!" Rebecca yelled, still rocking. "No, no, no!"

"Rebecca, it's going to be okay," Dolly consoled her, going to her side. She refrained from touching her, knowing that that would just make things worse.

"I want to go to my room," Rebecca spoke suddenly. She leapt to her feet and dashed to the door, pacing in front of it. "I want you to leave me alone!"

Dolly quickly followed her, swiping the key card that opened the door and Rebecca was off like a shot, bolting down the hallway to her room, slamming the door behind herself. Dolly stared after her despairingly as Katherine slipped out into the hallway after her, letting the door to the common room slowly close behind them. "What happens now?" Dolly whispered.

"Now…I call back the officer who has Ronald's phone," Katherine answered. "And then I talk to my boss."

CHAPTER 4

"DAMN IT!"

The Texan drawl was plainly audible in the curse exclaimed by Special Agent in Charge Roger Jackson as he suddenly dropped the pile of papers in his hand, a paper cut having stung his finger. He let out a sigh, looking around at his new office. It wasn't in complete disarray since many things were still in boxes, but it still had a long way to go to reach 'organized'. He grabbed a tissue from his pocket and the Scotch tape from his desk, which luckily he had already unpacked, and taped a makeshift Band-Aid over the blood slowly leaking from his dark brown skin.

When he received the promotion to SAC, Jackson had had about ten years in the field. It was invaluable experience; he couldn't be a handler for trackers without it, or at least he couldn't be a good one. But his job for the past fifteen years was a better fit. It was difficult to explain to someone who felt stifled sitting behind a desk, but Jackson felt more fulfilled when he was overseeing the day-to-day assignments of his agents. When he was guiding his agents in their missions, he felt he was accomplishing more than he ever could out in the field.

So he now found himself at the main Los Angeles field office, an imposingly large, white building on Wilshire Road, trying as best he could to make his new office a mirror image of his old one rather than planning a whole new layout.

Picking up the papers he'd dropped, Jackson put them in the file cabinet he'd been transferring things into from the box to his left, but stopped as his cell phone rang. He glanced at the caller ID and smiled before answering. "Colebrook. How're things coming along in your part of LA?" he spoke.

"I'm actually back in San Diego for the moment," Katherine replied. "I was here for court testimony and then Dolly Hanford called for a favor." She explained the situation. "I'm mostly concerned about the man Rebecca had a vision about. It's likely that he's the assailant that killed Ronald. I was hoping you could pull up the case file and get me some background."

"Uh…hold on." Jackson went over to his desk, where his computer had already been set up by the IT department, the screensaver sliding fish across his screen like it was an aquarium. He moved the mouse to dissipate it and brought up the necessary program to do a search. "Okay…. All right, ah, I'll email it to ya…. It'll be in your inbox in a second. Yeah…. Ronald Wilson. Body was found yesterday in an alley next to his car, in South Central, gunshot. His buddy Patrick was dead on the ground a few yards away, same cause of death."

"I spoke to the M.E. and she determined Ronald was killed by a psychic vampire," Katherine said. "Likely his friend was too. It's probably not in the official report yet.

And it's probable that...this thing would have come after Rebecca next," she murmured. Jackson tensed, immediately recognizing the anxiety coloring her tone. "So he told her to run. She stumbles into a restaurant, overwhelmed by her surroundings, and the police find her. She was in a public place, which is likely why the vampire didn't pursue her. And she's psychic, so there's a good chance the vampire couldn't push her to do what he wanted."

"If Ronald's a dealer and he was doing business with a psychic vampire, likely it was ecstasy," Jackson noted, typing away on his computer and holding the phone with his shoulder. "I'll put that in the case summary. So you're thinking this guy went after her–?"

"Because she's psychic," Katherine finished. "Was in the mood for a delicacy, so he caught her scent–"

"And since he caught her scent, he'll still be on her," Jackson muttered. "We're lucky you got there 'fore he did. You stay on her."

"I'll brief the guards on the fact that something with persuasion might be stopping by for a visit," Katherine said. "At least I think it's the vampire that's coming for Rebecca. It's hard to read things off of her. Her brain works differently, it's oddly organized, and some parts are shielded from me, like she's protecting herself. Like there are a few things she just put in boxes and locked up."

Jackson looked around his office, rubbing his thin goatee. "I know the feeling."

Katherine made a noise of vague amusement. "You keep starting work on new LA cases and you've still got a dozen half-emptied boxes around your office, don't you?" she asked, a knowing smile in her voice.

"I am…multitaskin'," Jackson told her. "Listen, call if you get any trouble."

"Thanks, Jackson. Will do."

Jackson hung up the phone, staring at it. Katherine would always be the tracker that was, if not his proudest achievement – he couldn't exactly take credit for the woman she had grown up to be – the one he was proudest to work with. She was one of two trackers that had followed him to Los Angeles when he'd gotten the promotion to the larger field office, but two others had remained in San Diego to be reassigned to another SAC. Jackson knew that Katherine would move to LA with him because when he got the transfer offer, her partner at the time, John Sweeney, had gotten the opportunity to retire and took it.

Part of it was that Jackson knew Katherine would be interested in a fresh start in LA. San Diego and her home held some memories that weighed on her. But in the end, Jackson and Katherine just came as a pair. He was her boss, and always had been, and if Sweeney was retiring then there wasn't anything keeping her in San Diego. Jackson knew they still had many more years of trouble to get into ahead of them.

But in order to get there, Jackson thought with a sigh as he looked around the room, he needed to be able to find his way around his own office.

CHAPTER 5

ALEXANDRA TUGGED ON THE CORD beside the window to signal that her bus stop was approaching. Her hair starting to stick to the back of her neck even on the air-conditioned bus, she took a hair tie from her wrist. The brown hair she'd inherited from her mother was long enough by just a few inches to put up in a ponytail. Pulling a strap of her backpack over her shoulder, she stood up as the bus came to a gradual stop.

Getting off the bus, and giving a smile to the driver as she did so, Alexandra walked down the sidewalk, taking in the bustle of Saturday afternoon Los Angeles. Her smile widened at a Shih Tzu pulling slightly at his leash being walked by an old man who was shuffling along, with no interest in attempting to keep up with the energetic dog. She pulled the other backpack strap over her shoulder and headed down South Grand Avenue before turning onto West 5th to head toward the Los Angeles Public Library.

At the library near their old house in San Carlos, just outside San Diego, Alexandra had been nearly as recognizable as the employees, and she could see that the librarians here were already starting to give her smiles of recognition when she entered. By her third trip she had memorized where all her favorite sections were. There was a library closer to where she lived, actually there were several between her and this one, but they were no match for the immense diversity of the books in stock at the Central Library. Shortly upon arriving for her first visit, she had decided this would be her second home. Alexandra had checked out and quickly finished a particularly good book on pùca biology, and it had been quite a feat. She hadn't understood a great deal of it, but most of what she'd understood, she'd retained. And she would rather understand some of an advanced book than all of a book from which she would learn little new information.

Grabbing a few books that looked interesting, Alexandra headed downstairs to the children's section, where there were two comfortable couches, and made herself at home. She started on the book at the top of the pile, fidgeting absently with a loose thread on her cargo shorts. An hour passed, and then two, and Alexandra startled out of a trance as her cell phone buzzed in her pocket. A text from her mother, saying she would indeed be in San Diego for a while, and to please call when she got home from the library. Alexandra replied and then went back to her book.

After another hour, Alexandra stretched and got up from her seat, leaving the mostly-finished book on the couch and stopping at the front desk to check out the rest. She then headed for the exit, but slowed down as a sign caught her eye, which read quite plainly, 'Parasapien Outreach'. It was next to a large conference room, where one of the double doors was propped ajar with a doorstop, giving an open invitation. It seemed as if the festivities were coming to a close though, as there wasn't anyone sitting down and only about half a dozen people left.

A young woman in her mid-twenties was talking with a young man just outside the doorway and there were some others chatting inside, as well as a middle-aged man picking up pamphlets and information packets that had been left behind.

The young woman noticed Alexandra and gave her a smile. "Hey. I'm Ellie. You here for the outreach? Sorry, it just ended."

Alexandra shook her head. "I actually just came to the library to pick up some books," she said. "I didn't realize this was going on, though. I'm sapien, but I'm really interested in parasapien science and culture and all that."

"Want a packet or something?" Ellie asked. "We hold events here every couple months."

"Do your parents know you're here?"

Turning around and blinking, Alexandra looked up at the woman standing a few feet away. "I'm sorry?"

A middle-aged Korean woman stood with her daughter, who was about Alexandra's age, both angled toward the exit. In addition to her striking, immaculately tailored clothes, her glaring red lipstick gave her an even more overbearing presence, and Alexandra could smell her perfume from five feet away. The woman stood with an iron grip on her daughter's shoulder and gazed at Alexandra worriedly, as if Ellie, who Alexandra had known immediately was a pùca, was going to drain her of energy on the spot until she dropped dead.

"Ma'am, my name's Ellie," she introduced herself. "If you'd be interested in talking about–"

"No, thank you," the woman answered. "And I don't think you should be here, interacting with kids."

Ellie, to her credit, didn't react as if the woman had just slapped her, though Alexandra knew that's how she felt even without using her psychic abilities. "I've never hurt anyone," Ellie responded. "I'm not sure how much you know about parasapiens–"

"I know enough," the woman snapped.

"I'm a pùca," Ellie continued, ignoring the interruption. "That means that I'm part fae, and that I need energy from other living things to survive. So, like humans eat some animals, like cows and pigs, I can touch them and take energy from them. But I don't do that with people."

Alexandra saw the woman's grip on her daughter's hand tighten. "You just shouldn't be around humans," the woman said. "You're a loaded gun."

Ellie took a breath. "I'm not a weapon," she said.

"You can kill someone without a weapon, so that makes you one," the woman said, prompting Alexandra to roll her eyes.

Ellie shook her head. "It's just prejudice. A full-grown man could kill a child, but we're not worried about that happening. It's just because I'm different that people are scared."

"So as long as a few of you behave well, the rest can roam the streets looking for their next kill?"

Ellie mostly failed at holding back a scowl. "We have to register," she said. "We don't just roam the streets. Remember?"

Alexandra grimaced and shook her head quickly. "Oh, no, don't do that," she said. "You were great up until that."

Ellie blinked and looked to Alexandra, startled out of the conversation. "I'm sorry?"

"You just lost her," Alexandra said. "The facts just aren't there to support the idea that pùcas are roaming the streets looking for their next kill. But, if you remind her that you have to register, it's like saying that you might be dangerous, but don't worry, the government is keeping an eye on you. That's ridiculous though, since registering doesn't actually do anything aside from put you guys on a list like sex offenders. Except it's worse, because you haven't actually committed a crime yet."

Ellie stared at Alexandra for a long moment before smiling. "That's, ah…really smart, actually," she said.

"Just talking points," Alexandra said with a shrug.

"Do your parents know you're down here cavorting with nonhumans?" the woman behind her spoke up suddenly.

"Cavorting? Seriously?" Alexandra snapped, turning around to face her. "My mom knows I'm down here, yeah, and she's fine with me 'cavorting' with whoever I want. And my dad's dead. He doesn't know much of anything. He was killed by a pùca, by the way, which should tell you that I'm not exactly ignorant on the possibility of dangerous pùcas. And my mom's a tracker, so maybe you don't want to assume that I'm the naïve little girl that's going to be drained and left in an alley behind the library by what is quite obviously a *vicio*us pùca," she said. Alexandra motioned to Ellie. "I mean look at her, with her…beaded bracelets and colorful, flowery shirt. Pink and green. Those are totally gang colors, right?"

The woman gaped at Alexandra for a long moment. "Well, I don't know how your mother can see what she sees at her job and then let her daughter interact with such dangerous *things*," she said.

Out of the corner of her eye, Alexandra caught the woman's daughter glancing from her mother to Alexandra, somewhat embarrassed. The statement struck a nerve and Alexandra's gaze narrowed furiously. "My *mother* teaches me martial arts to defend myself. My *mother* teaches me about what parasapiens can and can't do if one attacks me. Facts, not useless prejudices. And my *mother* would walk through *fire* for me, and kill anyone who harmed a hair on my head," she said. "So. You tell me who you think is the better mother. You, or her."

The woman stared at Alexandra, stunned and completely still, before abruptly pulling her daughter by the hand toward the exit.

Alexandra let her anger fade, knowing the ignorant woman wasn't worth it. She snorted, turning back to Ellie. "Anyway," she muttered. She held out her hand, which Ellie shook. "Alex Colebrook. Nice to meet you. I've actually gotta get going," she said. "I'm new in town, so I'd like to look up your meet-ups online. I'll try to make one sometime."

"Great, thank you," Ellie said absently, still smiling from the encounter that Alexandra had simply brushed off.

Alexandra took out her cell phone as she turned and left, dialing her mother's number. "Hey. I'm on my way to the bus station. Just had a really interesting encounter at the library. Didn't you say Los Angeles was *more* liberal than San Diego with parasapiens?"

CHAPTER 6

AFTER HANGING UP WITH HER daughter, Katherine stood in the hallway of the psychiatric ward in silence for a long moment, turning over events in her mind. She finally looked back to Dolly, who was patiently waiting for instructions on their next step. "You think Rebecca would be willing to talk to me again?" she asked.

Dolly pursed her lips and shook her head. "I'm not sure. Worth a shot, I suppose."

Dolly led the way down the hallway and into Rebecca's room, Katherine right on her heels. They walked into the room slowly. "Rebecca?" Dolly asked, shutting the door behind them. The teenage girl was sitting on her bed, legs pulled up to her chest and her arms wrapped around them, rocking back and forth. Her face was crushingly sad and stained with tears. She stared at the wall, not saying a word.

Katherine sat on the edge of Rebecca's bed, waiting for a minute to see if she would acknowledge her presence. "Rebecca, I need to talk to you about Ronald," she finally spoke. No response. Rebecca's mind clearly expressed she didn't want to talk about it, knowing Katherine would pick up on her feelings. "I know you prefer to communicate psychically since we can, Rebecca, but it's better for me when we talk out loud, so I can get details." She paused. "I think the parasapien that killed Ronald is after you," she said carefully. "I think you're in danger. I'm going to keep you safe, though. Okay?"

Rebecca slowed to a halt, going perfectly still aside from the movement of her eyes and the slightest tapping of her fingers. The lack of motion was unnerving, since Rebecca had barely stopped moving since Katherine had first set eyes on her. "Ronald keeps me safe," she suddenly muttered.

Katherine nodded. "I know, Rebecca. I think he died keeping you safe."

"Ronald says it's good to talk about our feelings," Rebecca told her. "So that we can fix ourselves if we hurt. My chest is sore and my whole body feels tired. I don't want to hurt anymore. Can you fix it?"

Katherine became hesitant as she gazed at Rebecca. "Did Ronald talk to you about how sometimes it's good to feel pain?"

Rebecca shook her head, sliding her legs down and folding them, starting to snap her fingers rhythmically, to the beat of a song that only she could hear. "No. But I've read about it. Animals evolved to feel pain so they know when something is wrong. I understand that."

"This is kind of like that," Katherine murmured. "You miss Ronald and your body knows that he was important to you. That he protected you. So it's important that you feel that he's gone. That's why you feel pain." She paused and blinked a few times, pushing back the burning sensation emanating from behind her nose. "It never really fades.

But...you learn to live with it." Katherine focused on differentiating the grief weighing on Rebecca's chest from that which she herself was feeling. It could get overwhelming if she let too much of other people's emotions slide in. It went double for something she could truly empathize with.

Rebecca nodded, still snapping her fingers. "I understand. How long was it until you learned to live with it?"

The breath Katherine had just inhaled remained in her lungs for a few moments before she slowly forced it out. She felt Dolly's eyes on her back. "Ah...." She blinked rapidly again. "It's...inconsistent person to person. It's not relevant," she murmured. As she expected, Rebecca accepted the logical answer and, gratefully, Katherine moved on. "Rebecca, did you see what happened to Ronald's friend, Patrick?" she asked. "Where were you?"

She nodded again. "I saw. I was in the car. In the back seat. Ronald sits in the front. I'm not allowed to drive the car. I tried once. Ronald got mad," Rebecca said, her mouth twisting in confusion.

"Did you see what happened to Ronald's friend?"

"Patrick was giving the man a medicine," Rebecca told her. "An illegal medicine. I'm not allowed to touch them. And he gave Patrick money. But he started to talk to Patrick about me. And he started to get angry. Ronald did too. And the man grabbed Patrick's head and started to...." Rebecca swallowed, her eyes continuing to look around like she was watching the path of a fly. "Patrick died. It made me scared."

Katherine continued to stare at the girl, waiting as Rebecca kept on snapping her fingers, the beat speeding up just a bit at the recollection of the disturbing event. "What happened next?" she asked.

"Ronald was scared too. And he told me to run. And I tried." Rebecca's face contorted in frustration. "I tried to run home. But I got overwhelmed. And so I hid in a restaurant. The police found me there. I didn't like them," she muttered. "They touched me. I told them I don't like to be touched."

Katherine nodded. "All right. And...you said someone is coming to find you? They're going to kidnap you?"

"I had a daydream and I saw it happen," Rebecca said. Her voice softened as her mind went to the memory. "It was the man that killed Patrick. My daydreams hurt my head. I don't like them. I want to go home. Can I go home?"

"No, honey, I'm sorry," Katherine muttered. Rebecca's gaze lowered and she frowned but she didn't say anything.

Katherine stood up, her eyes remaining on Rebecca for a moment before she turned and gave Dolly a small nod as she walked past her. She took her phone from her pocket, dialing a number stored in its speed dial as she exited into the hall.

"Yeah?" Jackson asked.

"Hey, just spoke with Rebecca," Katherine said as the door to Rebecca's room shut behind her. "Listen, my best bet to take out this vampire is to wait here and kill him when he tries to get to Rebecca, since we know he's on his way. Once that's done...." Katherine's voice trailed off and she let out a sigh, leaning against the wall, pinching the bridge of her nose. "In Rebecca's file, does it say if she has any family?"

"Ah…that's the thing, darlin'. We can't figure out who exactly she is."

Katherine's spine straightened, her gaze narrowing. "What do you mean?" she asked. "We have her name. What else do you need?"

"Rebecca's last name ain't Wilson. Not according to any government database." Katherine remained silent, mulling over that information. "Seems there's something she and her brother were running from. At least, that's my best bet. But that's a problem for another time," Jackson muttered. "Safe to say, she ain't got no backup."

"I just think it'll be important for Rebecca to…."

Jackson let out a breath, rustling the line with static. "You're worried about her," he murmured.

Katherine snorted. "Of course I am. The one person she relied on is dead. She's powerfully psychic. And smart. She got her GED over two years ago. And she does a decent amount of grey hat computer hacking, so it would help if she had a good place to propel that passion of hers. She needs someone that can take care of her," she said.

"I know," Jackson spoke. "I'll make some calls, ask around. And I'll put in a special request with the HHSA. There has to be someone that could take her in."

Katherine fell silent. "I…." She shook her head. "No. She can come live with me."

Jackson paused. "With you? Colebrook, I know this hits close to home for you—"

"Okay, for the record, this isn't close to home; this is the exact city, street, building and apartment number," Katherine spoke. "And this isn't just about her being psychic, or about her having no one to turn to, or needing somewhere she can feel safe. Rebecca has a past that we don't know anything about yet. If she and her brother left home and changed their names, there's a reason why. That would not have been an easy thing to do, considering her abilities and autism. So they were seriously desperate. Sticking her with a foster family just isn't good enough. Honestly, even Randall wouldn't be good enough, because Rebecca doesn't just need a home like I did; she could need protection."

"You've already got Alex. How are you going to take care of another teenager? Especially one like Rebecca?" Jackson asked.

"However I have to."

Jackson let out a long sigh. "All right. Okay, fine, I'll make the arrangements."

"Thank you." Katherine hung up the phone, staring into space for a moment before going back into Rebecca's room. "Rebecca?" she asked. The teenager was still sitting in the same spot on her bed, snapping her fingers. "I know that it's overwhelming to think about everything that's going on right now. But I was wondering if, at least temporarily, you'd like to live with me."

Dolly looked to Katherine at the offer, her eyes widening, and her gaze went to Rebecca for her reaction.

Rebecca pursed her lips, considering the offer. "I'd like that," she finally spoke. "But I need my computer. I do a lot of work on my computer."

Katherine smiled. "I know," she said. "We'll get it for you. We can go back to Ronald's apartment and bring all your things over to mine."

"And I have a schedule," Rebecca continued. Her stance

gradually relaxed and she ceased snapping her fingers. "I wake up at 8:15 AM. And I use the toilet, I get dressed, I have breakfast, I brush my teeth, and then I watch cartoons. SpongeBob. And that's just in the morning. I do a lot of things."

"How about we write them down and put them up on the wall, so I know exactly what they are?" Katherine asked. She sat down on Rebecca's bed opposite from Dolly, clasping her hands in her lap.

Rebecca nodded. "That's a good idea," she stated. "I remember everything, but other people don't. They need to write things down. I think that'd be annoying, having to write things down to remember them."

"It sort of is," Katherine admitted with a nod and an amused smile. "But all this has to happen later, Rebecca. We need to talk about what happens next. Do you remember if you saw anything that would tell you what time of day it was during your daydream?"

As her eyes trailed around the room and around the blanket on her bed, Rebecca shook her head. "No. But it felt like today. And it was light outside. So it was before 7:16 PM. That's when sunset is tonight."

Katherine let out a long breath and nodded. "Okay," she muttered.

CHAPTER 7

CURTIS WALKED THROUGH THE FRONT doors of the large hospital, making his way toward the mental ward. He went directly over to the young woman at the front desk, his back straight with implied authority, and he gave her a wide smile. She smiled back, shyly and predictably, as most women did when he smiled at them. "Hi. I'm here to see Rebecca Wilson."

"Are you family?"

"No. I'm with the police," he spoke. He held out his empty hand. "This is my badge. Can you tell me where she is?"

The receptionist nodded, checking her computer. "Of course. Ah…third floor, room 303."

"Any key cards or codes I might need to get up there?" Curtis asked. "You can trust me."

"There's a pin pad at a few doors. The code is 2-5-2-5 this week. All the guards have key cards that will get you in to wherever you need to go."

"I appreciate it," Curtis said, winking at her once. "Let me through. You never met me." He went over to the door to his left, which opened when the receptionist pressed a button on her desk. He walked straight over to the security guard. "Hey. I'm with the police. You need to give me your key card."

"Sure," the guard answered, handing it over. "Something wrong? You here to talk to the FBI?"

Curtis froze. "Who's here from the FBI?"

"A woman. Special Agent. Don't remember her name."

"Why is she here?"

"She's with Rebecca Wilson, a patient here. Said she was here as a bodyguard."

Curtis worked his jaw, his eyes sliding around the hallway before looking back to meet the guard's gaze.

————◆————

The hospital security guard shifts his weight on his feet. He looks at the clock. A nurse smiles as she passes and he smiles back. His attention is drawn to a young man that walks in and up to the counter.

The young man is handsome, and the receptionist smiles at him fondly. He needs information, and the question–.

She gives him the information. He's very nice. And he's a police officer. There's something going on–.

What was she doing? The young woman looks back to her computer, continuing her work.

Katherine quickly jumped to her feet, startling Rebecca, who had been sitting next to her in the common room working on another puzzle. "Dolly, take Rebecca and go sit in her room," she spoke tightly through the window partition to her right. Dolly looked up in alarm from the small room adjacent to them, where she was doing paperwork. "Something's going on."

Dolly promptly did as she was told. Katherine went over to the door, feeling that the guard on the first floor was going after someone that had made his way into the building. She swiped the key card she'd been given, prompting the door to unlock and open. A sinking feeling started to form in her chest, though, as Katherine realized she couldn't feel the vampire itself. This was a psychic vampire that was able to mentally shield itself, like she was able to do.

"Brilliant," she muttered.

Bursting into a stairwell and descending quickly, using the key card to get through the doorways that were locked, Katherine found the guard frantically darting down a hallway, looking for the intruder. "Hey," he snapped, stopping in front of her. "There's someone here."

Katherine nodded once. "I know. Where'd he go?"

"He shoved me and ran past me into the hospital to the first floor. He was wicked fast," he said. "I've got no clue where he went."

Katherine reached out mentally to the guard to try to get a feeling of the intruder's appearance, but there was a stutter in her abilities. She blinked, feeling like she had reached the top of a staircase and mistakenly thought there was one last stair. Her eyes slowly narrowed at the man. "Say that again?" she said.

"He shoved me and ran past me into the hospital to the first floor," the guard repeated. "He was wicked fast. I've got no clue where he went."

Her heart sinking, Katherine suddenly turned and bolted back the way she'd come.

There were many times she'd spoken to people that had

been influenced by the persuasion of a psychic vampire. First of all, it had a certain feel to it. Their mind felt somehow fuzzier than normal, but at the same time they were convinced of what they were saying. That was unusual, since real memories weren't as solid. When recalling things that really happened, people made mistakes, they misremembered, they paused to think. And a pointed feature of their speech was that they said exactly what the vampire had told them, because it was that version of events that their brain thought was real. And they'd say it word for word.

Katherine quickly took the stairs back up to the second floor, two by two, rushing to Rebecca's room. Dolly was sitting on the bed. And Rebecca was nowhere in sight.

"Dolly?" Katherine asked, clapping her hands in front of the woman's face. Dolly blinked a few times and looked up to her, confused, as if to her Katherine had appeared out of nowhere. "Where's Rebecca?"

Dolly blinked, perplexedly. "Katherine? Who-Who's Rebecca?"

Katherine's lips parted in shock as her chest tightened. She spread out her feelers as she dashed back into the hallway, her eyes widening at the feeling of a nearly unconscious Rebecca being carried down the hallway by the psychic vampire.

Katherine let out a growl of frustration. "Damn it." She drew her gun as she ran quickly to the first door, bursting through and entering the second room on her right. Curtis had broken the bars on the window and was just about to leap out of it, with Rebecca over his shoulders in a fireman's carry.

Katherine didn't bother with pleasantries. As soon as her weapon sighted on the young man, and he turned at her entrance, preparing to calmly use its persuasion to assure her that everything was okay, she fired a single bullet through his shoulder.

The vampire shouted in surprise and pain, falling to the ground, Rebecca with him. Katherine bolted over to her, pulling her away from her attacker. "Rebecca," she murmured, putting her gun back in its holster. She tapped the girl gently on the side of her face a few times. "Can you hear me? Rebecca?" Rebecca struggled to open her eyes and Katherine drew back, sensing the girl's dislike of the contact. "Sorry, sweetheart. I think he drained you of energy. That's why you're tired. But you're safe now."

Rebecca opened her mouth, attempting to speak, blinking rapidly. "I...I don't...."

"You can rest," Katherine told her softly. "I'll keep you safe." Rebecca's eyes twitched a few times before she slowly, reluctantly, let herself relax and drift off to sleep.

"You...bitch," Curtis gasped.

"Oh you ain't seen nothin' yet," Katherine whispered. She walked over to him and shoved a foot into his sternum.

"Get off me," he wheezed, attempting to shove at her leg as he forced persuasion into his words.

Katherine drew her weapon and aimed it between his eyes. "Stop moving."

The fact that his persuasion had no effect on her prompted him to freeze. He stared her down for a long moment. "What are you?" he finally muttered.

"Pissed," she snapped. "Let me into your head."

"Go screw yourself."

Katherine shifted her foot to his shoulder, which was already healing but had a ways to go, and shoved. He screamed, fumbling back from her along the ground, his back hitting the wall. "Let...me...in," she growled.

"What's going on?" called a voice as rapid footsteps came down the hall and the security guard abruptly stopped at the threshold to the room. "Was that a gunshot?"

"Shoot her," Curtis barked.

Katherine immediately turned as the security guard attempted to draw his weapon, darting forward and kicking him in the chest, throwing him back into the hall and collapsing to the ground. She swiftly holstered her gun and grabbed him from behind, wrapping her arm around his throat and squeezing, grasping her wrist with her other hand to hold the pressure. He struggled for only a few long moments before going limp, and she immediately let him go.

Katherine swiftly handcuffed him before going back into the room and shutting and locking the door behind her, breathless. "Now we won't get interrupted," she said. Katherine took her gun back out of her holster. "I'm not gonna ask again."

Curtis grimaced in pain as he slowly pulled himself up by the window frame, pushing himself up to his feet and leaning back against the wall. "You're killing me anyway," he muttered, trying to catch his breath.

"But how long will it take?" Katherine whispered.

Curtis stared her down for a long moment before she felt the walls around his mind disappear.

The girl is so powerful and so sweet, he had a hard time just taking enough to make her tired. He wants to kill her, drain her dry. Take every drop of life from her mind and body. She's his. She's all his. Hatred, pure loathing for the woman keeping him from her. The best meal he's ever had, and it had to bite him when he tried to take advantage. Those stupid bastards—.

A pang of concern hit Katherine in the chest. "Who told you about her?"

"I got a call," he said. "They told me I could get a bonus from some dealer. I went to him for some molly and sure enough, she was in the car. Needed to chase her down, but...the payoff would've been worth it."

Katherine's upper lip twitched. "Who were they?"

"I got. A call," Curtis repeated. He took his cell out of his pocket with a grimace, the movement jostling his shoulder, and tossed it to Katherine with his good arm. She caught it with her left hand, not looking or moving the aim of her gun as she slid it into her pocket. "Saturday afternoon. They didn't exactly advertise why they were serving me dinner."

Katherine continued her search of Curtis's head for a long moment before she eventually came up empty, realizing that actually was all he had. Then she aimed her gun at his chest and motioned to the ground. "On your stomach."

Curtis frowned. "What?"

"What, you thought I was going to execute you? I'll take you to local lockup and they'll figure out what's next."

Curtis stared at her for a long moment before he scowled and shook his head. "You know I'm as good as dead for what I did. I'm not going to prison."

"I won't ask again," Katherine growled.

"Fine. Don't ask again." Curtis suddenly lunged at her gun and Katherine took an abrupt step backwards and fired her weapon multiple times.

Curtis collapsed into her and she threw him to the side as he fell to the ground, bleeding profusely from his chest wounds. He gasped a few times and stared at Katherine wide-eyed, but one of the bullets had hit his heart. It wasn't long before he died.

"Damn it," Katherine muttered. "Asshole."

CHAPTER 8

After Katherine put Rebecca in the ambulance
and gave instructions to the police that came to the
scene on how to handle the case, Katherine headed back
inside the hospital. She'd left Dolly sitting with the security
guard in a break room after the two employees had given
their statements to the police. Katherine knocked on the
door and the security guard opened it, currently on the
phone. She gave him a nod and he gave her a smile that was
more like a grimace as he left the room.

"How you doing?" Katherine asked.

Dolly fidgeted with her hands on the table in front of
her as Katherine sat down across from her. "I'm all right,
I think," she murmured. "I just…I'm still so confused.
Everything's so fuzzy. Who was she, exactly?"

Katherine smiled. "Just someone who needed my help,"
she said. "You called me, which was very much the right
move, when you realized she was psychic. And when I went
downstairs for the psychic vampire when he got here, he
bypassed me and found Rebecca with you. I'm not sure
exactly what he said to you. Probably, 'Forget you ever met

Rebecca,' or something akin to that. And your brain just did what it was told."

Dolly folded her arms tightly as a shiver slid through her. "It's just...horrifying," she whispered. "Just like that? I remember calling you, walking around the hospital, but not why. Nothing about Rebecca. I mean, just like that, and it's all gone."

"Not gone," Katherine spoke carefully. "There have been many successful cases of those affected by vampire-induced amnesia recovering their memories. Especially with people and events that are more significant to them. It's sort of like putting things in the recycle bin on your computer, but not emptying the recycle bin. Your brain just doesn't have access to the information."

"I see."

"I'm actually quite glad things turned out as they did," Katherine murmured, prompting Dolly to look up to her with a confused expression. "Could hardly have asked for it to go any better. The vampire didn't hurt anyone, and I killed him without much fuss. My only problem now is... how he found her."

"What do you mean?"

Katherine shook her head. "That's my problem. Don't worry about it."

Dolly let out a long breath. "Well...you can take a shower before you go to the hospital after Rebecca," she said. "I know you're far from home."

"Oh, it's fine–"

"I insist, sweetheart," Dolly said with a gentle smile. "You look like you could use it."

Katherine glanced down at herself, realizing that she

should indeed take her friend up on that offer. There was some blood spatter she'd gotten on her shirt when Curtis had fallen against her. It wasn't much, but the level of blood that required a change of clothes to her was higher than the average persons. It was something she'd had to be reminded of before.

"Yeah, a shower actually sounds like a nice idea," she finally answered.

Katherine locked the door to the locker room, pulling open the curtain on the shower, stripping down and turning on the water. Testing it until it got hot, she slipped in and let the water pour back across her head. She slid her hands back along her hair let out a long breath, trying to focus on absorbing the warmth and let go of some of the tension that her shoulders had taken on. After letting the water rhythmically beat against her back for a minute, she picked up the soap.

Once she'd cleaned herself off of the blood that had soaked through her shirt and stained her stomach, Katherine pushed the handle a little further, nudging the water toward that perfect temperature on the edge of searing her skin. She massaged the back of her neck with her hands as she stood under the steaming water for a minute before finally shutting it off. Stepping out and grabbing the towel and wringing out her hair, Katherine turned on the fan to vent out the room and got her brush from her bag. She wiped the mirror of the steam that had started forming on it and paused for a moment.

Katherine smiled as David came up behind her, wrapping

his hands around her stomach. "I'm all wet," she giggled as he pressed himself against her, his shirt and pants absorbing the moisture from her skin.

"Mm," he murmured, kissing her shoulder. "I don't care." His fingers grazed the scar on her right hipbone. "What was that? A knife?"

Katherine slid her left hand over his. "Yeah. Just a memory of one now."

"You've got a startling amount of memories scattered across your skin," he said. His eyes examined her reflection in the mirror and guided his right hand to her shoulder. "How many times have I seen these, and I only know the stories behind a few? We've got…a bullet over here…a burn from what looks like a cigarette…what I could only assume was either claws or the world's biggest fork—"

Katherine laughed and turned around in his loose embrace, stretching out her arms and resting them on his shoulders, clasping her hands behind his head. "World's biggest fork would've been a more interesting story, probably."

"I'm pretty sure claws is a more interesting story," David contradicted her. "It's either, 'He turned around at the barbeque and accidently stabbed me,' or 'I was being chased by something that looked like a cross between a gorilla and a cougar—"

"I grimace to think at what that sex must've been like," Katherine told him.

"Really acrobatic. Speaking of," he said, coaxing her forwards as he walked backwards.

"Oh come on, I cannot be late on the first day," she objected.

"The first day?" David repeated, narrowing his eyes and coming to a halt. "You've worked at the FBI for years."

"Not my first day; I've got a new boss," she clarified. Katherine pulled away and went back into the bathroom, picking up her hairbrush. "ADIC Watkins. Today, he could show up anywhere. I won't have it be my cubicle and not be there."

David sighed, leaning against the door jamb. "Mommy is such a hard worker," he said.

Katherine smiled at that. "Speaking of that, Alex didn't wake up once last night. How did you do that?"

"A magician never reveals his secrets."

"Made me love you even more."

David scoffed as he turned and walked away. "Not possible."

Katherine's fingers danced across the claw marks on her hip before shaking her head to bring herself back to the present and pulling her brush roughly through her hair.

<hr />

Katherine stared at Rebecca, lying in the hospital bed in the Rady Children's Hospital ER. Her IV drip and the oxygen nose-buds made her condition appear worse than it was; she was just tired and drained of energy. But the appearance had still sent a pang through Katherine's chest.

The curtain to her left pulled open and Rebecca's doctor walked up to them. "Agent Colebrook?" he spoke. Katherine looked up at him. The fifty-odd year-old man appeared almost as tired as Rebecca did, actually, and his comb over had long ago turned into a messy clump of hair. He gave Katherine a small smile. "You can go home, if you'd like," he said. "I spoke with the Marshals, and they said they'll be coming to stay with Rebecca until tomorrow, when they pick up her things and bring her to your home."

"Thank you," Katherine said. "I was hoping she would wake up before I left, but I know she needs her rest and it's better if she sleeps anyway." Katherine stood up, taking a business card from the bunch in her wallet and handing one to him. "But if she does wake up and she's disoriented or suspicious of the people here, feel free to call me and put me on the phone with her. She's been through a lot, and a familiar voice will probably help."

"I'll let the nurses know. Thank you," he replied.

Katherine gave Rebecca a final glance before she turned and walked down the hall, taking out her cell phone. She hesitated before letting out a small smile and checked out the lecture schedule on the FBI's website for the next morning, pressing the button for the elevator. It was almost 11PM, which was a valid excuse to get a motel room rather than make the two-hour commute home. And two days in back in town meant she had to make a certain surprise visit.

CHAPTER 9

J OHN SWEENEY SLOWLY WALKED BACK and forth across the stage in one of San Diego University's moderately sized auditoriums, speaking into the microphone in his hand, finishing up his lecture on his experiences with pùcas and their talents and limitations of shape shifting. He was dressed in slacks and a shirt that he'd ironed, which was as far as he was willing to go into business formal, even for lectures. His Irish heritage was responsible for his graying red hair, including a small beard, and freckles. He was just short of six feet tall, and probably would have had a slight Irish lilt to his voice, learned from his parents, if he hadn't been born severely deaf.

After four decades of working for the FBI as a tracker, Sweeney had recently retired and promptly become bored. He'd started giving the occasional lecture at SDU to criminology students, among others, and was now doing it several times a week, having found that he was definitely enjoying himself.

A few minutes earlier, he'd seen some people start to get up and walk over to the microphones set up on either side of the room for questions. The sign language interpreter stood off to the side of the stage to translate for Sweeney, since it was a bit of a distance to lip-read from. "I hope everyone learned a lot. Ah, if we could get the house lights up and turn down the ones glaring fiercely at me, we could get those questions started," Sweeney spoke.

The lighting shifted and Sweeney blinked a few times, his eyes adjusting. There were two lines that had formed and Sweeney's eyes landed on the person first in line at one of them and he smirked.

"Yeah, I've got a question," Katherine spoke and signed, smiling innocently. "If, say, you were on a plane with your partner, and she was telling you some *extremely* important information on a case, would you ever close your eyes and take a nap?"

"Ah, no, no, I'd never do that," Sweeney said, folding his arms and shaking his head, his face tense. "But if my partner was being extremely irritating and talking so much it bordered on a lecture, that might be another story. And I had a partner for a while that could really grate on my nerves." Katherine grinned. Sweeney motioned to her. "Ladies and gentlemen, Special Agent Katherine Colebrook," he spoke. Some applause echoed through the auditorium. "Colebrook, sit your ass down and let the kids ask their questions." Laughter echoed through the crowd as Katherine smiled and took a seat.

About half an hour later, Sweeney walked off the stage and took Katherine in a tight hug, which she returned. "Good to see you," he said, pulling back and looking her over. "You look…." He blinked. "Stressed. Are you in town for a case or something?"

"Yeah. Thought I could stop by and say hi while I'm

here," Katherine said. "And I thought I could mention that it looks like I'm adopting a teenage psychic."

Sweeney folded his arms. "This sounds like it's gonna be good. Walk with me? Need to refill my water bottle."

"Yeah, lead the way."

———◦◇◦———

Sweeney and Katherine walked along the sidewalk through college campus, occasionally dodging someone on a skateboard or smiling politely at someone offering a pamphlet for the newest, coolest club in town. Sweeney shook his head and stared at her with a smile. "You just can't stay away, huh?"

"It's only two hours from LA, and Dolly knows she can call me anytime," Katherine replied, accompanying her speech with sign language. "And it's not like I ran away from San Diego. Just got a bit of a promotion."

"You going to take after Randall?" he signed. "Adopt kids in need like he did for you? You'll need a bigger apartment if you start adopting kids at the rate he does."

Katherine's eyes widened. "No way," she told him. "It's enough of a handful being a mother to Alex. I saw how much of a full time job it was for him when I was growing up, and I've already got one of those. Rebecca is just… special."

Sweeney curved their path and sat down at one of half a dozen tables outside a building they were passing and Katherine followed his lead. She stared at him curiously, his demeanor suddenly serious. "Why are you here?" he asked.

Katherine raised her eyebrows. "I'm not allowed to visit?" Sweeney raised his eyebrows in reply. She sighed, leaning back in the uncomfortable chair, and her gaze went distant as she fell silent for a long moment. "I've had you on my six for twenty years," she finally said. "I mean longer if you count…everything." Katherine stopped talking again, staring at the table in front of her. She shook her head and looked up to him. "I can do this on my own. I can be a tracker on my own. But now I'm supposed to bring in someone new. I've got to take on a probie."

Sweeney's face relaxed in comprehension. "Look. Rome wasn't built in a day," he told her. "We weren't either. And neither will you and your new partner. I know what's going on in your head right now, but you can't let it in. You've got a job to do. You need a partner in LA, and the sooner you get one, the sooner you'll be able to build trust and build a history with them, just like you had with me. There's only one path to take here. There's no shortcut."

Katherine smiled at him and nodded. "Unfortunately."

"So is this going to become a regular thing?" Sweeney asked. "Calling on Yoda whenever you need advice out in the world? Bother me every time you're in town, or text me or hop on Skype and talk my eyes off?"

Katherine chuckled. "I'll do my best to survive without you. I know you're extremely busy in retirement."

Sweeney shook his head. "So busy. So, so busy."

CHAPTER 10

S PECIAL AGENT IN CHARGE JACKSON sat back down at his desk, putting a folder of papers down in front of him, holding his phone with his shoulder. "How's Rebecca handling things?" he asked. "She all right with you being back in LA?"

"She's fine," Katherine answered. "She knows the plan and that she'll see me again soon. Did you talk to WitSec?"

"They're writing up a file for her as we speak," Jackson replied. He flicked the bobbing woodpecker on his desk to start bouncing up and down and he leaned back in his chair. "And I got everything in order for the foster situation. Permanent foster, we're calling it. For now."

"Thank you."

"So what's your guess on her case? Any brilliant ideas?"

"I...have too many theories and not enough evidence to really nail one down in particular," Katherine muttered. "The biggest thing here was that the people that called Curtis didn't want anything in return. At least, they didn't tell him they did. They might've asked him for something in the future. So maybe they wanted a psychic vampire to owe them one. Or maybe they wanted Rebecca, and they wanted someone else to do the dirty work for them. And considering she might have a past, since her brother changed their last name, who knows who that could be?"

Jackson let out a ragged sigh. "All right. It'll take a day or two to get the paperwork in order and then they'll bring her here. And I'll keep a few agents looking for anything on who she is."

Katherine paused for a long moment. "Yeah. Sounds good," she finally muttered.

Hesitating, Jackson smiled. "How's Alex?"

"She's good," Katherine answered, her tone predictably shifting toward the happier end of the spectrum. "We're going to the range later, but she's still down at the library right now."

"Again?"

"What can I say? The kid's a sponge," Katherine replied.

"Sharp as a tack, too," Jackson noted. "A sharp, pokey sponge." Katherine chuckled. "All right, well, keep in touch."

"I will. Talk to you later, Jackson. Thanks again."

———⟡———

Katherine waited patiently for a homeless man to push his cart across the entrance to the parking lot before she drove in, finding a spot not far from the shooting range. If she were honest, the fact that there was a parking lot, however tiny, at the range was a huge plus when she'd been shopping around. Katherine glanced to her daughter sitting shotgun beside her, bringing her mind back to their conversation. "You sure you'll be okay with this?" she asked.

Alexandra nodded. "Of course," she replied. "Rebecca

can't just get lost in the foster care system. For so many reasons. Besides, it'll be cool having a genius for a sister."

Katherine chuckled as she turned off the car. "Good. I do still want to have the guest room available for impromptu visitors, so I'll be clearing out my office and putting my desk in my bedroom and my file cabinets in my closet." She got out of the car, Alexandra following suit, and locked it. "You can come shopping with me this evening for supplies for her new room."

Alexandra's expression brightened. "Awesome! What kind of décor do you think she'd like? Maybe a poster of computer circuitry or something?"

Katherine smiled as she unloaded her Glock, putting the magazine in her jacket pocket and removing the chambered round. "I'm sure Rebecca will appreciate any homey touches you help me put on the room," she said. She left the slide back on her firearm to show that it was empty before heading inside with Alexandra.

Katherine nodded at the man behind the register, an older man named Richie who owned the store, whom she'd met the other day when she'd stopped by to check the place out. He smiled back and waved at her familiar face before turning back to his customer.

"Here you go," Katherine said, handing one of the forms on the counter and a pen to Alexandra. They each filled one out, and then both went over to the counter once Richie was available.

Katherine had, for the past five years, been taking Alexandra out to a friend's ranch for their shooting practice. Alexandra's aim now rivaled that of her mothers, even though she was only sixteen years old, but she'd wanted to start shooting at a range like her mother did. So, with her passport in hand, the only ID she had aside from her birth certificate, Alexandra had commenced begging her mother to take her. Eventually Katherine relented.

"We're here for some target practice," Katherine answered, handing over the forms. "Both of us."

"I see," Richie spoke. "Well, you know the rules and I'm sure you've told her, but I've got to lay them out again anyway. All weapons brought onto the property must be unloaded, slide back to show there isn't a chambered round. There is no rapid fire permitted; shots must be at least one second apart. Protective glasses and earmuffs must be worn at all times inside the range…."

Once Richie was done with his spiel, Katherine nodded once. "I've got my Glock, so I'll get four boxes of ammo for it, and I'll need to rent one for Alex."

"All right. She know what she wants to try?" he asked.

"Smith and Wesson, .40 caliber," Alexandra said, looking up to her mother.

Katherine nodded once, looking back to Richie, and he took the firearm off the wall behind him, giving Alexandra a brief once-over of the weapon.

"Can I have an extra magazine?" Alexandra asked him.

Richie nodded once. "Sure."

Alexandra smiled at him in thanks as she took the gun, pointing it down, and went over to the glasses and earmuffs. She took one of each as her mother got ammunition for each of them and the extra magazine for Alexandra.

Once they were settled in the booth they'd been assigned, Katherine handed a box of ammunition to Alexandra and placed the rest on the wide ledge. She hung up a target, a piece of paper with the silhouette of a person, and pushed the switch to slide it back twenty-five feet, taking a step back to give Alexandra some room. The teenager blinked at the occasional shots sounding from a nearby booth as she emptied a row of rounds into her hand. She smoothly ejected the magazine from the gun, putting the weapon on the ledge and loading the rounds in the first magazine, then the second. Katherine smiled at the effortless, efficient handling of the weapon by her daughter, watching as Alexandra loaded it and chambered a round.

Then Alexandra took a step back, shifting her grip to two-handed, feet shoulder's width apart, arms locked, aimed at her target, and fired. She went through the magazine, and Katherine could feel the tension Alexandra felt, on the edge of just firing off round after round, unaccustomed to the mandatory full second of pause between shots. But she managed to obey the rule, if just barely, and after the next-to-last bullet had been fired, Alexandra pressed the button to release the magazine. She dropped it on the ledge, grabbing the second and thrusting it into the grip with a *snap*. Alexandra was instantly back into her stance and went through the next magazine just as effortlessly, finishing off the bullets this time.

Once she'd gone through the second magazine, Alexandra looked up to her mother with a smile, who grinned back at her, nodding at the impressive accuracy. "Very nice," she said, prompting Alexandra's smile to widen.

Removing the empty magazine, Alexandra left her gun on the ledge and stepped back, letting her mother take a stance and start firing.

Rebecca looked around Katherine's kitchen, examining the wood paneled floors, the granite countertops, the organized rows of spices on a small shelving unit. Katherine knew she was taking in all the details, fascinated by things which Katherine had probably never paid more than a moments notice. She'd given the teenager a thorough tour of the apartment, and they'd lingered on Rebecca's new room, though it only had the basics in it for now.

Katherine had paid particular attention to Rebecca's room at her former home when she'd gone to help the agents in charge of packing and bringing her things over. The whole apartment was sparing in décor and belongings, but it was home and that was important to anyone. Rebecca had the only bedroom, a bed and a computer desk the only furniture in it, and it appeared Ronald had slept on the couch in the living room.

When deciding how to put together Rebecca's new room, Katherine attempted to emulate some of the small things in the teenager's bedroom that probably meant more to her, and even the ones that didn't consciously register but might help her feel more comfortable. She'd removed one of the shelves from the closet so she could hang her shirts up as she had in her old room. She'd brought over the blackout curtains to Rebecca's new room and hung them up first, knowing they were for a better atmosphere for computer work. And Katherine had spotted a Febreze air freshener on Ronald's coffee table so she'd stopped and picked up several identical ones. Nothing made something feel like home like familiar scents.

"I'm often gone for work, and Alex is at school for seven hours a day, so you'll have the place to yourself a lot of the time," Katherine spoke, spreading peanut butter on a slice of bread. "I'll talk to some of my contacts at the FBI and see if there's something they could contract out to you. Keep you busy. What kind of work do you usually do?"

"Coding and hacking computers," Rebecca answered. "It's complicated. I talked to Ronald about it sometimes, but he wouldn't understand. I don't think you would either."

Katherine smiled as she finished making a peanut butter and jelly sandwich. "I'll take your word for it."

Even though it was complicated to understand Rebecca's mind, Katherine did find it helpful to be able to find out things directly rather than having to ask her. And she knew Rebecca preferred it because she felt words took too long when you had the option of expressing something mentally. Plus it was easier to understand feelings, which was something important to Katherine if she was going to help ease such a huge transition period. Rebecca was still aching inside from the loss of her brother, still trying to digest it. She had to now adjust to a new home, a new family, new schedules. It would be overwhelming for anyone, much less a kid.

"When's my computer getting here?" Rebecca asked.

"About an hour. The rest of your things, too. Do you like your sandwich cut into squares or triangles?" Katherine asked.

"Um…fractals," Rebecca said. Her face suddenly split into a grin as her eyes darted from the plate on the counter to her hands fidgeting on the table.

Katherine laughed. "Not sure I can do that. Second choice?"

"Triangles, please. Thank you. And I appreciate you making me lunch, but I know how to make myself a sandwich. I'm not a child."

Katherine cut the sandwich and brought it over to the table. "I know. I'm just a mother, so I like mothering people," she said.

"That's acceptable," Rebecca said.

Rebecca started in on her lunch as Katherine glanced toward the living room when the front door opened. Alexandra walked into the kitchen, her backpack slung over her shoulder. "Hey."

"Our guest is here," Katherine said. "This is Rebecca."

"Cool. Hi, I'm Alex," she said with a smile.

"My name's Rebecca Wilson. It's nice to meet you," Rebecca said.

"You too."

"Do you like to play Scrabble? I really like Scrabble. I played all the time with Ronald. And poker."

Alexandra shifted her backpack on her shoulder. "Yeah, um…Ronald was your brother?" she asked.

"Yeah. I beat him every time, but he still liked to play with me."

Alexandra smiled. "Sounds like fun. We have a board, so we can play after dinner tonight." Rebecca didn't respond, but smiled. Alexandra turned to her mother. "I'll be on the roof. I've got a book I want to start on," she said, taking a few slow steps backwards.

"When don't you?" Katherine asked, grinning. Alexandra made a face. "I'll be leaving for court soon."

"Okay, good luck," Alexandra called over her shoulder as she went down the hallway. Katherine listened for the sound of the front door closing as she stretched out her feelers.

Alexandra goes down the hall, her mind bouncing around from her new school to the library, to the parks closest to their new apartment. A desire for a good hamburger. Pressing the elevator button. A reminder to herself to do a search online for good hamburger places within biking distance. Realizing she needs to get a new bike soon. But mom won't let her ride her bike that much around Los Angeles, considering how careless drivers could be around bicyclists. Bright sun as she walks outside onto the roof. She's confident she'll never get tired of the beautiful weather of this town....

Katherine let her focus on her daughter fade and disappear. Her abilities of clairvoyance came in handy in many areas of her life including, obviously, at the FBI working as a tracker, but nowhere was she more grateful for them than as a mother. And the fact that her abilities had been passed on to her daughter gave Katherine comfort, knowing that in addition to the training she received from her mother, Alexandra had another advantage to protect herself.

Katherine went down the hall toward Rebecca's new room, stopping in Alexandra's room when she saw that her daughter had finished unpacking most of her things. Alexandra's bookshelves were filled with her paperbacks and hardcovers alike that had been read multiple times, the content ranging from children's classics to weaponry to young adult fiction to werewolf biology. Dotting another bookshelf were martial arts trophies, school certificates of academic achievements, and the box that housed Alexandra's knife collection. There were also photographs, and Katherine's eyes landed on the picture that her daughter had placed on her bedside table: a photograph of Alexandra, Katherine, and her husband David.

Katherine walked over and picked up the picture frame. "I think it's a nice place," she murmured. "I know you would've liked it."

When they'd been on vacation in Florida, David had gotten someone who was a local, probably irritated with constant onslaught of tourists, to photograph them on a boardwalk in Daytona Beach. David stood with one hand clasped in his daughter's over her shoulder and an arm around his wife, grinning like a fool. Katherine's head tilted toward him as she smiled at the camera, with her hand resting on her daughter's shoulder.

Aside from her wedding ring, Katherine seldom ever adorned herself with jewelry. The only things on her person aside from a wallet and such were folding or throwing knives, a gun when she had a holster to put it in or a jacket to disguise the bulge in the back of her jeans, pepper spray, and a laser pointer that emitted UV lights. Though she'd left the gun in her safe at home for the vacation, at David's insistence.

A perceptive person would see the difference in her appearance today from the photograph Katherine held in her hand. Ever since she was a child, she'd had an air of what David would call suspicion, though she called it wariness. It was composed of her visibly athletic body toned by years of judo, the confidence of reflexes honed by jiu jitsu, and the calm control she got from tai chi.

Alexandra's brown hair was much longer at six years old, perpetually pulled back into a ponytail or a braid, revealing the green, wide set eyes that she had inherited from her mother. Katherine's gaze into the camera, even with her open smile, was piercing and keen, full of wisdom from decades fighting back against the monsters of the world, and heavy with the onslaught of knowledge she consistently felt from those around her. It was another two years after the picture was taken that Alexandra's eyes had begun to take on that appearance. Katherine's chest clenched at that fact. A memory of the moment that had turned her child into an adult at too young an age made her want to put down the photo face down on the table.

Katherine's heart ached from the harsh, cruel reality of the world that Alexandra had had thrust upon her, but it had made her stronger. It had made her more able to protect herself. And that helped settle the constant niggle in the back of Katherine's mind that she felt whenever her daughter left her line of sight or the reach of her feelers. Not to mention Alexandra now held herself with confidence and determination, knowing she could protect herself from dangers out there.

It had also made her tenacious, but Katherine could handle that. Most of the time.

Staring at the framed photograph for a minute, Katherine finally blinked herself out of her daze and went over to Rebecca's room, getting to work assembling the pieces of the new bed.

CHAPTER 11

A FTER ONLY A FEW MINUTES of searching for parking, since it was early, Katherine pulled into a spot on Sunset Boulevard. She took her phone from her pocket, looking over the shopping list of herbs she'd written up to see if anything she'd forgotten sprung to mind before getting out. Glancing at the clock, which read 8:48AM, she put her phone away, paying the meter in front of which she'd parked and heading toward the store down the road.

As she approached the store, though, Katherine's pace slowed. She stopped one store away, glancing up at the sign above her destination that read *Altar of a Mystic*. Hesitating, Katherine reached out toward something that had jumped out at her from an occupant of the store. The young woman that owned it, Cassandra Lively, whom Katherine had met a week or two back, was speaking with two men about something that was making her feel extremely uncomfortable, if not downright vulnerable. And as Katherine gathered some information, being an FBI agent wasn't the best way to enter this store.

Slowly taking a few steps backwards, Katherine turned around and headed back to her car. After locking her gun and badge in her glove compartment, Katherine approached the store.

The hanging sign on the front door had been flipped to Closed, but the door wasn't locked, so Katherine ignored it and confidently strode inside. The bell above the door rang at her entrance and all three sets of eyes went to Katherine as she picked up a small basket next to the door to collect the items she needed. Although now, she had decided to strategically add to her shopping list.

Altar of a Mystic was one of the best shops Katherine had found in her area for supplies she might need, stocking a selection of hundreds of herbs that far surpassed most other stores. The most common spells Katherine did were scrying for someone or something, or increasing or decreasing the effects of her psychic abilities (which depended on whether her talents needed a leg up for some reason, or she was on vacation and wanted some quiet time). But there were loads more supplies stocked in this store than she had the time or need to learn to use.

Lining the store's shelves were dozens of kinds of leaves and roots, spices, and herb blends and extracts, as well as some oils, incense, and supplies like mortars and pestles. There was also a small section of books, some with instructions, some biographies of noted spell casters, some simply informative on the types of supplies you might find in this kind of store.

Since spells only worked if you were either a parasapien, psychic, or a witch, most customers fit in one of those categories. There were of course the occasional clear-cut sapien who insisted on trying a spell, and sometimes even insisted they worked, so there was a significant amount of stores whose owners had no problem selling those supplies while knowing full well that they were useless to the buyer. Altar of a Mystic was no such place though; Cassandra Lively was a psychic and a witch and had grown up in the Wiccan community, so she took her work and her store very seriously. That had given her a reputation of a powerful person, however, and this was what had created the two problems currently standing at her counter.

The middle-aged men, who were now glaring at Katherine, were Frank Calabrease and Rick Lazos. Calabrease was someone that Katherine was familiar with mostly through water cooler conversation, though also from the occasional newspaper article. He was a mobster, known for being a ruthless businessman and for stepping up to do his own dirty work, at least when it came to the important things, which told Katherine quite a bit from his presence here. Lazos was his second in command, about ten years Calabrease's junior, willing to carry out any order his boss gave him.

Katherine gathered some information from the two criminals. Lazos was a formidable man, in his late thirties and always up for a fight, which was why he had made it so high in the ranks. He had jet-black hair that was slicked back in a way that was sleazy, wore an expensive suit, and had a gun tucked in his holster, as she knew he always did. Calabrease was about ten years older, graying at the temples and also wearing a pricey, tailor-made black suit. They had the appearance of any other professional businessmen, and Katherine's abilities were the only reason she could tell they were there for something more nefarious. That and recognizing Calabrease's face from the papers.

As Katherine picked up the shopping basket, she met Cassandra's eyes for a moment. Barely a second, but it was heavy enough to prompt Cassandra to reach out mentally toward Katherine. Cassandra blinked and she was careful not to shift her expression.

Lazos glared at Katherine. "Hey," he spoke up. "Didn't you see the sign? The store's closed."

Katherine glanced at him indifferently. "I'm on a schedule." She went over to the shelves against the back wall, skimming the extensive selection of bottled and bagged herbs and making her selections fairly quickly.

"Katherine is a very good customer of mine," Cassandra said. She unconsciously picked at her nails as she stared at Katherine. "I'm sure she won't take very long."

Lazos glanced to his boss, brushing his jacket back just slightly to reveal his holstered firearm. Calabrease looked thoughtful for a moment before shaking his head.

Katherine spoke, not turning around, continuing her shopping. "I really have no time for guns, Cujo," she said.

Lazos's eyes shot to Katherine and Calabrease's gaze narrowed. "I'm presuming you're a psychic as well?" Calabrease asked.

"Wow, you graduated top of your class, didn't you?" Katherine muttered. She took one more thing from a shelf and put it in her basket before heading over to the register. She ignored Calabrease's heavy glare and began putting her items out on the counter.

"Much better psychic than I am," Cassandra said quietly as she started ringing up Katherine's purchases.

"Cassie, I'm busy," Katherine said. "Sorry, but this job's all yours. Besides, it seems boring."

"I don't appreciate the fact that you're digging into our business," Calabrease said.

"It's nothing personal. I don't care about your business. I don't care about your mole or the fact that Cassie's gonna do a crappy perusal of your employees' minds later today because you can't hire decent help. I just find it really funny," Katherine said with an amused smile, glancing briefly to Calabrease. She looked back to Cassandra. "Do you have three more ounces of saffron?"

"I do," Cassandra said, turning and going into a cabinet on the wall behind her. She took out three carefully packaged brown bags, bringing them over to the counter and ringing them up as well.

"Are you local?" Calabrease asked, unwilling to be ignored. "Who are you?"

"Busy," Katherine muttered, keeping her gaze steadily on Cassandra.

Calabrease gnashed his teeth and took two small steps closer to Katherine. "If you're new to the neighborhood, you're not going to want to alienate a potential new client, are you?" he asked pointedly, something malicious coloring his tone.

Katherine looked mildly irritated, but sighed in resignation. "Kathy Moore. I've mostly worked out of Sacramento. I travel when the job requires it."

Calabrease met Lazos's gaze briefly. "I don't suppose this job you're so busy with could wait for a day or so?" he asked Katherine. "I'd be very grateful to take advantage of your services while you're in town."

"It can barely wait an hour," Katherine chuckled, looking over to him as Cassandra put Katherine's purchases into a large brown bag. "And I'm not going to be available until 4PM. So since this is time sensitive–"

"Not so much that I don't want it done well," he told her. "A few more hours is fine. And that will give me time to look into you. How much would you charge for this job?"

"It's gonna be ten grand."

Calabrease froze, staring at Katherine. "Ten thousand?"

Katherine smirked. "You think it's expensive to hire a professional, wait until you hire an amateur."

Lazos stared at his boss, his demeanor revealing nothing, but Katherine knew he was awaiting orders. Cassandra finished ringing up Katherine's purchase, trying to make herself blend in with her surroundings.

"Fine," Calabrease muttered. "Ten grand it is."

"Fine. And save the tough-guy threats," Katherine told him. She took a piece of scrap paper from the cash register and jotted down a number of one of her burner phones, handing it over to Calabrease. "Keeping my mouth shut is how I keep my clients happy. Cassie, how much do I owe you?"

"Seven hundred forty-nine," Cassandra responded.

"Put it on my tab," Katherine spoke, picking up her bag. "I'll have the cash for you tomorrow."

"Okay. Thanks," Cassandra said with a small smile. The emotions flowing from Cassandra were much stronger than her smile revealed, but Katherine just nodded in reply.

CHAPTER 12

CALABREASE'S OSTENTATIOUS LINCOLN SEDAN DROVE along with Lazos driving, Calabrease sitting shotgun, and Katherine alone in the tan leather back seat, cruising along secondary roads into north Orange County. After about twenty minutes, the nicely trimmed residential lawns and yuppie condo developments eventually gave way to dirt driveways, horse farms, and some long-abandoned, rusted industrial parks. There, Calabrease's vehicle finally turned onto a gravel road leading to a well-maintained brick warehouse.

Katherine had parked at the diner where they had decided to meet and they'd picked her up and driven around for a while. Calabrease had to give his employees some time before they had to be at the meeting point and he didn't want to arrive early. Plus they'd needed time to pick up Katherine's payment.

The Lincoln parked and Katherine exited the car, following Calabrease and Lazos across the parking lot and into a warehouse. The warehouse was wide and empty, boxes piling in the corner, some obviously empty and some piled high and definitely packed with goods. Nothing criminal though, Katherine found when she probed further; they wouldn't have brought a new employee into a base of operations, no matter how much they were paying her.

The building had a musty odor to it, the smell of nonuse and griminess that discouraged anyone from looking too closely at the small furry things in the corners. A thin layer of dust covered pretty much everything, though some of it had been disturbed and created several path options. They took the one furthest left, going into another, smaller room.

There was a long table in the middle of the huge storage room they walked into, surrounded by folding chairs. Katherine counted fourteen men seated there, though they stood up respectfully when Calabrease walked in. He didn't sit down, but motioned for the rest of them to do so, instead electing to stand at the head of the table, his hands clasped behind his back. His second in command stood a few yards away.

"Gentlemen, this is a friend of mine," he spoke, motioning to Katherine. His voice echoed through the huge room. "She's here about the mole. I know not all of you have been in on the hunt for this rat, but that was for security purposes. I'm sure you understand." Calabrease paused. "If the rat would like to give himself up before the rest of the theatrics, that would be greatly appreciated. And…rewarded," Calabrease said. Katherine gathered from that that the guilty man's death would be quick rather than long and drawn out from his betrayal. No one stood up, though, so Calabrease turned to Katherine.

"How do you do your work?" he asked.

"In silence," she answered, taking the seat at the head of the table. No one said anything else after that.

She spreads her feelers out through the men, searching for guilt, anxiety, fear, or a combination of them. Goosebumps spread over her arms at the crimes she feels these men had committed. Intimidation. Assault. Murder. Two men are just muscle, some work racketeering, prostitution, gambling, extortion....

They're all worried. They don't know what Katherine is doing aside from slowly moving her eyes from one of them to the next. Could be a scare tactic. Could be something serious. Fear for their very lives is not plentiful, but they have small secrets. One runs a gambling racket on the side that he hasn't told his boss about and it's quite profitable. The second has been dabbling in selling drugs for some extra cash, which Calabrease has forbidden.

Then oddness. A slippery, unsure character. It solidifies, though, and Katherine examines the personality and structure of the man. Nervous like the others, but a good employee, loyal to Calabrease, and confident in his abilities.

Katherine didn't let her eyes linger on the guilty man any more than the others. After she'd gone over all of them, she stood back up, looking back to Calabrease. "You've got a problem," she told him.

He cocked an eyebrow. "Oh?"

"If you've got a mole, he isn't in this room. But you've got one guy running drugs, which apparently you're not keen on? You might want to get on top of that."

"Which man?" Calabrease asked, his jaw clenching.

Katherine shook his head. "That was just a bonus. I'm not signing a death warrant if I don't have to. But I don't like knowing that coke is circulating the high schools thanks to some jackass here. Now that you know, either he'll drop the side business or he'll keep going and you'll catch him."

Calabrease's gaze raked over his men, hesitating before he nodded. "Fine," he said curtly. "Everyone here can go about their day," he spoke loudly to the rest of the men. He turned and walked from the room, prompting Lazos to follow him, and Katherine took that as a cue to follow them both.

———❈———

Finally back at home base at the Los Angeles FBI Headquarters, Katherine walked down the short hallway to the security guard in front of the large door that led to the LA FBI's Evidence Control Unit. She handed over her ID and badge and he glanced at it before scanning it into the computer, which beeped once, and then handed it back. She had put the envelope that contained her $10,000 payment in a plastic evidence bag as soon as she had driven a few miles from where Lazos had dropped her off, and now handed it over to the guard.

The bag was labeled it with a sticker that read LATENT, letting the evidence technicians know to check the bills and envelope for prints. Katherine had purposefully not taken the money out of the envelope when Calabrease had handed it over, giving the impression that she assumed he hadn't shorted her, but mostly to not handle the cash unnecessarily. Before she'd come down to the ECU, Katherine had submitted all the appropriate electronic paperwork on the incident with Calabrease, and she also now handed over a few stapled papers to the guard. It sometimes felt like paperwork, on actual paper or on her computer, was half her job. Apparently, if it wasn't written down in at least three different places, it hadn't actually happened.

Once she was finished, Katherine headed toward the other side of the building and over to Jackson's office. Katherine knocked on his door, not waiting for an answer before she opened it. She glanced at the few boxes that were still half-empty around the room and several bookshelves that were already full, and then over to him.

Jackson was sitting in his desk chair, leaned over a large box and with a pile of papers in his lap. Looking up to her, his eyes widened. "To what do I owe this pleasant surprise?" Jackson asked. He put the papers aside and stood up, his six-foot-six frame a considerable presence in the room.

"A tip and a bribe," she replied, sitting in one of the chairs in front of Jackson's desk.

"You spoil me."

"I just stopped at Evidence to drop off ten grand that Frank Calabrease paid me to tell him who of his employees is the mole currently digging him a nice deep grave."

Jackson cocked an eyebrow. "You went and got drafted by Frank Calabrease," he repeated as he slowly sat back down behind his desk, "to find a mole."

Katherine nodded once. "And I found him. I would've checked in with you first, but it was a matter of safety for a civilian. It's all in my report. Once I was in, I didn't want to risk contact until I was free of Calabrease. Anyway, he doesn't know I found the mole. I'm sure he'll call it in as soon as he's got a free moment, but the LA gang unit should know about it ASAP. It's not just an informant; it's a Bureau agent. He was given a solid identity, I couldn't get past it, and I only figured out he was the fake because of my extensive experience with psychic covers. Don't know why they started a mole hunt, but we should get him out of there. Calabrease will probably try again."

"Yeah, I'll say," Jackson muttered. "I'll get the tip over to Gangs pronto."

"Good," Katherine said. "Make it anonymous? As much good as that'll do. I used Kathy Moore from Sacramento, but I am local, so even in a city of four million, this could mean trouble eventually. And Moore is probably burned."

"Of course. And I'll stay in the loop with gangs about anything going on with Calabrease. He ain't gonna be happy when he figures out you screwed him."

Katherine chuckled and shook her head. "Serves him right for not properly vetting the help."

"Sure, but I doubt he'll see it that way," Jackson said. "So you get everything wrapped up with ECU?"

Katherine gave a mock sigh, pushing herself to her feet. "Of course. No good deed goes unpunished. All the paperwork is on Sentinel waiting your approval. But that's not the only reason I'm here. Also, this is for you," she said with a smile, handing him the plastic grocery bag. "For your new office."

Jackson curiously took out his gift, his face softening into a wide smile at the custom nameplate for his desk. "You know, they give me one of these. You don't gotta bring your own. They even nail it right to the door for you."

"Well, tough luck, cause once they dig your name into that, you can't return it," Katherine told him. "You'll just have to deal."

"Thank you, Katherine," Jackson said as he placed it at the edge of his desk, in front of some picture frames.

"You're welcome."

"How's your move-in going?" he asked.

"Pretty well," Katherine replied. "All of the important stuff was unpacked right away, and we've still got a few boxes here and there, but it's starting to feel like home. How about you? How's the zoo adjusting?"

Jackson smiled at Katherine's affectionate term for his pets. His house was home to a ball python named Venus, two cats named Gilbert and Charlie, a red ackie named Arnold, and a dozen fish of various species, including Alexandra's favorite, a small catfish she'd gotten him a few years back for his birthday and dubbed Kitty.

"They're adjusting pretty good," he answered. "Charlie and Gilbert are having the hardest time, obviously, but they've got all their toys and such, so they settled in fine eventually. Hey, before I forget, you pick a probie yet?" he asked, sitting up straighter.

"I've got two or three in mind. I'll start the vetting process soon."

"Looking forward to it?"

Working her mouth a bit, Katherine shrugged. "I guess."

"Hey, don't you gimme that," Jackson told her with a shake of his head. "You had a hell of a partner to work with when you hit twenty-one, and you damn well better put your heart into this."

Katherine smiled. "Yes, sir." Jackson's face split into a gentle smile and he made a shooing motion with his hand. She left, shutting the door to his office behind her.

CHAPTER 13

THE FOREST IS QUIET, BUT *alive. The wind rustles gently through the brush around him and strokes his fur, bringing him the scents of the territory. The smell of the pack is long gone. He gathers instead the smell of others, the prey. The rabbit, the deer, the fox.*

He runs.

The forest is his territory. All of it. He rules over the acres with strength that can take down anything in his path. His paws hit the ground rhythmically and propel him forward with a graceful strength, leaping over fallen trees and easily descending or ascending steep hills.

Coming to an abrupt halt, he catches a scent. A meal cooked by humans. It's burned flesh, but it's prey that has been caught and slaughtered for him already. He bolts forward, darting through the trees, leaping smoothly over a bush as he goes, and following the scent that was as apparent to him as if it were a path of neon lights. He comes to a slow stop eventually, his head lowering to the ground as he gradually moves in on his target.

There are two humans. They move about so clumsily. His eyes take in the scene in front of him, easily discerning his surroundings in the dark, and with annoyance he realizes they've finished the meal. The wonderful smell of cooked meat is fading, and the flesh he had wanted so dearly to dine upon has gone. All that are left are scraps.

But there is more. The humans will give more meat for him than their puny meals anyhow.

Without hesitation, he bolts forward and ignores the scream from the female human as he attacks the male, his teeth sinking into his prey's throat as he crashes to the ground. He tears out the flesh, blood pouring out into his mouth and across the ground, and the human flails helplessly, his attempts to survive desperate and futile. The wolf turns on the female then, who is already running, and he jumps, his teeth sinking into her shoulder and ripping out a wonderfully fresh mouthful of meat.

He devours his prey.

⸎

Alexandra sat in class at her new school, her eyes occasionally sliding around to the other students, taking notes every once in a while as her teacher went over that day's topic. At her old school most of the other kids in her class had thought she was weird. Knowing things without being told them? Random absences with no explanation behind them? Having some kind of seizure-like headache in class? She was never the cool kid. And she'd grown up there, so even in the large schools of the highly populated city San Diego, everyone pretty much knew who she was within the first year.

However, over the past few years, increasing her martial arts training as she grew older, she started carrying herself with more confidence. It seemed that somehow the other kids at her old school had picked up on that. And one particular fight during recess didn't help her image much. Or maybe it did, depending on how she looked at it. At her new school in Los Angeles though, the other kids had easily gotten comfortable enough around Alexandra to just treat her as the average weird kid, so to speak. And that was, oddly enough, a role she was happy to slip back into.

Which made it somewhat irritating when she ran into a werewolf on the way to the bathroom.

Alexandra glanced at the clock when she got up and left the classroom, grabbing the pass from the hook on the wall as she went, and headed down the hall. A young woman came out of the main office, speaking to the secretary, and Alexandra froze almost in mid-step.

Wild, a breath of fresh air, strong and powerful, and yet a part of her that is soft and gentle. Wolf slides through her veins.

The woman seemed to sense someone was staring at her and looked around, sliding her gaze over to Alexandra, her eyes locking on her. She didn't falter in the conversation she was having with the secretary, though, looking back to her after a moment as if nothing had happened.

Alexandra slowly started to continue down the hall, her eyes staying on the young woman as she turned the corner, the hair on the back of her neck prickling a bit as she ducked into the empty bathroom. A werewolf wasn't necessarily danger, of course, but as a general rule, they didn't hang around public schools. If there was a werewolf on public school property, it was possible she was looking for trouble, but her demeanor with the secretary hadn't given that impression. The only thing that irritated Alexandra was that she'd been caught staring.

Then Alexandra's eyes widened when she felt the young woman walking toward the bathroom. She slid her hand over the knife in the back pocket of her jeans to assure herself that she had a way of protecting herself if the woman became a threat, and she went over to the sink, turning on the water and quickly washing her hands.

The door opened and the woman let it close behind her, staring at Alexandra with a single cocked eyebrow. Alexandra looked over to her, drying her hands with a paper towel, carefully avoiding meeting the woman's eyes, her spine stiff but to all appearances looking relaxed. Alexandra put the werewolf's visual age at around thirty, and as she examined the young woman's light brown skin and her thick brown, wavy hair, she guessed the woman had Native American heritage. Her outfit of tan pants and a long-sleeved blue shirt was clean and presentable, but her worn hiking boots indicated that she preferred to be high in the mountains of California rather than at a stylish, pricey restaurant. She wore no earrings or bracelets, not uncommon for werewolves if only for convenience, though a gold chain hung around her neck, on the end of which Alexandra happened to know was her wedding ring.

"You weren't just staring at me cause you didn't recognize me, were you?" the woman murmured.

Alexandra blinked innocently. "Why are you here?"

"Kinda private business. My name's Allison. Allison Thatcher."

Alexandra nodded. "I'm Alex. Nice to meet you Allison Allison Thatcher."

Allison smiled at that and paused for a long moment. "You're very tense, but at the same time you're relaxed. And I have a feeling if I were to attack, you would attack back."

Once she said that, Alexandra dropped all pretense of being the innocent sixteen-year-old, smoothly snatching the small HideAway blade from the sheath in her back pocket.

"Guess that answers that question," Allison murmured. "A knife on school grounds? A little risky, isn't it?"

"Not as risky as not having one."

"Didn't expect a kid here to know what I can do."

"I'm a psychic," Alexandra muttered. "So yeah, my feelers can tell that you're a werewolf."

Allison smiled. "That's what you call them? Feelers? Like an ant?" she asked. Alexandra didn't respond. "I'm not going to change and attack you," Allison told her, exasperated.

"Werewolves aren't hired as teachers and can't attend public high schools, which means you don't have a kid here, so sue me for being suspicious of you following me into a bathroom," Alexandra told her.

"Come on. If you're a powerful enough psychic to know I'm wolf, then you're powerful enough to feel that I don't mean you any harm. Go ahead," the werewolf told her, tapping her right temple a few times.

Alexandra raised an eyebrow at the stranger giving her the go-ahead for a thorough lie-detection test. But she reached further into Allison's mind and motives, and after a few more long seconds she slid her knife back in her pocket.

"I'm just here to talk to the principal and sign some paperwork. It's about a member of my pack. My mate and I are the pack leaders in Los Angeles. Do you have a relative who's a tracker?" she asked. Alexandra remained silent. "I'm hoping...you won't tell them. Because I'm keeping everything in order and just don't want to make any trouble."

Alexandra shook her head. "She wouldn't make trouble."

Allison hesitated. "You seem sure about that."

"I am." Alexandra paused. "When do you shift?"

"When I have to. Once a month, my body changes—."

"Completely to a wolf, on the first night of menstruation, accounting for mass, your human consciousness just slightly able to give impressions to the wolf," Alexandra finished.

Allison lifted her chin a bit, apparently impressed, before she nodded. "Yeah."

"Only when you have to?" Alexandra repeated.

Allison hesitated and nodded. "Yeah. I had a bad day once...so I went running. But that was it."

Alexandra had found that out already, with a cursory exploration of Allison's mind. It had only been the one time, a bad day, as she'd said, that she'd slipped up. What Alexandra had wondered was whether the werewolf would tell the truth if she'd asked.

The door suddenly opened and a girl Alexandra vaguely recognized walked in. The girl smiled and Alexandra smiled back as she started some small talk with Allison.

Once the girl was gone, Allison resumed their conversation. "So. Are you going to tell your...?" She let her voice trail off.

"Mother," Alexandra decided to answer.

"Mother. You going to tell her?"

Alexandra hesitated, not because she was deciding

whether she was going to tell Katherine, but whether she was going to tell this young woman the truth. "Yeah," she finally answered. "My mom'll probably like to meet you, but it won't be to make trouble. Seriously. It just seems to me like you could use some help."

Allison nodded once in acknowledgment. Alexandra sensed anxiety in her, but the alpha in her wouldn't let it show. She was strong, protective, and on a mission here. "All right," Allison finally spoke quietly.

Alexandra nodded slowly before nodding toward one of the stalls. "Well, I'm sorry to be blunt, but...I did actually come here to use the bathroom."

CHAPTER 14

THAT THURSDAY NIGHT, KATHERINE, ALEXANDRA, and Rebecca enjoyed what Alexandra knew was a rare occasion of Katherine being home from work to all have dinner together, making small talk about their day's events. Eventually Alexandra noticed a lull in the conversation and spoke up.

"So I met an alpha werewolf of LA at school today," Alexandra stated.

Katherine coughed out an astonished breath into her grape juice, choking on it slightly, and cleared her throat before glaring at Alexandra, who smiled back at her. "You did that on purpose."

"Maybe," she murmured.

Katherine paused. "Huh. An alpha at your school?" she echoed. "Allison or Joshua?"

"Allison."

"And you talked to her?"

Alexandra nodded again and explained what had happened. "She seems like a good person. And she was telling the truth about the fact that she was doing the right thing, whatever she was doing. But...she is hiding something and she could use some help. I didn't dig that much, though, so I'm not sure with what."

"All right, well, I'll go talk to her tomorrow," Katherine said, nodding. "See if there's anything I can do. I wanted to get in contact with the local alphas anyway. It could come in handy to have already met them."

"Alpha is a Greek letter," Rebecca stated as she walked into the kitchen. She sat down at her place at the dinner table. "How can you be a letter? Who is an alpha?"

"A leader in a werewolf pack is an alpha," Katherine explained as Rebecca started in on her spaghetti. "There are alphas in every city."

"Werewolves scare me," Rebecca said quietly. "I don't like dogs either. I can't tell what they're thinking. Their thoughts are jumbled and messy."

Katherine smiled just slightly as Alexandra snorted. "Have you ever met a werewolf?"

Rebecca put her fork down, pausing, before shaking her head. "No. So werewolves don't scare me. Just the concept of werewolves scares me."

"It's an important distinction," Katherine noted.

"True," Rebecca said with a nod. "If you work with werewolves, I suppose they can't be that dangerous."

"See, if everyone could be as reasonable as you, we'd have a lot fewer problems," Katherine murmured.

After dinner, Katherine went down to Rebecca's room, where the teenager was emptying one of her last boxes, carefully placing a ceramic elephant on her bookshelf. "I wrote down my schedule for you and left it there on my desk," Rebecca spoke. "You said we could put it on the wall."

"I remember," Katherine replied. "I'll type it up and put it on the fridge tonight. By the way, Alex likes to head out to the library or down to hang out at the La Brea Tar Pits, if you'd like to accompany her."

"That sounds nice," Rebecca said. "I like going to the park. There's a lot of grass there and it feels cool on my hands. And Alex is nice."

Katherine nodded. "She is. Finds her fair share of trouble, though," she muttered with an exasperated smile.

Katherine took some sheets from one of Rebecca's boxes and opened up a pillowcase. Once she had put the pillows in and put the fitted sheet on, Rebecca suddenly took the other sheet from her hands. "I'll make my bed," Rebecca told her.

Katherine's eyebrows rose as the teenager spread the sheet across the bed. "Sounds good. I'm sure you have a certain way you like to do it, right?"

"Right," she answered with a nod.

Katherine gave her another smile. "Well...I know you don't know me very well, but if you ever want to talk...I'm here."

"Ronald said talking is good," Rebecca told her. "So I'll talk to you about how I'm feeling. And I know you're worried about me because I don't have Ronald anymore, so I'll make sure to talk to you about that too."

"That's good. That makes me happy. And I should get a call from that friend of mine about a security job tomorrow," she continued as Rebecca tucked the sheet under the mattress. "Remember what I said about that?"

"You said, 'Rebecca, you're not allowed to break laws. If you need or want to go somewhere restricted online, you need to get permission from the FBI,'" she echoed. "'I will not have a SWAT team breaking down my front door because you hacked into the Pentagon.' And I told you I don't know how to hack into the Pentagon."

Katherine's mouth split into a grin. "Exactly. So we'll make sure you have plenty to do to keep you busy."

"I like that plan," Rebecca told her. "I don't like breaking laws, but sometimes I do it when I don't mean to. It's just a place and I just go there because I can. Ronald got mad at me when I did that. He was worried I was going to get in trouble."

"We'll make sure that doesn't happen," Katherine told her. She watched as Rebecca carefully spread the quilt on the bed, folding it down just so. She then pulled the sheet down over it, smoothing it and examining it to ensure it was symmetrical. Katherine took a slow breath. "Rebecca…I was hoping to talk to you about your past," she said. "Because I know your last name isn't Wilson."

Rebecca paused for a moment before continuing to tuck her sheet and quilt under her mattress. "My name is Rebecca Wilson," she objected.

"Not legally," Katherine murmured. "And I get the feeling that you have something in your past that Ronald got you and him away from. Something he told you to never, ever talk about," she said. Rebecca continued to ignore her. "And that's okay. But I want you to know that I want to keep you safe. I'll be warding against scrying spells for people trying to find you, and we'll make sure you keep a low profile. But if you ever think I should know something about your past, you can tell me. You can trust me."

Rebecca snapped her fingers for a few moments as she walked around to the other side of her bed. "My name is Rebecca Wilson," she repeated, her voice quieter this time.

Katherine let out a long breath and nodded. "Okay."

CHAPTER 15

KATHERINE EXITED THE ELEVATOR ON the first floor of LA's FBI headquarters and walked to her left, past security in the lobby. She nodded to the security guard she passed on her way out and went over to Allison Thatcher, who was standing near the double doors at the front.

Katherine's path toward Allison curved a bit, her posture relaxed, and she kept her gaze on Allison's chin. Allison's stance responded in kind as Katherine offered her hand in greeting.

"Hi, I'm Katherine," she said with a smile. "It's nice to meet you."

"Hi," Allison said, smiling back. "Nice to meet you too. Ah, that was impressive. And polite. Not that many people take wolf manners seriously. Do you have wolf friends?"

"In my life, I've been around just about everyone at one point or another," Katherine said with a serious smile. "Speaking of, I figured I'd spare you an elevator ride and we could find a bench outside."

"You're getting brownie points all over the place," Allison said, following Katherine outside. "Alex mentioned you were a tracker when we met. She was instantly protective of herself when she realized I knew she was trained. Did you train her?"

Katherine nodded. "Yeah."

"And she's a psychic. So she inherited her abilities from you?"

"Yes. Though we do try to keep that quiet," Katherine explained, her voice subdued. "Easier for Alex to go about her life without widespread knowledge of her abilities, especially since she's still just a kid."

Allison nodded. "I understand."

Katherine and Allison sat down on a bench near a large grassy area and Katherine nodded to her. "So. You're paying visits to local schools for a reason."

At that, Allison tensed. "Yes. Do you know why?"

"Not yet." Katherine paused, waiting patiently for Allison to continue.

"I've lived in Glendora for a long time. My pack heads north to turn. There's a pup that recently joined, but during a run two days ago he shifted and...took off," Allison murmured. "I'm pretty sure he's still in the Los Angeles National Forest, but in addition to spending our time tracking him down, Joshua and I are covering our legal bases. Joshua's out there right now, but we haven't had any luck yet."

Katherine nodded. "So you're worried you're going to lose him to the wolf," she muttered.

The difficulty with new wolf pups was that they were still finding themselves, so to speak. Like teenagers. If they had a strong family, a stable pack, it was almost easy for them to manage their life as a wolf once a month. At least, easy compared to how it was if they didn't have a pack, or at least other werewolf friends. But it was important to strike a balance, to know that even though it might feel like you weren't a person anymore, that instead you were a wolf, that wasn't the case. The parasapien subconscious only needed to actually come out to play once a month. And the rest still belonged to the sapien.

"Does he have family?" Katherine asked.

Allison fell silent for a moment, staring at a spot on the ground in front of her. "A younger sister. She's still in high school. She doesn't know. He was attacked by a rogue and he didn't figure out what happened until the first time he turned," Allison muttered. "He knew that something was wrong. Something was coming. So he said he started walking to clear his mind. Just didn't stop. Eventually he got into a rural area and headed into the forest. Felt like he should. Felt right. And then later that night...." Allison let out a long breath. "He ran into our pack. It was surprising, to say the least. Finding a rogue in our territory. But I handled it. Or rather, my wolf did, with a little coaxing from my human side not to kill him."

Katherine blinked. "You handled it? So you're...?"

Allison nodded. "I'm above Joshua. I know, it's unusual," she said with a smile. "Anyway, since Devon was terrified and it was his first time shifting, his wolf submitted pretty easily and he let me take him under my wing. He's been with us for three months and I thought he was doing well, but...."

"Could he attack?" Katherine asked quietly. "If he comes upon some campers?"

Allison gnashed her teeth. "I don't know. He knows how to hunt in a pack but I don't know how he'd do without backup. So he might be hungry. He might be...confused. He and his wolf will be clashing."

Katherine pursed her lips before nodding slowly. "And your worry is that he's too far gone into the wolf to come back."

"I don't even know if he's changed back all this time," she whispered. "If he's stayed wolf...."

Katherine let the silence stretch for a moment. "Allison, you know what has to happen if he's mentally gone," she told her. "If he attacks someone, they won't be able to fend him off because they won't be packing silver, so it would be my job to take him down."

"No," Allison said tightly. She looked up to Katherine, not quite meeting her gaze. "It's my job. If I failed as his alpha, if there's no other choice...I'll do it."

———— ✦ ————

Short of pleasantries, Katherine remained silent in the car after Allison Thatcher picked her up in her Jeep. They were headed to the area of forest just east of Lancaster that, through her research and an extensive amount of time on Google Maps and a moderate amount of scouting from Joshua and several other wolves, Allison had predicted Devon would currently be cutting through. Or if they'd missed him, she would be able to pick up his scent and determine how long ago he'd passed through. Katherine had a pack full of camping supplies in case they had trouble tracking Devon, enough for a few days or so, which she would share with Allison. Allison couldn't bring any supplies herself, as it would be difficult to carry a backpack in her wolf form.

"So. Two days," Katherine murmured after about an hour of silence.

Allison tensed. "Yeah."

"What are your expectations? Did you know him well enough to make a prediction?"

"Not really. Only known him a couple months. And the fact that he hadn't been educated on this life for that long…I really am worried that he's too far gone."

"If you can take him down, we can restrain him," Katherine told her. "Take him back to your place. Wait for him to shift back."

"He won't," Allison said. "If he's too far gone to shift back with me there and a gun in his face…he's too far gone," she whispered.

Katherine sighed softly, staring at Allison's tight, tired expression. She fell quiet for a little while longer until Allison spoke up again. "How long have you been tracking?" she asked.

"Ah…technically? Since I was about fourteen."

"What?" Allison asked, glancing to her.

"Legally, since I was twenty-four," Katherine continued.

Allison stared at the road in front of her, sparing a glance to Katherine. "Were your parents also–?"

"My parents were gone," she muttered. "My dad left, I barely remember him, and when I was ten, my mom…."

Allison chewed on her lower lip for a few seconds. "If you don't want to–"

"It's not important," Katherine muttered. The two lapsed into silence and Katherine kept her gaze staring steadily out the car window.

CHAPTER 16

KATHERINE TOOK HER HIKING PACK from the back of the car and shut the trunk door.

"So, I don't suppose you've ever actually had a werewolf as a sidekick?" Allison asked with a grin.

Katherine grinned back at her. "Other parasapiens and the occasional werewolf, yeah, but a wolf in wolf form? No, this is new. You ever done this before?"

Allison shook her head. "Not really. My wolf's been around the pack when they were still in human form, but no one else. And since she's much more satisfied hunting rabbits and running with the rest of the pack, she never goes near humans that are camping, on the off chance there's someone nearby."

"That's what I've heard about most of your kind," Katherine replied.

They walked about half a mile into the forest before Allison looked around, stretched, and nodded. "Okay. I think we're good." She looked to Katherine. "You sure you want to do this?"

"Ask me in five minutes," she replied.

Allison shook her head. "You're the most open-minded

tracker I've ever met," she muttered. At that, Allison slipped out of her sneakers and jeans and pulled her shirt over her head, putting them in the plastic bag she'd taken with her, followed by her underwear. Katherine averted her eyes a bit to allow for some modesty, even though she knew that this was commonplace in werewolf culture since naked was kind of the norm when you ran around as a wolf. But she couldn't help looking back when Allison started to shift.

Kneeling down with a long breath out and a slight grimace, Allison's bones rippled under her skin with an uncomfortable sound, like cracking knuckles, as her hair melted back into her skin like it was un-growing and dog hair sprouted all over her body. Her arms and legs reallocated their mass in a flowing process and within about twenty seconds Katherine found herself staring at a beautiful light gray wolf with a white oval of fur on her stomach.

Katherine kept her stance relaxed and her gaze away from Allison's eyes as the wolf's ears twitched forward toward this fascinating creature that it was rarely exposed to. "So. Friends?" Katherine asked, reaching out toward her with her feelers.

The sensation is odd. The wolf is clear, but the sapien impresses her feelings. Comrade, the sapien tells the wolf gently. The wolf wags her tail a few times. She understands. She approves. Pack. Pack pup is near. Needs to come home. Her nose sniffs the air, dismissing the human as she looks around, her posture straightening. Rabbit. Coyote. Mountain lion. Territorialism is sharp in her mind. She puts her nose to the ground and walks to the left, then sniffs the air a bit more.

"You got something, Lassie?" Katherine muttered,

walking after her as she continued. The wolf paid her no mind and abruptly took off.

Katherine picked up her pace as she followed after Allison, but going quickly through a forest wasn't like traversing a hiking trail. Her hiking boots were solid and she watched her steps, but would've easily fallen behind if the werewolf hadn't stopped occasionally. When the wolf started to get out of eyeshot from Katherine, she came to a halt, looking back and waiting like any dog on a hike with her master. Though she seemed a bit impatient with the comparably sluggish two-legged animal following her.

They kept going for about an hour and then Katherine needed to take a break. She took a long drink of water and poured some into a bowl she'd brought for Allison, which the wolf lapped up eagerly. Then they continued on. It was about three hours and two more breaks later that Allison suddenly stopped. Her body tensed more than it had been before and her tail wagged just slightly. Katherine reached out mentally and her eyes widened, realizing that Devon was just a few hundred yards from them.

Wolf pup. They are downwind. She stops and she looks around, takes a deep breath of the air, the smells, her gaze alert. Walks slowly toward the pup. Her muscles tense, she is ready to move, ready to react to however the pup responds to her appearance, as they get closer.

And then suddenly, there he was. A dark gray wolf, lying on the ground, about midway through eating a rabbit he'd caught. The motion of Allison approaching caught his eye and he quickly rose into a crouch, his hackles rising, before he recognized her. He then settled a bit, though he backed up a few steps, lowering his head and cocking it a bit at Katherine's presence. He was confused at her arrival. But then he gathered himself and his posture relaxed more, trusting his superior.

His demeanor is friendly and he quickly goes to his rabbit and grabs it in his powerful jaws, bringing it over to the alpha, putting it at her feet. She is alpha, so she can have it. She can leave him what she wishes.

But Allison would have none of it. Her posture was angry and she snapped at him. Katherine grimaced as Devon flinched, backpedaling and scowling in confusion. Katherine felt the human side of Allison pressure the wolf and she shifted back, now towering over Devon. He lay down, rolling over on his back and exposing his stomach to her, apologizing for whatever he had done wrong.

"Don't give me that," Allison growled at him, a bit of her wolf giving her voice a deeper timbre. "You ran off from the pack. You know you get one night a month. You know how this works. Don't play dumb."

Devon slowly got back to his feet, taking a few uneasy steps back as a low, rumbling growl slid out of his throat.

Don't want to go back. Don't want the human life. The human doesn't want the human life. His eyes slide to the new female human. His emotions turn bitter. Angry. Alpha wants to be this other thing. Wants him to be this other thing. Wolf is better. Wolf is free. Hunt and run and live and sleep and the forest was our whole life. How could she want to walk on two legs? To live in a world that wasn't made for them?

"You are not a wolf," Allison muttered, seeing Devon's resentment for Katherine. "You are part wolf. The human owns that body. You're just renting it out." Devon's hackles started to rise again. "Shift back. Shift back to human now, Devon," she told him, taking a few steps toward him.

Devon took a few steps backward in reaction, growling again.

"He's not going to do it," Katherine muttered. Speaking prompted Devon to flick his dark eyes to her instead. "He doesn't want to go back."

Allison kept her gaze on him resolutely. "I am your alpha and you will listen to me," she spoke, the words just an emphasis of her posture.

Suddenly Devon snarled at her, pulling his lips back to reveal his teeth, prompting Allison to immediately do the same.

Who is she to order him around? The other thing? The human part? His human is gone. His human had bled into his wolf and is no more. Because he enjoyed the wolf more. He wanted to be the wolf more. A runner, an animal, a hunter. No master. Just him. Killing. Feasting. Humans are weak. He killed two so easily. So weak.

"Oh god," Katherine breathed.

And suddenly Devon leapt at Allison, jaw opening and snapping at her, and she swiped her arm at him, smacking him with a hard force that propelled him into the ground. But he just rolled over once before he jumped to his feet again, crouching his hind legs to leap at her again as Allison's wolf pulled at her to turn, to be able to defend herself properly.

Katherine drew her gun from her holster. And as he leapt, she pulled the trigger.

The wolf let out one short whimper and fell to the ground, tumbling a few times limply. Allison let out a wail that echoed out from her wolf into a howl, taking a few steps and falling to his side. She took in and let out short, sobbing breaths.

"No…. Why didn't you listen to me?" she breathed, crouching down and nuzzling her nose in his fur. "You stupid…stupid pup…."

"He killed two campers, Allison," Katherine muttered.

Allison stilled and choked out a sob.

Devon slowly shifted back to human, and Allison leaned forward and laid her forehead against his shoulder. She took a few shaky breaths, sobbing as she slid her hand down his arm, interlocking her fingers in his.

Katherine swallowed, putting her gun back in her holster. It was rare to feel this guilty after killing a werewolf that needed killing, but as an alpha, Allison had developed an attachment to Devon. A pack member quickly became family and a family member that she couldn't save was devastating. And yet Katherine knew Allison couldn't be angry, knowing what Devon had done and what he would have done in the future. Knowing that there was no going back for one of their kind after murder.

Katherine didn't move for a long while, allowing Allison the time she needed. To feel tired and empty, to stare at the inside of her eyelids before she gradually forced herself to remove her hand from that of her dead pack mate and push herself to her feet. She paced back and forth a few times, as if she had a sudden urge to turn and run, forget everything, but then she took a breath and settled down. Katherine pulled back mentally from Allison, feeling like she was prying as she felt overwhelmed with the woman's grief. Allison looked over to Katherine, tears sliding down her cheeks.

"I'm sorry," Katherine whispered. Allison nodded slowly, walking over and taking the plastic bag containing her clothes as Katherine offered it to her. Then Katherine took her cell phone from her pocket and dialed the second number on speed dial. "Hey. I need some backup and an M.E.," she murmured. "I just killed a werewolf in the Los Angeles National Park. I can give you coordinates."

Katherine finished briefing the first police officer that had been sent out to the park to secure the crime scene just before several other police cars and various FBI agents, including a coroner's van and CSU among others, started arriving. As a tracker, Katherine handled any cases involving parasapiens, but there was a significant amount of cooperation with local police departments for various reasons. She'd had a pretty good working relationship with San Diego PD and knew it would take a while before she started to know officers in Los Angeles by name. The fact was, though, that killing a werewolf in a case that was pretty much tied up in a bow was a good introduction. It was an unfortunate and macabre fact, but it was true.

Allison was sitting on a nearby bench talking to someone on her phone and Katherine waited out of earshot, giving her some privacy until she ended the call.

"Was that Joshua?" Katherine asked as she took a seat beside Allison.

"Yeah."

Allison stared at the crime scene technicians and

Katherine followed her gaze, realizing that they had come out of the forest with the gurney that held Devon's body in a black body bag. The two young men carrying it extended the wheels underneath and rolled it over to the M.E. van.

"You doing okay?" Katherine muttered.

"I think so. I just…his sister is going to be devastated," she whispered, still staring at the van. "I've done it before and every time I hope it's the last. And it never is." Katherine nodded slowly. "Do you think werewolves go to heaven?" Allison asked suddenly.

Katherine blinked. "Ah, that's a bit of a loaded question. I don't think heaven exists."

Allison tore her eyes from the crime scene techs and looked to Katherine. "Really?"

"Yeah. I pretty much think this is it," Katherine said with a shrug. "No heaven. No god. All we've got is each other."

"That's kind of scary," Allison mused.

"Maybe. But I think it makes this life a lot more special. Since it's the only one we get."

"It's just sad to me that if that's the case, Devon wasted the only life he had. I do think he's in heaven," she murmured, looking back to the M.E. van as the doors were shut, locking his corpse inside. "That he got a second chance. And that the gods will help him make peace with his wolf. At least, I hope so."

"Allison, that would be his third chance," Katherine told her. "His second came from you, when you found him that night." Allison's gaze slid down to the ground. "You are a great alpha. And you did the best you could to help him. I hope you know that."

Allison swallowed hard and paused for a long moment. "Yeah. Yeah, I guess I do." Her gaze flicked to Katherine's momentarily. "Thanks." Katherine nodded in silent reply.

A while later, the M.E. van left, the officer Katherine had been chatting with gave her a nod before leaving in his cruiser with his partner, and the two were left alone. Katherine leaned back against the bench, letting the momentary stillness and peace of the forest wash over them. They sat in silence for about ten minutes, an empathetic, comfortable silence that only wolf culture could create, before Allison finally got up and Katherine followed her back to the car.

CHAPTER 17

ALEXANDRA WAS WALKING DOWN THE hall of her
school, going to grab some books from her locker
before heading home, when she felt eyes on her back and
stopped, turning around.

A girl about Alexandra's age had been staring at her
and slowed her pace as she'd walked by, but when she was
caught she quickly looked away and walked the remaining
steps to her locker. Alexandra walked toward her, looking
the girl over, realizing that she recognized her. She wore
blue jeans and a t-shirt with a design embroidered in
sequins, matching dangly earrings that sparkled under
her shiny black hair, and had a manicure with pink nail
polish, a getup that gave her an ability to blend in among
other girls their age that Alexandra severely lacked. Not to
mention that her manicure was still impeccable, which was
impressive to Alexandra, who remembered getting one for
a wedding a few years ago and managing to make it about
five minutes before ruining it.

"Hey. I've only been going here for like a few weeks.
Usually takes longer for people to start staring," Alexandra
noted.

The girl looked back to her, her eyes wide. "Hi," the girl said quietly.

"We met," Alexandra said with a smile, shifting her backpack on her shoulders. "Well. Ish. I remember you staying pretty quiet as your mom attempted to ream me out about the company I keep."

"She's not like that," the girl protested. "I mean…she is, but…."

"But she's your mom," Alexandra murmured. She shrugged. "Whatever." She stuck her hand out. "Alex."

"Jessica," the girl replied, shaking Alexandra's hand tentatively. "So…you really…all that stuff you said…."

"Yeah, my mom feels better knowing I can protect myself," Alexandra said. "And so do I, of course."

"So you've, like, met nonhumans and stuff," Jessica said, obviously fascinated by the topic. "Not just the girl at the library."

"Yeah. But the word they're actually using now is 'parasapien', not 'nonhuman'. Cause, I mean, they are human."

Jessica blinked. "What do you mean?"

"Genetically. They're human. They're just different. I mean, sapiens can have babies with parasapiens, so we almost have to be the same species. It's surprising how many people don't realize that." Jessica looked confused and a bit thoughtful at this. "But yeah, my mom actually has a good friend who's a pùca who lives in San Diego," Alexandra replied. "And she works with parasapiens for her job all the time."

"Wow," Jessica breathed, her eyes wide. "I've just seen them on TV. Hey, I was gonna go get some ice cream on the way home. You want to come?"

"You sure your mom would approve with you hanging out with a delinquent like me?" Alexandra asked.

Jessica scoffed. "She doesn't have to know."

Alexandra nodded, grinning. "All right. I'm always up for ice cream."

CHAPTER 18

CALABREASE LOOKED UP AT THE knock on his office door. "Yeah," he called out. The door opened and Rick Lazos entered. Calabrease sat back in his chair, staring at Lazos. "You don't look happy," he muttered.

"No sir," he answered quietly, slowly lowering himself into the chair opposite Calabrease's desk. Lazos hesitated. "Colt is in the wind."

Calabrease shut his eyes and slowly lowered his face into his hands. He rubbed at his eyes and shoved himself to his feet abruptly, and Lazos barely managed to keep himself from flinching. "I paid that bitch ten grand...and she screws me like I'm some punk–"

"That's not it, boss," Lazos said quietly.

His face twitching with anger, Calabrease turned back to Lazos. "What do you mean, that's not it? How could one of my men turning stoolie not be it?"

"Cause he didn't turn stoolie. He was a fed."

Calabrease blanched and a long moment passed before his jaw clenched. Then he suddenly let out a morose chuckle, walking slowly over to his liquor cart, pouring himself two fingers of scotch. He looked over to Lazos, who had fallen silent. "You've been with me longer than anyone, Lazos. When was the last time I fucked up like this?"

"We had to do something," Lazos muttered. "You know we were at the end of the rope with the mole. Hey, at least he's gone."

"Yeah, and now they're gonna take down every operation they were gathering intel on," Calabrease said, shaking his head. He walked back over to his desk, sitting down, and mulled over the situation for a while. "She thinks she's so smart," he finally spoke again, drawing Lazos's gaze. Calabrease gnashed his teeth. "I don't care who the fuck she is or why she did it; nobody screws me like this. I run a business. I paid for a service. And I didn't get it." He downed the rest of his drink. "I'm getting what I paid for if it's the last thing I do."

Katherine rolled over in bed and leaned toward her bedside table with a yawn, picking up the latest book she'd been reading and opening it to the bookmark. She frowned and put the bookmark back in, though, when her cell phone rang. Recognizing the number, sitting up straighter and putting the book aside, she answered the phone.

"Yeah?"

"Katherine?" Cassandra whispered.

"Cassie. What happened?" Katherine asked.

There was a long pause before Cassandra spoke, her voice tearful. "I-I need you to come over. To-To my store."

Nearly leaving skid marks on the pavement as she came to

a stop, Katherine parked her car in a handicapped spot on the street directly in front of Altar of a Mystic. She shoved the car into park and yanked out the keys, bolting to the store and pushing the door open. The two glass cases to the right of the register had been smashed, but that was all the damage Katherine could see. Her hand twitched toward the gun in her holster, but she didn't draw it, sensing that the coast was clear.

"Cassie, you okay?" Katherine asked, walking quickly around the counter. Cassandra sat on the floor, her knees up to her chest, staring at the floor, her face stained with tears. Bruises had started to form on her face where she'd been hit. "Shit," Katherine muttered. She went to the young woman, kneeling beside her.

"They're long gone," Cassandra muttered.

"Cassandra, I am so sorry. I never should have–"

"I went along with it," Cassandra interrupted her. "And for good reason. There's a man alive right now because Calabrease hired you, isn't there?"

Katherine stared at Cassandra silently for a long moment. "An FBI agent, actually. Even still. This shouldn't have happened."

Cassandra blinked, still not meeting Katherine's gaze. "I told them, Katherine. I told them who you are. I'm sorry."

Katherine didn't react for a long moment. "And the other option was, what?" she muttered. Katherine gently squeezed Cassandra's shoulder. "Don't you dare feel guilty, Cassie. I can take care of myself. All right?" Cassandra remained silent. "Come on. We'll go in and I'll take your statement."

"No," she murmured. "I'm not pressing charges."

Katherine stared at her. "Did you recognize who it was?" Cassandra just stared. "Was it Calabrease himself?"

"No."

"It was Lazos."

Cassandra finally looked up to Katherine. "I'm not getting into this any further," she whispered. "They won't come back here. For anything. This place is toxic now that they know about you, and that's all I could hope for."

"They'll know you can be intimidated now though–," Katherine started.

"They don't know that," Cassandra told her. "Because this isn't about me anymore. It's about you." Katherine's face twitched in a grimace. "If it had been about me...I know how to protect me and mine. I don't know what I would've done if you hadn't shown up, but it wouldn't have been doing as I was told. I don't lead a carefree life, Katherine. I have trouble of my own. So this is me picking my battles."

Gnashing her teeth, Katherine nodded. "Fine. Fair enough." She motioned to Cassandra, helping her to her feet. "Let's get you cleaned up, then."

CHAPTER 19

KATHERINE FOUND A COMFORTABLE POSITION in her seat in the courtroom's witness chair and folded her hands in her lap, making sure she wasn't in a position to fidget.

The case with Arnold Pastoret and Nicholas Hubbard was a small case in the scheme of things, but Katherine knew technically it was much more than that. At least it was to the werewolf community. Because they had been running.

To a sapien, running was something you did for exercise. A chore. Few actually enjoyed it for its own sake. To a werewolf, it was like a breath of fresh air in a claustrophobic world. It was their safe place, their place to be free, their place to let out part of themselves that was caged up most of their lives. The forest was a sanctuary from the rest of the world. It was a place to be that part of themselves. And these werewolves had been murdered there.

Katherine knew Nicholas had watched two of his friends die excruciating deaths from silver poisoning. When she'd first spoken to him, she'd felt his fear and his rage from when he'd attacked their killer, saving his mate

Samantha from suffering a similar fate. Even the sapien side of his mind hadn't been thinking in the slightest bit about the repercussions of attacking a sapien. Nor should he have had to. They were murdered in cold blood. All Nicholas should've had to do was explain the travesty and put Arnold Pastoret in prison. But that wasn't how these things went. Katherine still held out hope for a guilty verdict, but despite how good Jacqueline Harkins was, she knew there was a lot more to a case like this than the facts.

Arnold Pastoret's lawyer, Dennis Austin, went through a long series of basic questions before getting to the real questions, as Katherine thought of them. Most of which the jury could probably deduce the answers to on their own. That was another of the things Katherine found so frustrating about being in court. The pomp and circumstance. The procedure. The boredom of it all. But it turned out she preferred the boredom, and wished they could go back to it, once they started getting into some of the questions he had lined up.

"Several days ago, a werewolf that went rogue killed two campers in Los Angeles National Forest and you were assigned to the case, correct?" Austin asked.

Katherine tensed, but did her best not to let it show. She nodded once. "I was."

"When you found him, did you kill him?"

"Yes."

"Does the wolf in wolf form have the same mind as when they're in sapien form?" Austin asked her.

"…No," Katherine answered. "The wolf does most of the thinking."

"I'd like to direct the court to a segment from a paper

118

titled, 'Werewolf Culture: An Examination of Territory,' written by Katherine Colebrook approximately six years ago," Austin spoke, glancing to the judge, as he took a couple papers from the folder in his hand, giving them to Katherine. "Could you read the highlighted portion on the first page please?"

Katherine kept her face blank as she found the segment and read it aloud. "'When the sapien form of the werewolf is in control, the wolf gives impressions, but can rarely overrule. The case is the same when they are in wolf form; that being, the sapien mind is in the background, but rarely overrules the wolf.'"

"And please read the portion on the second page."

Katherine fought against gnashing her teeth as she flipped to the next page of the stapled papers. "'Much like Canis lupus, the werewolf is fiercely protective of their friends and family, of their pack, and of their territory. While they tend to avoid sapiens since they know they can be dangerous, if they feel threatened, they will not hesitate to attack.'"

"Thank you." Austin took the papers from Katherine, putting them back on his table, before turning back to face her. Katherine wanted desperately to snap at the lawyer that the exact point here was that they *had* been threatened, with a gun to be precise, and that's why Nicholas had attacked. But that wasn't the way things worked in court. She could very well derail the entire case if she spoke out of turn.

Austin slowly walking back over to her, hands clasped behind his back. "Are you of the opinion that my client deliberately went into werewolf territory in order to kill werewolves?" he asked

Katherine stared at him, not having been expecting such a question. It took her a moment to answer. "Yes."

"You said before that 100% of those surveyed buy silver bullets at least partially, and usually entirely, for only one purpose. To kill werewolves. Correct?"

"Yes."

"And you're aware that my client's sister was killed by a werewolf four months ago in Wisconsin?" he asked.

Katherine narrowed her eyes. "Yes."

This was part of the motive, of course, and something the federal prosecutor had made apparent. The jury couldn't know his previous crimes, including the hate crimes, but his bigotry toward werewolves after his sister's death went to motive since Katherine and Sweeney had discovered it during the course of the investigation. Katherine had a feeling that wasn't why Austin was bringing it up, though.

"So is possible that, as someone who regularly went camping, my client could have been concerned he would be the victim of a werewolf attack, and bought the silver bullets as protection?"

Katherine hesitated. "Yes."

"Werewolves have killed people before. Do their relatives always go on to become bigots who hate all werewolves?"

"...Not all of them."

"Just yes or no please," Austin told her. He didn't bother to coax her to continue. He just went on. "In fact, you are an FBI agent of high moral standing. Weren't you attacked by a werewolf as a child?"

Everything in the room seemed to slow around Katherine, and she felt like her mind had slid underwater.

The question was completely out of left field. Katherine wasn't often stunned, because she tried to know what was going on around her at all times, but in a situation like this she kept her abilities tightly constrained, especially when it came to opposing counsel. The last thing she wanted was to know something she shouldn't when her testimony on a case was at stake. So being caught completely unaware on the topic the lawyer had decided to tackle was more than just unusual; she wasn't used to it, and it was uncomfortable as all hell.

Hawkins's voice brought Katherine back to the moment. "Objection. Beyond the scope," Hawkins said, standing up and locking eyes with Katherine. Her face conveyed a sense of apology, though obviously she had nothing to apologize for, and an irritation with the opposing counsel.

"Goes directly to my client's motives, your honor," Austin told the judge.

"Overruled."

"Were you attacked by a werewolf family member as a child?"

Katherine paused, something heavy weighing on her chest. She took a deep breath against it. "Yes."

"Who?"

"It was her first time and she was drunk," Katherine muttered.

"Ms. Colebrook, please, just the question."

"…My mother." At this point, she was no longer attempting to keep eye contact with the jury or to direct her answers to them. She just stared into space.

"And do you regularly work with werewolves?"

"Yes."

"Including on that case where you had to kill a rogue werewolf last week?"

"Yes."

"Who did you work with on that case?" Austin asked.

"The pack leader of Los Angeles," Katherine answered.

Austin nodded. "No further questions, your honor."

"Special Agent Colebrook, you're dismissed."

The ending felt abrupt, but Katherine slowly got up and left the witness stand. Nicholas caught her gaze, surprise in his expression. He hadn't known her past. Not many people did, unless they knew her background as an agent. Since she was a good agent, some others were familiar with her history, and it wasn't a secret. But working with parasapiens on a daily basis didn't exactly give great opportunities to tell a story like that particular night three decades ago.

Katherine gave Nicholas a small smile as she passed him and left the courtroom.

CHAPTER 20

REESE JOHANSSON WAS JUST ABOUT to fall asleep when he was startled back to full consciousness by the sound of his front door quietly opening.

His eyes flashing open, Reese narrowed his gaze toward the open door to his bedroom as he sat up straight, unsure if he'd dreamt the sound. Then someone carefully shut the front door and there were soft, gradual steps into his apartment.

Swallowing hard, being as quiet as possible, Reese slid out of bed and grabbed his gun from his bedside table drawer, checking that it was loaded properly before leaving his bedroom. His weapon up and at the ready, Reese went slowly down the hall, hearing muffled sounds of drawers and cabinets opening. He was wearing only boxers, which meant he'd be showing off his chiseled physique to the intruder, but it wasn't as if he had time to get dressed, so he ignored the vulnerable feeling it gave him.

Reese's training at Quantico flipped through his head like he was leafing through a manual. He hadn't heard of any break-ins nearby, and his apartment, while not covered in security in the Hollywood Hills, was on the third floor of an apartment building in downtown LA that was nice enough for him to only spot a cockroach once or twice a year. Not to mention his apartment was in what he'd consider a random location, halfway down his hallway. So this was completely unexpected.

He could call for backup. But likely the intruder wouldn't be there for more than a few minutes, so that was useless. He could announce that he was armed and order the intruder to leave. But then they would get away, and could hit an apartment down the street later that night. He wouldn't risk that. He could also wait until the intruder was in his sights, and then announce that he was armed and order him or her to get on the ground. That was probably his best option.

Coming to the end of the hall, Reese considered the angle around the corner that he was supposed to take to clear the room unaided. He paused for a moment to listen for the intruder, but realized that they had fallen silent. Or more likely, they had gone into the kitchen to see if there were any items of interest in there, since the only thing in the living room of value was his flat screen, and that was screwed to the wall. Careful not to flag his gun as he raised it, Reese sidestepped to the left in a wide-angled, circular motion around the corner to clear the room.

And was promptly relieved of his weapon and kicked backwards.

The air whooshed out of Reese's lungs at the kick and he hit the wall hard as the intruder ejected the magazine from the gun to her left and popped out the round in the chamber, then tossed the gun to her right. It was a woman. One that knew how to handle a gun, definitely. As his back throbbed from the impact of the wall and he blinked his vision back into focus, Reese recognized this piece of information as important. This wasn't just some druggie looking for loose change. But she also didn't want to kill him, at least right now.

That opened the door to other possibilities. Bad ones.

Reese barely paused before lunging forward and striking out at his opponent, light on his feet and ready for her to retaliate as soon as she chose to. After a punch whizzed past her face and she parried another punch and an uppercut, Reese attempted a strike at the side of her knee. Her leg came up to meet the hit with her shin and Reese blocked a punch aimed at his face and defended himself against a swing toward his already bruised stomach, which he blocked, but barely. And in that instant, Reese realized that he was outmatched.

Immediately, the woman leapt forwards again, her leg flying up and around in a powerful kick that Reese managed to block and duck in the direction he was thrown from the force. As he turned into the spin, he snapped out his left leg and swept at the woman's ankles. She attempted to dodge him, but since she had been coming back down from the kick, he knocked her off balance. She hit the floor.

Reese flipped himself sideways to bring his right heel down on the woman's stomach, but her right arm snapped up to defend and he bounced off. He let the energy take its course and used it to propel himself back, rolling up to his feet. But the woman was incredibly fast. He barely had a chance to get himself upright before a fist rushed toward his face and cracked against his cheekbone, sending a jolt of pain and white light slamming through his skull. The force drove him around to his right and the bottom of the woman's sneaker snapped hard against his back, throwing him into the wall, and collapsing him to the floor.

Reese wheezed in a breath that sent prickly pain radiating through his chest as dots danced in front of his eyes. He was on the ground. That was very not good. At any moment, the woman would land a kick under his jaw or stomp on the back of his head, and that would be it. He needed to get back on his feet.

But all of this sunk in in the span of less than a second after he hit the floor, and the strike didn't come. By the time his muscles cooperated a full second later and he shoved himself to his feet, an eternity in a sparring match, the woman spoke.

"Point, match," she gasped, taking a few steps to her left and flicking a light switch. Reese winced at the sudden onslaught of light from the three bulbs overhead in his ceiling fan. He blinked furiously as he took advantage of the lack of aggression, filling his lungs and moving backwards to gain distance from his attacker, his hands up defensively. But it seemed as if she were no longer interested in fighting.

"FBI," the woman told him. Her chest heaving as her lungs tried to keep up with the blood still pumping furiously through her veins. She took something from her back pocket and tossed it at him. Reese caught it instinctively. "Not bad at all. I'd say I was almost impressed. Though you need a better deadbolt. Standard five-pin tumbler is kid stuff."

Swallowing against his dry throat, his heart racing, Reese's wide eyes looked at the black leather wallet in his hands, flipping it open, revealing an FBI badge and ID card. His gaze darted back to her. "What...is wrong with you?" he finally managed.

"I said I'm almost impressed," the woman repeated. "It's a compliment."

"Why...? Why the hell didn't you knock?" he barked. "I came out armed! I could've killed you!"

The woman shrugged. "I doubt it. But your confidence in that possibility, even after getting your ass handed to you, is remarkable."

Reese's gaze became a glare as he threw the badge back to the woman none too gently. "You didn't hand me my ass," he muttered.

"Yeah, you're right. That's a bit harsh." She put her badge back in her jacket. "Anyway, I'm Special Agent Katherine Colebrook. I heard you're looking for a job."

Two things happened at that moment. One, Reese blinked a few times in surprise at the fact that apparently she had broken in to ask about a job. Then, he froze at the introduction she'd given herself. His breath even caught in his throat for a moment, even though he was still a bit starved for oxygen. "You're...Colebrook," he stated, realizing that he hadn't actually absorbed the name on the ID card, having only been focused on making sure it was authentic.

"That's what it says on my badge," she replied. "You know who I am, then?"

"Yes ma'am," he muttered.

Katherine grimaced. "Don't call me ma'am. It's Colebrook."

Reese blinked. "Okay."

"So. Are you?"

"Am I...?" he asked slowly, staring at her.

"Looking for a job," she repeated, a bit slower this time. "I'd hate to have wasted your time tonight. I don't actually break into people's apartments and scare the hell out of them for fun." She paused. "Well...not regularly."

Reese just breathed for a few moments, unsure of how to respond. "I...work in CID," he finally murmured. "Violent crime. But a couple weeks ago, I put in my Tracker application. As a probie. It's always been my goal."

Katherine nodded, examining his apartment now that the lights were on, already having briefly taken in Reese himself. It was difficult not to, considering his well-sculpted body, which she knew from his file was from an intense interest in both martial arts and swimming. She had also spotted a tattoo down the outside of his right arm, a quote she recognized from Edmund Burke, 'All that is necessary for the triumph of evil is that good men do nothing.'

Katherine's gaze now flicked over the mismatched couch and loveseat, a sketchbook leaning against the couch, the scratched wooden coffee table covered in mail and paperwork, and the huge, worn Foreigner poster hanging on the wall. "I got your file," she spoke, starting to slowly walk around the room. "Not bad. Twenty-four is pretty young to submit for an apprenticeship, but you're not the youngest, by far. And you've kept busy. Can I ask why you made the change from LAPD to FBI two years ago?" she asked, glancing back to Reese.

"Cause that's the soonest they'd hire me," Reese answered.

Katherine's smile widened. "I liked your test scores.

Not just cause they're high, but because I helped design the tests, written and physical, so I know you can't bullshit them."

"Yeah, I know," Reese muttered. "So...you're taking me on as a probie."

"A vampire's been kidnapping young men and holding them hostage for three days before dropping their bodies in dumpsters, drained," Katherine spoke instead of answering his question, turning back to him, her spine ramrod straight. "This happens three times, then he picks up the pace. Starts taking one person a day. You find his place a week later while you're scouting abandoned warehouses. There's a decent amount of blood on the floors. Then you turn the corner and there's someone sitting at a table at the other side of the room, his back to you. He hasn't noticed you yet. You see blood on his shirt. What do you do?"

Reese paused for a long moment, considering the question. "Reveal my presence, that I'm armed, and that I'm FBI. Tell him to get on the ground."

"He turns around, surprised. Then he looks despondent. You see blood on his mouth and chin. He doesn't get on the ground."

"I repeat the order."

"He lets out his fangs."

"I ask him his name."

Katherine stared at Reese. "Why?"

Reese shifted his weight from one foot to the other and stared at Katherine, pausing for a long moment. "Cause he's not the vampire I'm looking for."

"Why?"

"Because he was turned by the one I'm looking for,"

Reese muttered. "That's why there were more victims. He was feeding a newborn, and needed to feed himself too." He hesitated briefly. "And just last year, over a dozen vampires in California committed suicide through death by cop. Most were turned against their will."

Katherine continued staring at Reese, motionless, before she nodded once and turned around, walking over to a window, pulling up the Venetian blinds. "Decent locks. Locked at night, even though you're on the third floor." She motioned vaguely around the room. "You know this place in the dark?"

"My apartment? Uh…yeah, pretty much."

"A few weapons hidden in case of emergency?" Katherine asked. Her eyes skimmed the bookcase beside the television, going over and taking a book off the shelf.

"Hidden?" Reese hesitated, blinking a few times. "I didn't…. No, uh, just my service weapon. In my nightstand drawer."

"Your home is your fortress," she told Reese, glancing to him before looking back to the book in her hand, putting it back on the shelf. "Home base advantage. It's the one place you should have the highest confidence in being able to face off against an enemy. Because it's the one place you can most prepare. You've got no wards on this place either. We'll fix that too." Katherine smiled suddenly at a book on the top shelf, taking it off, noticing that the binding was quite worn. "The Parasapien Threat. Friend of mine wrote this." She waved it in Reese's direction before putting it back on a shelf. "You've got good taste."

"You know Jean Pearson?" Reese asked, his eyes widening.

"Met her as a kid. She taught me a lot. Sends me Christmas cards. So, do you have anything you don't want me to know?" Katherine asked, turning back to him.

Reese's expression turned confused. "Sorry?"

"I do not take chances with people that I trust with my life. Nor do I with the people I let into my home," she spoke, walking slowly back over to Reese. "You'll be both. So you will not have any secrets from me. This won't be a choice, because I can and will know everything. Not your moment-to-moment thoughts, cause I don't have that much time and I am familiar with the concept of privacy, and not anything classified that's been warded, obviously, but...the important stuff. Is there something in your head that you would rather keep to yourself than come on as my probie?"

Clenching and unclenching his fists, Reese averted his eyes and thought for a second before looking back to her and shaking his head. "No," he muttered.

"You know how thorough my background checks are?" Katherine asked, tapping her temple a few times with her index finger.

"...I do."

Katherine paused for a long moment. "You've got quite the chip on your shoulder from daddy," she murmured. "Serial bank robber, so you went the other way? Get as far as you could into killing the worst monsters you could find? Regular humans obviously wouldn't meet that standard. I get that." Reese paled, remaining silent, his jaw clenched tightly as he stared at her. "But you don't think in black and white. You dated a werewolf. Interesting. An animal in bed, I'm assuming?"

"Shut up," Reese growled.

Katherine let out a sigh at the flare of rage she felt in him. "You would've clocked me for that comment if we were in a bar and I was a guy," she muttered. "That's a problem. You're going to have to learn to keep your temper in check."

Reese blinked a few times, the anger dissipating from him instantly purely from surprise. "I–"

"Just saying," she told him. "Everyone has issues they need to work on. Impulse control is a pretty bad weakness, though. So you'll really have to work on that." Reese stared. The wheels spun in his head, trying to take in her demeanor and constant changes in the conversation topics. He was pretty sure he was doing a good job keeping up with her, but he wasn't sure. And of course, there was some residual irritation of her having broken into his apartment.

"So," Katherine said, glancing at the clock on the wall. "It's been almost ten minutes, and you still haven't offered me a beer. You're a somewhat crappy host."

"To be fair, you broke in and threw me around my living room, so you're a pretty crappy guest," Reese told her.

Katherine grinned. "But you do have beer."

"Necessary staple of any agent's diet," Reese replied. "I'm gonna go...get dressed. I'll meet you in the kitchen."

CHAPTER 21

"So why can vampires be around light bulbs?" Jessica asked.

"Well it's not the light that's the problem," Alexandra told her friend. The two girls walked down the school hallway quickly toward the cafeteria, the loud chatter of teenagers growing in volume as they went. "There are a lot of different kinds of light. The light that vampires can't be in is UV. I mean, otherwise they'd have to stay in the dark all the time. Even moonlight is fine, which is reflected sunlight."

Jessica's expression turned confused, and her mouth opened and shut. "But...wait, how?"

"UV light affects us too, just in a different way. If we're out in the sun too much during the day without sunscreen, our skin is damaged. We call that a sunburn. But we don't have that problem with moonlight, even if we're out all night with a full moon of light reflecting back at us."

"But vampires are *really* sensitive to it, so why don't they at least...I don't know, get itchy?" Jessica asked.

"Because the moon reflects about .0002 percent of

the sun's light that it receives," Alexandra replied. "That's nothing. They can't even get a tan." Jessica grinned.

The two girls got their lunch and found a spot at their normal table. Jessica, who apparently was on a mission that day, barely stopped her questions long enough to take a bite of her sandwich. "You know, you can find answers to every one of these questions online," Alexandra pointed out.

Jessica chewed and swallowed. "Sure, but you make it more interesting." Alexandra blinked, momentarily flattered into silence. Jessica didn't notice. "So how can I meet a parasapien? You said you've met a bunch of them. Like, where do they live?"

Alexandra narrowed her eyes. "Where do they live?" she asked slowly. "You mean...like which manhole cover should you look under or where are the burrows in the Hollywood Hills that vampires nest in?" she asked, cocking her head. "They're people, Jessica. They live in Los Angeles."

"Yeah, I know they're people. But, like, how do I find one?" Jessica asked insistently.

Alexandra took a breath. "Pretend I told you some foreign exchange student came up to me and said, hey, where can I find a Korean person? They're so exotic and I really want to meet one!" Jessica's sandwich stopped halfway to her mouth and her face went slack. Alexandra raised her eyebrows. "Got it?"

"Uh...yeah," Jessica muttered bashfully.

"Honestly...they're less likely to live in the more decent parts of LA unless they're on a reality show," Alexandra admitted. She blinked a few times, swallowing hard and trying to push back the beginnings of a headache. "When it's legal to discriminate against potential employees who are parasapiens, it's hard to find a job."

"Oh," Jessica said. "I guess I didn't think…." She let out a small sigh. "So I've probably met parasapiens a bunch of times…." Jessica continued talking, but Alexandra suddenly wasn't hearing her. Because the headache was quickly pushing forward with immense strength, and it was becoming apparent that it wasn't just a headache.

Alexandra grimaced, sliding out from the table and pushing herself to her feet. "Jessica," she managed, stumbling toward the door.

"Alex?" Jessica asked worriedly. "You okay?"

"Not really," Alexandra muttered. She tried to blink back the stars forming in front of her eyes, knowing that she couldn't but attempting to at least delay the onset. *Bathroom. Get to the bathroom. Or a closet. Something….* She grunted, squeezing her eyes shut and holding her forehead as she made it out into the hallway, right before her vision completely clouded over.

"Alex," Jessica spoke urgently from behind her, having followed her. "What's wrong?"

Alexandra's hearing became muffled as pain sliced through her mind. She cried out, leaning back against the wall and sliding down to the ground, clutching her head.

The young boy stares into the mirror of his bathroom, looking at his fangs and grinning. They are beautiful. His mother is right. They were made to tear flesh. To allow him to drink the life from any human he wanted.

He had started to crave fresh blood. His mother said soon. Soon she will hunt for them, and he will have the spoils. She said he can pick their target. He wants a boy his age. He will

work his way up to a target that was worthy of his mother.
Kill them himself. But he is still young. It will be a long while.

Find a target. Isolate them. Then kill.

He thinks about the target they are going after. The one he
has in mind. The one he's seen down the hall. They are hiding
from something. Someone is already after them. The boy likes
that, because now it is a race. See if he can get his kill first.

The younger brother. That is the one he wants. Then his
mother can have the parents. And he wants the older brother
for dessert.

He has the scent. He wants his kill.

Alexandra gasped in deep breaths, blinking away the
clouds and stars that had formed in front of her tightly
closed eyes. Jessica knelt next to her worriedly, staring, as
well as a few other kids in the hallway that had stopped and
a teacher that had been taking her pulse.

"Are you okay?" Jessica exclaimed.

"I-I'm sorry, I get migraines," Alexandra muttered to
the teacher. "They only last a minute, though."

"That looked like it really hurt," the teacher exclaimed.
"Do you want to go to the nurse? Lay down for a bit?"

"Ah, yeah. Let me just grab my lunch," she said quietly,
pushing herself to her feet.

As she gathered her backpack and her tray from the
cafeteria, Alexandra went over what she'd seen and felt from
her vision to report back to her mother.

CHAPTER 22

Alexandra took the elevator to the fourth floor of her building and headed down the hallway, shifting her backpack on her shoulders as she approached her apartment. She briefly met the eyes of a man leaning against the wall next to the door of the apartment across the hall from them, smoking a cigarette. It was instantly apparent to her that he was there for her. Not to grab her, though. Just to intimidate her. In a black leather jacket and with slicked-back dark hair, he was the epitome of the word 'goon'. He spoke just as she lifted her keys to her doorknob.

"Alexandra, right?" the man asked softly.

Freezing momentarily, gradually removing the key from the doorknob without unlocking it, Alexandra slowly turned toward him, sliding the key in between two of her fingers. "Who wants to know?" she asked.

The man shrugged. "I'm a friend of your mother's."

"If you were, you wouldn't be lurking outside in the hallway. She would've let you in," Alexandra told him.

"Actually, Katherine isn't here right now," he responded.

Alexandra's eyes narrowed at him. It wasn't so much

what he'd said, but how he'd said it. His tone. It was just barely threatening. Telling her that, in fact, she was alone.

"Is there a message you'd like me to give her?" Alexandra asked softly.

The man smirked. "Nah. I'll just wait."

Alexandra warily lifted her chin a bit before turning back to the doorknob, unlocking it, and glancing to the man briefly as she went into the apartment. Shutting the door and locking the deadbolt before resetting the alarm, also putting on the chain, Alexandra took out her cell phone.

"When did you get to Los Angeles?" Reese asked, taking a drink from his iced tea.

"Ah…a little over three weeks ago."

Reese blinked. "You work fast."

"I didn't follow Jackson to LA for the sun," Katherine said. "He was already bugging me to find a probie weeks before we started packing."

Katherine had told Reese to meet her at the diner not far from her new apartment building at which she'd started to regularly have lunch. Their menu was extensive and the waitresses didn't mind if she sat there for hours in the corner booth on her laptop, two big plusses. Katherine asked for her normal table when she arrived, and Reese had gotten there about ten minutes after her. It was still ten minutes early, which was a point for him. If there was anything she couldn't stand, it was someone that arrived late, no matter how casual the meeting was. It was just one more thing that she needed to find out on her own about Reese, rather than things she could learn with her abilities. One thing on a list of many.

"So what's Jackson like?" Reese asked.

Katherine paused as her mouth edged up into a smile. "Strong. Smart. Very experienced. Has almost a decade on me, which is saying something. You'll meet him tomorrow. Find out for yourself."

"Ah, fair enough. So, you said you have a daughter?"

Katherine nodded, smiling. "Alex. She's the best thing that ever happened to me. Takes after her mom in quite a few ways. Some I'm happy about, like being psychic and taking martial arts to protect herself, and some I'm not, like…getting into situations where those abilities come in handy."

Reese grinned. "I'd like to meet her."

"I'd like that too. You can come over for dinner sometime," she replied. "We actually also have a new houseguest–" Katherine cut off her response as her phone rang, and she pursed her lips as she saw her daughter's cell number pop up. "Speak of the devil," she spoke, answering the call. "Was just talking about you. You just get home from school?"

"Yeah, and we've got company," Alexandra answered. "Some guy loitering in the hall."

Her spine straightening, Katherine tensed, her full concentration suddenly on the phone call. "What kind of guy?"

"Tall. Thuggish. Creepy. Very pointedly made note of the fact that you weren't home."

Anger and protective instincts slid through Katherine's veins like ice. She clenched her left fist tightly, cracking her knuckles. "Did he try anything?"

Alexandra snorted. "No, or I'd be wiping his blood off my knife."

Katherine smiled. "That's my girl. Is he still there?"

"Yeah, said he's gonna wait for you," Alexandra said, her tone conveying just how odd she thought that was.

"Rebecca still in her room?"

"Yup. She doesn't see any reason to come out, so…."

Katherine glanced at her watch. "All right. I'll be there in…ten minutes," Katherine said, taking a twenty from her pocket and putting it on the table. "Wait in the safe room with Rebecca."

Alexandra hesitated. "Okay."

Katherine paused suspiciously as she made for the door, Reese quickly following her. "I mean it. Wait in there. I'll know if you don't."

"But I want to listen when you get here!" she protested.

"Alex, if he changes his mind–"

"I'll be on the other side of the door with my .45," Alexandra told her. "He won't get far."

"Go wait in the safe room," Katherine spoke. "Now."

Alexandra made a sound of annoyance. "Fine," she muttered before hanging up the phone.

CHAPTER 23

KATHERINE MENTALLY REACHED OUT AS soon as she drove up to her apartment building, slowing and pausing in front of the building, pressing the button on the gate door remote. Her eyes scanned up the wide steps of the pale yellow, five-story building, then down to the azalea bushes and small trees that dotted the frontage, not really seeing any of it, just concentrating on her feelers. She quickly found Alexandra's aura, faint and subtle, which meant she was in the safe room.

The building they lived in had been chosen by Katherine for a multitude of reasons, one of the most important being security. Precautions that most others who didn't know her would call paranoid were just instinct to her. Their hardwood floors came in handy for false panels to hide things like weapons or supplies, which gave them some additional comfort, but in this case was irrelevant because Alexandra didn't need to fight off anyone. It had security cameras that actually worked well and recorded decent video quality, but more importantly had the capability for Katherine or another FBI agent to watch the feeds from outside.

From her impressions from the man waiting outside her apartment, however, there was no need for her to do that. He was there alone. There were also several ways for her or Alexandra to get in or out of their apartment besides the front door. But in this case, none of the more extraordinary exits or entries, such as through their porch door, an air vent, or the door on the roof, were necessary. Going in through the front door and taking the elevator up to the fourth floor would work fine, because she wanted to feign obliviousness and fake a disadvantage.

"You want me to come in with you?" Reese asked as Katherine pulled into the small parking garage.

Katherine shook her head. "No, it'll be easier if you aren't there," she told him. "Just wait in the lobby and come upstairs in like…ten minutes."

Reese eyed her. "You're not gonna—"

"I'm not gonna kill him," she interrupted as she parked her car, exasperated.

Reese blinked, cocking an eyebrow. "I was gonna say *hurt him*, but all right, as long as you're not gonna *kill him*…."

Katherine rolled her eyes as they both got out of the car and Reese went through the doorway into the building's lobby as Katherine went for the elevator. The doors promptly opened and she selected the button for their floor, sensing the man waiting in the hallway. Taking her Glock from her holster, she slid the magazine out, tapping it once to seat the bullets against the back, before sliding it back in with a firm *click*. She double-checked the safety and then put it back in her holster, leaving it unbuckled.

The elevator doors opened and Katherine walked down

the hallway toward their apartment, rage simmering beneath the surface of her skin. Eyeing the man as she walked up to him, she observed that he seemed uninterested in her, presumably waiting until he was sure she was going to open the door he was watching. She waited until the last possible moment before swiftly grabbing her gun from her holster and lunging for him, shoving the weapon under his chin as she pinned him against the wall.

The man's eyes bulged, obviously not expecting this turn of events. His hand instinctively flinched toward his own weapon before rationality took over, telling him that he was definitely not faster than a bullet. She stared at his eyes, which were looking everywhere but down at her.

"Okay now, let's see," Katherine muttered. "You were sent by…Calabrease?" She stared at him, her eyes widening. "That son of a bitch."

"You lied about–"

"Hey, it's more fun when I figure it out," she growled at him, nudging the gun a bit further into his throat. He grimaced. "So…he's upset about the guy that turned out to be a fed, huh? Guess I made a boo-boo. The bigger question is, why send you here for intimidation? If he's pissed, I figured he'd just go for straight for violence." Katherine paused. "He wants to give me a chance to set things right, huh? Make up for the trouble I just made for him?" She paused again, this time for longer.

"I'm not…gonna say this twice," she murmured. "As you can tell, I take threats to my family quite seriously. You're pretty lucky. If Calabrease had told you to wait for me inside my apartment *with* my daughter, I wouldn't have been so nice. You probably would've ended up like the last guy that broke into my home, with a hole between your eyes," she whispered. A muscle in the man's jaw twitched restlessly.

"I'm sure Calabrease didn't get the kind of power he has without having a serious ego, but this time, he's gonna let it go," Katherine snapped. "If he gets pissy about not getting me on his payroll and decides to send someone else my way, I will put a bullet through their skull without hesitation. And after that, I will use every one of my law enforcement contacts to torpedo every single part of his business, down to the numbers operations run by eight-year-olds. And I have more connections than you can comprehend, starting with the LAPD and going up to the CIA, so I would *never* run out of torpedoes."

"Now. Do you think you can convey to your boss how sincere I am about this threat, and how bad a choice it would be to make me an enemy?" Katherine asked tightly.

"Yes, ma'am," he muttered, his eyes firmly on a speck of dirt on the wall.

"Good." Katherine twisted his arm with a force that caused him to grunt in pain and shoved him away from her. Keeping his eyes firmly averted, the man went quickly down the hall, foregoing the elevator in favor of the more immediately accessible stairs.

<hr />

"It's nothing I couldn't handle on my own, really," Katherine spoke into her cell phone. "I'd tell you if it wasn't. I just wanted you to know about it and possibly reach out to gangs, see if they could give me a heads up if there are any more goons heading my way."

"I'll talk to a few agents, yeah," Jackson grumbled. "This is just unacceptable."

"You're telling me. I'm considering paying the bastard a visit," Katherine muttered.

Jackson sighed. "You know you can't go doing that," he said.

"Shouldn't? Yeah. Can't?" Katherine shook her head. "This is a line, Jackson. It's a *big* line, and he waltzed right over it, and I am not going to let him—"

"He is a jackass and a moron, but you go after him without cause, you're dead in the water," Jackson told her. "Let gangs bring charges against him. They've got a laundry list from the agent they had in there."

"Right." Katherine paused. "Call if you get anything."

"I will. Stay safe."

"Always." Katherine hung up the phone, shoving it in her pocket a bit harsher than necessary.

"What kind of idiot is Calabrease?" Alexandra asked, walking out from the kitchen, holding a Pop Tart. Katherine looked to her, raising an eyebrow. "He's got to know how much this was going to just piss you off."

Katherine shook her head. "I can't pretend to understand the motives of human beings. Did Rebecca seem okay?"

Alexandra nodded. "Yeah, she's fine. Not like there was actually any excitement for her. She seemed a little confused at the fuss, actually."

"Good," Katherine murmured. "I'd rather her be bored with the theatrics of heading into the panic room than the opposite." She glanced to her left and walked over to the front door, unlocking it and opening it, revealing Reese standing in front of it, his hand raised to knock.

"I'm never gonna get used to you doing that," he told her as he lowered his hand.

Katherine smirked and moved aside, letting him in. "Reese, this is Alex, Alex, this is the new probie."

"Nice to meet you," Alexandra said, walking over and shaking his hand.

"You too. Your mom's talked you up quite a bit," Reese said with a smile.

Katherine saw Reese's gaze slide to the right as he took in her living room, fascinated by it. She knew he'd only met her two days ago, and before that she'd been only an abstract concept, a well-known, talented agent with more myths about her than Bigfoot. Her living room apparently looked far too normal for the Katherine Colebrook that he'd had in mind three days ago. As he looked closer, though, she knew certain things popped out.

The varnished brown coffee table had books on it that appeared to have been read many times, and the dozens lining the large bookcase looked similarly used, unlike the books in the homes of people who bought them seemingly just to fill shelves. Unusual trinkets and knick-knacks on the corner shelves such as ceramic icons from Greek mythology, a highly corroded iron knife behind glass, a small skull from an animal he couldn't identify, and what appeared to be a jewelry box lined with tiny seashells. Several photographs lined the mantelpiece as well, a personal touch to the room, including some of Katherine and Alexandra going back a few years.

A small smile surfaced on Katherine's face as she felt Alexandra mentally gathering information about Reese. Thoroughly. The way Katherine would expect to check out a boyfriend if her daughter ever brought one home. It wasn't surprising. Katherine's last partner in San Diego was someone that Alexandra had basically grown up with, since Katherine had started out as Sweeney's probie. A new face by her mother's side, a new person having her back, wasn't a role that Alexandra would consider just anyone good enough to fill.

"What do you carry?" Alexandra asked, nodding to the bulge under his jacket. Reese blinked at her, off-guard, before he glanced to Katherine for any support on how to react. But her expression was completely blank, giving him no help whatsoever, so he just looked back to Alexandra, who continued. "I usually prefer a Glock 27 or a Ruger LCR, but I'm sixteen. You'd use one of those for backup."

"The 27, actually, yeah," Reese replied, trying to force the surprise out of his expression.

"And what's your department-issue sidearm?"

"Glock 23."

"Why'd you go with that one?"

"Fits me better than the 22," he replied. "I considered the 19, but the 23's got better power for something like a vampire."

"Mounted tactical light?"

Reese shook his head. "I've got a handheld. Too much risk failure with it mounted."

"Tactical knives?" Alexandra prompted.

"Two Spyderco tactical folders. Both iron/silver, one DMF auto serrated, one mini covert auto serrated."

Alexandra paused before nodding her approval. "Nice," she said with a smile. She then turned back to her mother. "Can you wait here? I've got something for you."

"Sure," Katherine said with a blink. Alexandra headed back down the hall and Reese looked to Katherine with an expression that asked her why she hadn't given him a heads-up on the weapons quiz he would be getting.

Katherine grinned. "You're just lucky she didn't drill you harder on the knives," she said.

A few moments later, Alexandra came back down the hall with a three papers she'd stapled together, handing them to her mother. "Vampire."

Katherine's face went slack and she briefly looked over the papers, her stance tightening. "In class?" she asked.

"No, thankfully," Alexandra muttered. "Lunch. Passed it off as a migraine."

"Is that an FD-276?" Reese asked suddenly.

"Filled out by my daughter?" Katherine said, looking at him straight in the eye. "No. That would mean she'd need to come in for a debriefing, likely to last four to five hours." Reese blinked, looking to Alexandra, who gave him a thousand-yard stare.

After a long moment, Alexandra looked back to Katherine. "No problems. It was straightforward. I was thorough."

"All right." Katherine folded up the papers into thirds and stuck them in her pocket before stepping forward and taking her daughter in a hug. "See you later. Love you." She kissed Alexandra on her head before leaving, Reese followed quickly behind her.

Katherine glanced to Reese as she locked the door, turning and heading down the hallway, reaching out mentally to her daughter as Alexandra set the security alarm. "That FD-276 was typed up by me," Katherine murmured.

"It'll have my name on it when it hand it to Jackson. You mind driving so I can memorize it?"

Reese paused, then nodded. "Sure thing. Twenty minutes to headquarters. That enough?"

A shadow of a smile surfaced on Katherine's face. "It was a short vision. It's plenty."

"Does Jackson know?"

"Knows it happens sometimes and that I'll cover. And he's the only one. As a general rule, I don't lie to him about anything; he's not even particularly a fan of plausible deniability. But he doesn't often need to know about this," Katherine answered. "Like she said. She's thorough." She let out a breath. "She's a kid. She deserves to be able to have her life until rent and traffic and taxes take that away from her. Sometimes she can't, but with this, she can." Reese nodded, a small smile on his face.

CHAPTER 24

KATHERINE TOOK THE THICK FILE from Jackson as she sat in the chair in front of his desk. "Burglaries," was the single, quiet word Katherine spoke as she leafed through the file.

"*Seventeen* burglaries," Jackson spoke in reply. "The last one was three weeks ago."

Katherine looked up to him briefly before looking back to the file in her hand. "All of them were jewelry?"

"Every damn one. Mostly museums. Some were showing's of new pieces by wealthy entrepreneurs. The thief doesn't differentiate between cut, shape, color of stones. Sometimes it's a few, sometimes it's just one. And the burglaries were all over the country. But it's always jewels."

"And you're sure this is the same thief?"

"From what we gathered, yeah."

Katherine slowly narrowed her eyes as she read the case file summary before passing it to Reese, who was sitting beside her. "There's always a...hostage? Is that what you're calling this?" she asked, looking back to Jackson.

"Every time, someone with access to the item or items is abducted and killed and then after the burglary the body's dumped somewhere," Jackson answered. "Cause the thief takes on the person's appearance and takes their place in their life. We actually thought the thief was working with the hostages on the inside before they turned on their inside man or woman and took off with the goods, but the times of death just didn't match up." His tone deepened into something more grave. "Plus...a few times, the thief took and impersonated kids."

Katherine's eyes flashed. "What?"

"I assume that a kid is sometimes the best option to replace, cause no one's gonna look to them first as a suspect of a skilled burglary," he said. "We've found, not a pattern, but enough to establish an M.O. and predict the kind of targets the thief might go after. So far, tracking down fences and buyers hasn't panned out. This guy has just disappeared after every job he pulls. And he ain't stupid. We tried to go undercover, twice, but he didn't bite."

Jackson fell silent as Katherine looked back to the file and read over the papers inside it. Considering the amount of crimes, the entirety of it would make for a lot of reading, so she just skimmed, but she knew what she was looking for. She read the summary on each crime scene, on each victim, on each piece stolen, and only had to get about halfway through the burglaries before she slowly nodded.

"All right. Looks good," Katherine said, pushing herself to her feet. "We'll run with it. Check in with you once a day."

"It was great to meet you, sir," Reese said, getting to his feet. He held out his hand across Jackson's desk, which his boss shook firmly.

"Likewise," Jackson replied. "Good luck keeping up

with this one," he added, motioning to Katherine. She smiled as she turned and left the room.

"I'll do my best," Reese replied, heading after her.

———— ◦◦◦ ————

"Everyone that has access," Katherine repeated into the phone. "Whether it's a five-year-old or the president of the company. A complete security analysis to determine they are who they say they are, including standard parasapien scanning." She paused. "There is a pùca that's killed over a dozen people and stolen millions of dollars worth of jewelry and is currently preparing to do it again as we speak. Now will you be making sure this procedure is implemented or do I have to talk to my superiors?"

Katherine smirked. "Thank you. I'll wait on your call." She hung up the phone, turning back to her paperwork and crossing off the last name on the list of possible burglary targets she'd compiled.

Katherine and Reese were currently holed up in a motel in Oxnard. They needed a base of operations just for the day, a place to work on the information they were gathering on their case. Since there were several people out west they needed to speak to and some crime scenes they needed to check out, as a matter of convenience, they got a temporary crash pad.

The room could have been in any motel in the country. Plaid quilts on the two double beds that somehow vaguely matched the light green wallpaper, and a large picture on the wall that was, oddly, of the Chicago skyline. Katherine loved places like this. They were like mini-homes, a predictable pattern of strange décor and old, but usually reliable, appliances.

Of course, as much as Katherine enjoyed visiting new motels, she'd always check the reviews online first. Interesting new places was one thing, but bed bugs were another completely.

"So the lesson here is, get the information you need," Katherine muttered. She looked over through the files spread out on the floor, stepping delicately between them. She'd foregone putting any of the paperwork up on the wall as she usually did since she knew there wasn't much of a chance the pùca was still local. "Everything you don't know is another way you can get killed."

Reese looked up from the pile of papers he had on his lap. "We actually had paperwork in CID. We also had dangerous criminals. And difficult interrogations. And long nights. It might have more in common with tracking than you'd think," he said.

"Smartass," Katherine replied. "Definition: pùca," she spoke suddenly. "And your opinion of this one."

Reese glanced up to her. "Pùca: a fae shapeshifter that feeds on energy from living creatures. Some survive on small amounts of energy from many people or animals, but some think that isn't where the party is. Killing people is a lot more appealing, cause it's easier and more fulfilling, and obvious that's the kind of bastard we're after here. Because he could have killed his victims by draining them of energy, but he prefers not to. So he really likes to kill."

"Well done," Katherine said with a nod.

"Can I ask why we're in a crappy motel?" Reese asked, looking back to her. "That, I'd like to know."

Katherine grinned as she picked up the file she was looking for and went back over to her laptop. "It's not crappy; it has character. I could say it's habit," she replied. "When I was younger, I didn't make as much money. But bigger, higher-end hotels have better security, which only works against me. I can secure myself," she said pointedly, leaning back in her chair, meeting Reese's gaze. "Also, their housekeeping tends to be fixed on the idea of getting into my room to clean, whether I want them to or not. Plus there tend to be more people there, since nicer places are bigger, and there are times I want to stay invisible, or they could get in my way."

"But mainly, it's habit. They just feel uncomfortable," Katherine muttered, picking up a small pile of papers and leafing through them. "I'm used to the way small motels work. I prefer an atmosphere I've been in many times over to nicer surroundings. At least in the case of tracking. Vacations are a whole other story."

Reese paused, his expression bordering on confused. "Going out to a fancy dinner? Lounging by the pool? I seriously can't picture you on a vacation."

Katherine smirked, taking a pen from behind her ear. "Not for lack of trying?"

Reese's mouth opened and closed. "You-You said you don't peek in people's heads like that," he managed.

Katherine glanced up to him and slowly smiled. "I don't. That was a shot in the dark, Reese, which you just confirmed," she said.

Reese averted his eyes. "I still think it's easier to manage this stuff on a computer," he murmured.

"Oh wow, you are so green," Katherine said, shaking her head. "Do you even remember the days before Sentinel?"

"I barely remember the days before the Internet," Reese replied. "But I do know that paperwork was a mess before Sentinel came along."

"'A mess' is putting it lightly. It was chaos," Katherine told him. "And for the decade before Sentinel was implemented, everyone was skeptical that we could get it done. Agents didn't want to use it because they were worried it would crash and burn like VCF did. So even though you prefer it, I've only had it for a few years." She gestured to their setup. "This is just…how my mind works. Don't get me wrong, I love being able to type up everything and the fact that literally filling things out in triplicate is nearly a thing of the past, but I'm used to spreading it all out, memorizing everything, knowing where everything is. It's my own version of opening everything up in different windows and tabs on a computer."

"Well, considering your reputation as a legend in the FBI, if this is the way you operate, I'll go with all this over a computer any day," Reese said, motioning around the room.

"Very smooth brown-nosing."

"I try."

After a few hours of getting to know the case files and the psychology of the pùca, the two special agents had gone through its likely targets and called every one, putting them on alert. Now, they needed to reach out to contacts who might know the thief's patterns or next target. Katherine grabbed her jacket and her keys and checked her watch before heading out, Reese right behind her.

CHAPTER 25

"Now that is something you don't see every day," Katherine remarked from the other side of the glass counter. She looked over the shoulder at the man that was handling a taxidermy squirrel.

"Depends on your career choice." The man turned around and immediately grinned, laugh lines creasing across his face. "Damn. When'd you get into town? Been too long," Harold said, putting the squirrel on the shelf.

"I actually moved to LA recently. I'm just out west for business at the moment."

Harold, the owner of the pawnshop she was currently in, was someone that Katherine went to on occasion for information on the art world. It was a specialty of his, one that he'd done time in prison for, though one that he didn't participate in much ever since a certain bullet wound that he didn't like to talk about. He joked to Katherine that if he ever needed to get away from someone, it would be difficult with the steel rod in his leg, so he preferred not to make enemies he might need to run from.

"What kind of trouble you getting into these days?" he asked, leaning back against the counter.

"Same old. Wondering if I could steal you from the shop for a minute. It's important."

Harold ran his hand over his balding head thoughtfully before nodding. "Sure. Ah, Jim, I'll be in the back," he called to the employee on the other side of the shop, motioning to Katherine. He led her around the counter, his pronounced limp slowing their pace a bit, and through a door to the back of the store, taking a seat at the old wooden table pushed up against the wall. Katherine sat across from him in one of the other mismatched chairs. "You got something good to sell?"

"Nothing so lucrative. It's about a thief," she said, getting right down to business. "I'm here on business. I've got my probie with me, but I asked him to wait in the car."

Harold nodded once. "Appreciate that."

"The M.O. is to pull a job by impersonating someone, replacing them in their life, and killing them once they've got the goods."

Harold shifted in his seat uncomfortably. "I heard about this," he muttered. "Guy's like the wind. In and out of a crime, no one sees anything." He looked at her warily. "You're saying this is something up your alley."

Katherine nodded. "Yeah. So any idea of a pattern? The next target?"

Harold tapped his fingers on the table a few times before he sighed. "Well, the thief's been switching fences depending on where he ends up, but the last job I'm pretty sure he used a guy out in Santa Barbara. Name's Alan. He might know where your guy's at or how to get in touch with him."

Katherine raised her eyebrows at the promising lead. "Think you could put in a call to Alan for me?"

———◆◆◆———

Alexandra walked out through the school doors with throngs of other kids, squinting as she got out from under the shade of the large blue awnings. Turning right to go around the picnic tables, she passed a couple of kids playing hacky sack on one of several small patches of grass among what was mostly cement. She went down the stairs toward the sidewalk and spotted Jessica, who smiled back as she locked eyes with her friend.

"How was your math test?" Jessica asked.

"Okay, I think," she replied. "Won't know for a few days. You get your science essay back yet?"

"Nope. I'm pretty sure I got at least a B, though." They walked in silence for a few moments before stopping at a crosswalk. "But I'm kind of worried about the test. It's easy when you've got all your notes in front of you for an essay, but…." Her voice trailed off when she realized Alexandra wasn't listening, instead staring at something to her right. "Alex?" Jessica asked. She followed her friend's gaze toward a few kids that had started crossing the street adjacent to them. "Earth to Alex. What is it?"

"Come on," Alexandra muttered after a brief hesitation. She tugged Jessica's arm as she started to follow them.

"What's wrong?" Jessica asked worriedly.

Alexandra's eyes remained firmly locked on a girl that looked about fifteen, walking with a few of her friends. *Close. Something's close. The girl doesn't know, but Alex feels it. There's something.* "I don't know. It just feels like…."

"Like what?"

Alexandra hesitated. "Danger."

"How does something feel like danger?" Jessica asked as Alexandra sped up her pace. "And why are we following if it does?"

They closed the gap between them and the group of girls, which split into two groups of two as one pair of them stopped at a bus stop. The remaining two and Alexandra and Jessica all halted briefly at another crosswalk before continuing on.

They continued through a residential neighborhood, heading past small houses and several apartment buildings. Eventually they passed a car repair shop and a Denny's as the neighborhood transitioned to busy grocery stores and shopping plazas.

"Alex, I've got tons of homework," Jessica groaned. "Can you at least tell me where we're going?"

"Once I know, I'll tell you."

Jessica rolled her eyes. "Great."

"You can go home. I'll see you tomorrow at school."

Jessica fell silent, but continued walking alongside her friend, curiosity winning out.

Once they had gone another half a block, Alexandra's eyes narrowed at a black Jeep on their side of the street. "I don't like that car," she suddenly stated.

Jessica glanced to it and then continued looking at their surroundings. "What about it...don't you like?" she asked.

Alexandra swallowed hard as the feeling of dread in her chest grew and started to become more specific. And more recognizable.

An enemy is closing in on her. Or someone is scheming against her. Danger nearby.

"It's double-parked," Alexandra said quietly. "And idling."

The distance between the four girls and the Jeep closed from fifteen yards to about ten. Then the two girls said their goodbyes as one headed up a stairway to a brownstone. And Alexandra's pace increased. And she slid one of her arms out of her backpack.

"Alex, what's going on?" Jessica asked, her eyes widening. Alexandra realized Jessica had recognized the air she took on when she went up against a bully.

And suddenly they were close enough that, as she reached out desperately with her feelers, Alexandra got more information. It came in a wave, like she'd walked from a hot summer day into an air-conditioned lobby.

Girl in the photo. Right on schedule. Start the car. Check the street. Police scanner is on. Get out. Grab her.

Alexandra suddenly barked, "Get her out of here!" as she dropped her backpack on the ground. She darted forward as the girl passed the car and the back passenger door of the Jeep opened.

Katherine knocked loudly on the door to the small shack on the beachfront property, waiting and reaching out mentally. It was awkward knocking on the door of what used to be a large storage shed, but was now an efficiency and was rented out by this man from the owners of the million-dollar house behind it. She felt a man check a surveillance camera and she looked around, spotting it tucked under the awning, and waved. Reese eyed her for a moment before following her gaze and spotting the small device, prompting him to smile.

Footsteps sounded inside and the door was unlocked and opened, stopped by the chain. The best way Katherine could describe the man before them was 'squirrelly'. His head was a bit small for his body and he had glasses on that made it look even smaller.

Alan examined her carefully before speaking. "Yeah?" he muttered.

"Katherine Colebrook. Friend of Harold's. Looking for Alan."

His eyes slid to Reese. "Who's surfer boy, here?"

Reese glared at Alan, uncomfortably ruffling his dirty blonde hair as Katherine snorted. "My partner. You gonna make us stand out here all day?"

Alan paused, looking over his glasses at her, before he shut the door and took off the chain, opening it and moving aside. "Sorry for the mess. I'm not a very tidy person. But I make up for it in talent." Katherine and Reese walked in, opting to stand rather than take a seat on the couch that was almost covered in garbage and dirty laundry as Alan closed and relocked the door. "Harold said you're curious about a certain thief I might have had contact with."

"Indeed I am. I'm also curious why you wouldn't talk over the phone. Save me the drive," she asked, cocking an eyebrow.

Alan glared at her, folding his arms. "I don't like phones. Don't like not knowing who I'm talking to."

Katherine kept herself from reacting visually to that

one. *Wonder what your reaction would be to knowing this guy's a pùca.* "Fair enough. So?"

Alan remained silent in a heavy hesitation before narrowing his eyes. "So...what?"

"What can you tell me about this guy?" she asked, bordering on annoyed. Reese pursed his lips over a smile.

"Ah...what do you want to know?"

"Where he is."

Alan stared at her for a few seconds. "Harold said you were on the up and up. Why are you looking for this guy?"

"Because he's killed seventeen people so far, from age ten to fifty, in order to get the jewels he steals, and the police haven't been able to stop him. So they called us in."

Blinking a few times and taking a step back, Alan became a bit twitchy. "You're feds?"

"Trackers," she replied easily. Reese remained silent, glancing to Katherine and then back to Alan.

Alan's fists clenched and unclenched, knowing what that meant. "So you're gonna track this guy down and... what?" he asked.

Katherine paused, letting the silence stretch for a moment. "He's killed seventeen people, five of them children," she said softly. "Abducted them, kept them restrained without food and water for two or three days, and then strangled them to death. What do you think I'm gonna do when I find him?"

Swallowing hard, Alan shifted his weight and nodded slowly, letting out a breath. Katherine felt Reese staring at the man, fascinated at the approach she had taken, knowing that it had to have been helped by the background she'd gathered from him. Alan seemed to appreciate the honesty on her part and the malicious intent of the FBI. It appealed to his conspiratorial ideas of how the world worked. "This thief I might have talked to is about your height," Alan started. "Short black hair—"

"I'm not interested in what he looks like," Katherine told him. Alan blinked. "I need to know if you know where he is."

"I might have met with him about a piece of jewelry at the Ocean Bay Inn," he said with a shrug. "Room 205. And I might have a phone number for him."

"*Might* you be able to call him and say you have a client who needs something retrieved from a safe on someone else's property?" Katherine asked. "And that her reputation precedes her?"

Alan paused before slowly nodding. "I might be able to do that. Does this job pay well?"

"This woman might be willing to pay generously for this item she wants stolen."

Alan narrowed his eyes to slits and he paused before taking his cell phone from his pocket. "What do I call her?"

Katherine pursed her lips. "Debbie."

Alan nodded once and dialed a number. Katherine waited and listened to a conversation that she would have been generous to call cryptic and hypothetical. She glanced to Reese, who was managing to hold back his amusement. Barely.

Eventually, Alan hung up and turned to her with a nod. "He's in Vegas right now. He said he's got a colleague who can come meet with you to discuss this possible job in Laguna Beach. Six PM tomorrow. The Vortex on Moreland."

CHAPTER 26

As Alexandra picked up speed a man got out of the back seat of the Jeep, his face concealed under a ski mask, and grabbed the girl in a bear hug low around her waist. He hoisted her up and spun around to shove her in the car faster than the girl could comprehend what was going on. And in unison Alexandra took a flying leap and smashed her elbow into the man's nose as he turned, tumbling to the ground with the two of them. The assailant cried out, instinctively grabbing for his face, the girl briefly forgotten.

And, falling to the ground harshly and taking a sharp breath, the girl's eyes locked on the man with a mask and she let out a piercing scream.

Alexandra yanked the girl up and shoved her in Jessica's direction as she turned back to the man that had instantly shoved himself back to his feet. Jessica grabbed the girl's arm and pulled her into a run. Just as the man attempted to get back up, Alexandra snapped a leg out into the man's crotch, grabbing his wrist and yanking viciously downward, her knee slicing up into his chin, a cross-motion that would cut a hole clean in his tongue if he had the misfortune of biting it.

As it was, he was dazed, but reflex kicked in enough to backhand Alexandra. She cried out, flying back into the wall and hitting her head, collapsing to the ground. He assumed she was down for the count, she sensed, so she took a moment to gather herself and then flipped over as she spun herself to her feet, lifting her leg into a roundhouse kick, crashing her heel into his kidney. He collapsed to the ground and she rolled with the energy of the kick, coming back up into a crouch. "Shit—"

The man shoved himself backwards toward the car, his hand going to the small of his back and yanking a pistol out. But before he could aim it, Alexandra had leapt forward and grabbed it, snapping the gun from his grip and shoving him back with a front kick to his stomach.

Alexandra turned to face him, breathing hard, flipping the gun in her hand and locking her aim on his chest, double-checking that the safety was off. Aiming at his head would be more threatening, but considering he had an exit strategy behind him, she wasn't going to get cocky. She'd rather take the bigger target. The whole altercation had taken seconds, but by this time several people had ducked behind trees and stairways and started calling the police. None had attempted to intervene though, partially because a gun had been introduced to the equation and partially because it seemed like the sixteen-year-old girl had it under control.

The man's cold, wide eyes stared at her, slowly putting his hands out to his side. "Just…careful with that," he rasped.

"How long until you think your buddy in the car burns rubber?" she growled, cocking an eyebrow. She slid her cell phone from her pocket with her left hand, dialing 911 in her peripheral vision and lifting it to her ear as she kept her aim on him steady. The man shifted his weight anxiously.

"Get *in*," the driver barked.

"She knows how to *use* that goddamn thing," he snapped back. "I can tell. She'll plug me with holes." Alexandra sneered, her aim not wobbling a millimeter from where it was.

"Fine." At that, the car lurched forward, speeding down the street, the back door shutting from the momentum.

Still trying to get her heart rate to slow, Alexandra motioned curtly with the gun in her hand. "Down. Now." He swallowed tightly, slowly lowering himself to the sidewalk as he would if a cop had ordered him to. "Yeah, there's a black Jeep Patriot Sport headed west on Pico Boulevard," Alexandra spoke into the phone. "No license plate. It's a getaway car for an attempted kidnapping.... Yeah, I've got one of the assailants at gunpoint at Lincoln and Grand.... Yes, I know how to handle a gun.... I'm sixteen," she sighed. "Uh huh, she's fine. My friend got her somewhere safe.... Alexandra Colebrook.... And if you could put a call in to FBI SAC Roger Jackson about this, that'd be just lovely."

"So when you said it...*felt* dangerous..." Jessica murmured.

"I really meant it," Alexandra answered. She leaned back against the brick wall of the sidewalk café, letting out a long breath and folding her arms. "I just got a bad feeling.

I'm psychic. Like my mom is. I have visions. Matter of fact, that was the 'migraine' I had at school the other day. I feel things other people feel, know what they're thinking. But I don't snoop around people's heads," she added quickly. "Actually I spend most of my time making sure I *don't* know what other people are thinking, considering I'm surrounded by hundreds of other teenagers seven hours a day. I got enough problems. I don't need to know everyone else's." She examined Jessica carefully as the girl stared at her for a long moment. "Any…thoughts on this?"

"Aside from the fact that you're ten times cooler than I thought you were?" Jessica asked, her face splitting into a grin. Alexandra blinked in confusion. "You're, like, a superhero. With real superpowers, even. How could you not *tell* me this?"

"Uh…it's kind of not something I like talking about," Alexandra said. "Just…I'm weird enough already. I don't need everyone at school thinking I'm even weirder."

Jessica shook her head. "I'm not gonna tell anyone," she said earnestly. "It's like your secret identity. You can totally trust me." Alexandra let out a small smile, skeptical at Jessica's ability to keep such a secret, but giving her the benefit of the doubt for the time being. "I mean, we talked about psychics. You never even hinted. It's not even like you're a parasapien; you said psychics are just sapiens, right?"

"As far as we know," Alexandra said with a shrug. "Go back ten or twenty thousand years, maybe some fae got with some humans and came up with psychics. Like I said, we're all people. Someone somewhere just decided psychics were more human than others." Jessica fell silent at that.

"You trying to put the cops out of a job now?"

Alexandra turned toward the familiar voice and smiled dryly. "Just doing my civic duty," she replied, meeting Jackson's gaze.

The officer that had taken Alexandra's statement walked up to Jackson. "You here to pick them up?" he asked.

Jackson nodded. "Just the brunette. You got everything you need from her?"

"Yeah, I'm good. You know the little ninja?"

Jackson smiled. "Ya. I'm her mom's boss," he said, showing the officer his badge. "I'll make sure she gets home."

"All right then," the officer said with a nod, turning and leaving.

Jackson folded his arms. "So?" he asked. "How've you been?"

Alexandra let out a laugh. "Didn't the cop that called you tell you what happened?"

"Yeah, but I wanted to make sure it was the whole story," Jackson told her.

"Ah," she said, smiling knowingly. "No parasapien stuff. But those guys were pros. I don't know why they wanted that girl, but I'm assuming they'll try again."

Jackson nodded. "She's in protective custody and her parents are coming down to the station. It's their job to keep her safe her now," he said with a wink.

"I know."

"Called your momma. She ain't happy, but she's glad you're safe," Jackson said, giving Alexandra a look.

Alexandra gave him a tight smile and looked to Jessica, who had fallen silent. "Jessica was walking with me when it happened. And apparently takes orders well," she said. Jessica smiled timidly.

"You got yourself a keeper here," Jackson said, motioning to Jessica. "You ready to go?"

"I am," Alexandra said with a tired sigh. "Kicking ass is tiring. But Jessica's mom is coming to pick her up. Should be here any minute."

"All right. So we can hang out 'til she gets here," Jackson said with a nod.

"You should probably go," Jessica told Alexandra, lowering her voice. "If my mom knows that I was hanging out with you…."

"She's gonna know anyway," Alexandra told her friend. "I'm pretty sure the police are gonna tell her. My name's in the report."

"Her mom doesn't like you?" Jackson asked Alexandra, his eyes narrowing. "No accounting for taste. Just saved some girl from being kidnapped. You'd think she'd be grateful to have a mini-bodyguard hanging with her daughter."

Alexandra snorted. "You'd think. But she thinks my opinion on parasapiens seriously leaves something to be desired. That being, I don't think we should kill them all."

Jackson grunted. "I see. Well, can't win 'em all. But I think Jessica waiting for her momma with another officer's probably the best move. No sense in waiting for a fight you know's coming."

"Fair enough," Alexandra agreed. She glanced to Jessica. "I'll see you at school."

Jessica smiled. "See you tomorrow."

"We'll head straight to the hospital then," Jackson said, taking out his keys.

Alexandra walked after him, speeding up to keep up with his naturally fast pace. "What? I'm fine," she protested.

"Try again," he spoke, tapping the spot on his head where Alexandra had a nasty bump on hers. "I see blood. You get a knock on your head, you go to the ER."

"They've got better things to do than waste time on me," she scoffed.

"This ain't a negotiation," Jackson replied.

"After that, could we go back to your new place?" Alexandra asked. "I haven't seen the zoo in ages."

"Sorry, but I gotta get back to work after this," he told her. "We'll visit another time."

Alexandra put her backpack in the back seat of Jackson's car before getting in shotgun. He started the car and pulled out onto the street, remaining quiet as he drove.

After a few minutes, Alexandra spoke up. "You think Jessica's mom has a point about Jessica hanging out with me?" she asked.

"Now you know I don't think so," Jackson replied. "So what're you really asking?"

"I don't mean about parasapiens all being vicious killers. I mean…maybe Jessica would be safer not hanging out with me," Alexandra said quietly, staring steadily out her window.

Jackson sighed, hesitating, rubbing the graying scruff on his chin absently. "World's a dangerous place," he muttered. "Isn't gonna do Jessica any good to try to stay away from anything she thinks could hurt her. Just cause you find more than your fair share of trouble, doesn't mean she'd be safer keeping her distance from you. Having a friend like you, though…. That's nothing but positives. In my humble opinion."

A small smile pulled at the edges of Alexandra's mouth, and she remained silent.

CHAPTER 27

"I DON'T NEED AN MRI," ALEXANDRA said, exasperated. "Give me a break."

"The doctor'll be the judge of that," Jackson told her. He finished and sent his text to Katherine, his phone emitting a small *whoosh*. He put his phone back in his pocket, looking around the small curtained-off section of Cedar Sinai's emergency room that the nurse had brought them to. A small, plain clock was perched high on the wall and ticked away silently, informing Jackson that they'd been waiting for the doctor for about ten minutes. He went over to the chair beside Alexandra, taking a seat. "You should probably sit on the cot."

"I've got a headache, not a broken ankle," she told him.

Jackson shifted his gaze to her with a small smile. "I know. Just…the doc'll probably want you up there."

Alexandra suddenly looked to her right as the curtain was pulled aside, revealing a middle-aged man in pale slacks and a white coat, which had the name Doctor Hamid Rashidi embroidered on it. He had a full head of dark brown hair, a goatee, and attentive brown eyes, and he gave her a smile as he entered, glancing at the chart he'd just picked up.

The doctor is about halfway through a long shift, which means he is still wide-awake. He's had several easy patients so far and is glad to have another that seems straightforward. He is good at his job, good at handling the long days, the overprotective parents and their injured children, the strung-out druggies and the horrific accidents, the police investigations and the complex diagnoses. He has confidence, not ego, and that prompts her to immediately become more comfortable in his care.

"So, which one of you's Alexandra?" he asked.

Jackson raised his hand, prompting Alexandra to elbow him. "The nurses fixed me up, and I promise I'm not seeing spots," she told Hamid. "I'm fine."

"Let me do my thing anyway, hm?" he asked, motioning to the cot. "You her father?"

"Nah, I'm her mom's boss," Jackson replied as Alexandra hopped up on the cot. "Katherine's over near Oxnard today, so she asked me to help out."

Hamid nodded once as he took out a small Maglite from his pocket. "I see. All right, follow my finger without moving your head," he told her, holding up his index finger. Alexandra did as she was told. "Want to tell me what happened?"

"I foiled a kidnapping," Alexandra replied.

"Ha ha," he said, smiling.

"I can vouch for her," Jackson said, sounding a bit resigned.

Alexandra's expression turned sour as the doctor

lowered his hand. "Is it because I'm sixteen, or because I'm a girl?" she asked.

Hamid blinked once. "I apologize," he responded. "Not every day I meet someone as awesome as you just proposed you were." Alexandra smiled in amusement as he held up his finger again, moving it from left to right as she stared at it. Hamid flicked on his flashlight and put his hand on her head to hold it in place as he shined the light carefully in each of her eyes. "You experience any disorientation, nausea, ringing in your ears?" he asked.

"No, I would've mentioned that," she answered.

"Good." He picked up the chart again, writing a few things down before he put it aside again, going back to her and parting her hair to take a look at the wound. "Since you didn't need stitches, I think I'll call it," he said, looking back to her with a smile. "You can go home."

"Thanks," she replied, hopping down off the cot.

"Clean the wound carefully; don't wash your hair like normal. And let your mom know to be on the lookout for any of the things I mentioned–"

"She knows the signs for a concussion," Alexandra told him. "As do I, thank you very much."

Hamid held up his hands. "My apologies, again. Hopefully by your next trip in to see me, I'll learn not to underestimate you." Alexandra smirked at him as Jackson pushed himself to his feet.

"Don't even joke," the FBI agent said wearily.

CHAPTER 28

KATHERINE DOUBLE-CHECKED THE BULLETS IN the magazine in her Desert Eagle before tucking it into her holster, settling into her seat in her rental car. She had gone to the bar that morning and scouted it and the surrounding area and then had come back in the evening to wait for her guest of honor. The bar had conveniently situated parking spots against the wall of the opposite building, so she could keep a good view of it in her rearview mirrors. It included an interesting mix of customers, some regular but most just passing through. Among other things, she also noted that there were three exits, including those reserved for employees, no security cameras, and the owner kept a pistol under the cash register.

Katherine knew her best bet was that the pùca would come looking like someone else, pretending to be an employee of himself. It was smart, actually. Create an imaginary middleman. Reese had been disappointed when she'd told him to stay behind, but in addition to wanting to get a better feel for working with him before they went after a violent parasapien, this was actually a job she knew she'd be better off doing on her own. She didn't need backup, so

Reese would've just been unnecessary. Of course she usually didn't need backup, but when it was a job that counted on the element of surprise, Katherine much preferred to do it on her own. She wore a full-body leotard under her normal clothes, standard gear when going up against a pùca in order to make skin-to-skin contact more difficult, and had a handful of iron weapons on her person as well.

The minutes ticked by slowly, and Katherine's mind drifted briefly to the conversation she'd had with Jackson that afternoon, a tight pang sliding into her chest. Stopping a kidnapping was a new one to add to Alexandra's list of the times she had found trouble. Taking a slow breath in and letting it out, Katherine tried to push her mind back to the case at hand, knowing that she would have plenty of time to be overwhelmed with concern for her daughter's safety later.

Fifteen minutes early, a nondescript sedan drove into the lot and parked, the glare of the neon signs in its window giving the pale car a colorful glow, and Katherine smiled as she felt the pùca in the driver's seat. Katherine ducked down in her seat as he locked his car and went inside, keeping her feelers out to sense where the pùca was and what he was doing. As he headed inside, Katherine slid back up in her seat, getting a look at him. He had taken on the appearance of the most unremarkable man she could've imagined: Caucasian, short brown hair, a dark blue shirt and blue jeans. Not attractive. Not ugly. The kind of guy you would never remember.

The pùca ordered a beer that he nursed for nearly an hour as he waited for the client that would never come. Katherine waited for him to run out of patience, the occasional patron exiting and letting the combination of several televisions blaring a sports game and drunken customers spill out into the parking lot.

When the pùca headed back out to his car and took off, Katherine followed at a safe distance, keeping track of his emotions and feelings, and pursed her lips at his train of thought. Greed had prompted him to take a meeting with a new client while he was already knee-deep in a job, especially the way Alan had talked her up, but caution and suspicion had made him concerned about the timing now that she had failed to show. And now he was taking out his cell phone and calling his current client, reporting that he had gotten itchy and he was taking evasive measures, and that he would need additional time to complete the job he'd been assigned.

Katherine ended up following the pùca to a wealthy neighborhood and he entered a code on the front gate of a housing complex to gain entry. Passing the gate and parking down the street, Katherine surveyed the area as she climbed over the fence and speed-walked down the street to the house the pùca had gone to, glad she had the cover of night on her side but wishing she'd had more time to do recon. The large houses, most of which probably had swimming pools, all had beautifully kempt lawns garnished with colorful foliage and flowering trees, and most had topiaries and even fountains. In the minds of the residents, the gates kept out anything dangerous. They had potluck barbeques on Sunday and their kids rode their bikes in the street. No one knew the dark secret that was kept by the pùca occupying this particular house, and the idea that someone like him could live in this area was ridiculous to them, which was why it was the perfect place to hide.

Katherine gathered the layout of the house from the pùca's mind and she headed around to the backyard. She quickly made it to the back door, picking the lock as she felt the pùca closing the garage door and walking into its house and into the kitchen. The lock clicked and opened and Katherine put her lock pick back into her pocket, taking out her gun. She silently and swiftly made her way into the house, keeping her feelers on the pùca, and walked down the sparsely decorated hall to the kitchen. The pùca had gone through a set of folding doors that usually would have lead to a laundry room but instead led to a security setup.

Her gun up in front of her, Katherine sped up, sensing the pùca scanning his cameras, looking for anything out of the ordinary, and suddenly his eyes landed on her.

Katherine swore under her breath and as she turned the corner into the laundry room, her gun up and at the ready, the pùca shifted to a cheetah and leapt at her. A gunshot sounded and a bullet cracked into the glass of one of the CCTV screens as Katherine was thrown to the ground with a cry. Claws sank into her shoulders and the pùca suddenly screeched as the iron threads in her jacket burned him. He leapt off her, shifting back to human, and she pushed past the pain, lifting the gun to aim at him, but he grabbed it on its way through the air and twisted it of her grip, tossing it into the hallway. He seized a hold of her ponytail and hoisted her into the air, but before he could pin her to the wall or start draining her, Katherine twisted and flew her right leg up, shoving the creature away with her shin.

The pùca screamed at the iron contact, his grip slipping from Katherine's neck as they crashed to the ground. Katherine yanked a blade from its sheath on her belt and attempted to stab the creature in the stomach, but he promptly morphed to a small beagle, escaping from her grip. He darted into the hall at full speed and Katherine shoved herself to her feet, snatching her gun from where it had fallen and bolting after him. The pùca took a few quick turns through the house as he made for the back door, shifting to a greyhound as he ran, and Katherine focused on trying to catch up with him.

When she finally got him firmly in her sights in the den, where she'd broken in, Katherine raised her gun and fired just as he closed in on the door. With a yelp, the pùca tumbled a few times and stopped, blood pouring from the chest wound. Katherine immediately got closer and fired two more bullets into the greyhound's head.

Her chest heaving, Katherine took a moment to gather herself, slowly holstering her weapon. A few seconds passed and she gnashed her teeth, almost letting out a growl. "Really?" she snapped. "A dog? I'm gonna have nightmares where I'm murdering puppies."

Katherine took stock of her wounds soaking blood into her shirt, finding that they weren't too deep since the pùca hadn't had much time to make serious gashes before he leapt away. Putting her injuries aside for the moment, she quickly walked back the way she'd come down the hall and opened the basement door, descending the stairs.

In the corner was a teenage boy, exhausted and half conscious, his ankle chained to a bed.

The boy's eyes fluttered open and he whimpered and

drew back as she came down the stairs and over to him, kneeling at his side. "My name's Katherine," she said, taking the small water bottle from her jacket and opening it. She sat carefully on the edge of the bed. "I'm with the FBI. I'm here to take you home." Relief flooded the boy's exhausted face and he gratefully drank the water that was offered to him. "Easy, slowly…. What's your name?" Katherine asked once he'd drank his fill.

"Gareth," he whispered. He put his head back down on the bed. "Gareth Moore. What about the guy that took me? He changed so he looked like me. Did you–?"

Katherine nodded as she took out her lock-pick set. "It's okay. He's dead."

Gareth swallowed hard and let out a long breath, eyeing Katherine as she started to pick the lock around his ankle. "You're bleeding," he said.

"I'll be fine." Another twenty seconds or so passed and the shackle fell open. "Come on," she murmured, helping him to his feet. "Time to go."

<hr />

Reese looked over the railings on the second-floor hallway of the motel, taking in the palm tree that was situated between two lawn chairs around the swimming pool, focusing on his surroundings since the main subject of his sketch had gotten out of the pool. He finished the outline of the tree, moving the piece of scrap paper between his palm and the sketchbook that he was using to make sure he didn't smudge his work. It was just pencil, nothing as extravagant as charcoal, but smudges were smudges and he always worked meticulously to avoid them. Turning the pencil sideways, he swept the tip skillfully along the body of the tree, patterning the bark.

It had been after about an hour of reading one of the books that Katherine had left on the table that Reese had given up on trying to do something productive and instinctively reached for his sketchpad. He'd understood why Katherine had elected to go after the pùca on her own, but it was still irritating because he knew he would be a valuable addition to any assignment Katherine went on, including one that featured a psychopathic serial killing pùca. He could group half a magazine's worth of bullets in a parasapien's chest just as efficiently as Katherine could, and the fact was, he was a probationary agent for a reason. That reason was to learn from her. And he learned nothing sitting on his ass back at their motel.

"So my friend wants to know why you're leering at us," spoke up a voice to his right.

"You want to see?" Reese mumbled, not moving his gaze from his work as he continued.

The young woman paused. "You're drawing us?"

Reese looked up with a smile. "Well, most of what's down there, but you happened to be there too."

Biting her lower lip, she came forward and motioned with her hand, taking Reese's pad when he offered it. Her face suddenly turned serious and she blinked. "Wow, ah…. I didn't actually expect this to be…. This is really good."

Reese watched a drop of water trail down her collarbone for a long moment before forcing his gaze up to her eyes, which were studiously taking in his sketch, rather than allowing himself to look down to her golden, toned legs. "Thanks. I'm Reese, by the way."

The young woman handed the pad back to him with a smile. "Melinda. You want to join us?" she asked.

"I...didn't know there'd be a pool, actually," he answered. "No suit."

Melinda pursed her lips and shrugged delicately. "Don't necessarily need one. Not like they post security in a place like this. Especially for a night swim."

Reese smirked. "Ah, interest of full disclosure, I'm actually a fed," he confessed. "And if my partner came back here and found me skinny-dipping...."

Melinda's smile widened. "A fed?" She chewed on her lower lip. "You have handcuffs?"

Reese choked out a laugh, briefly looking down to the pool, where Melinda's friend was lounging in one of the chairs, before looking back to her. "I do. You thinking of someone I might need to arrest?"

Melinda shrugged one of her shoulders. "Maybe. I can be really naughty sometimes."

Reese finally let his gaze slide down Melinda's body and let out a small moan, letting his head drop to his chest before sitting up straight. "As much as I...would love to party with you and your friend," he forced out, "I gotta... stay here. In case my partner calls cause she needs me to swoop in and save the day."

Melinda pouted. "Well you're no fun."

"I'm a complete buzzkill," Reese muttered, nodding in agreement.

Melinda spun on one heel and headed back the way she came, leaving Reese to stare after her, enjoying the contours of her body before she turned the corner into the stairwell. Reese gnashed his teeth, falling back into his chair with a ragged sigh. After staring into the distance for a long moment, he shoved himself to his feet and went back into his room to take a cold shower.

"He'll make a full recovery?" Katherine spoke into her cell phone as she checked her blind spot, switching lanes.

"Yeah, he'll be fine. You did good."

"Thanks," Katherine said.

"Any injuries on your end?"

"Yeah," she muttered in annoyance. "Got some cheetah claws to my shoulders. I'll clean up when I get back to the motel. Reese and I will probably wrap everything up and drive back tomorrow afternoon."

"You shoulda gone to the hospital," Jackson grumbled.

"I'm fine," Katherine assured him.

"Like mother like daughter," he sighed, prompting Katherine to frown.

"Speaking of, I'm gonna have to have a talk with her when I get home," she muttered.

Jackson fell silent. "So the...thief?" he asked eventually. "Any idea who he was? Or she. Whatever. Cause we ran his plates and got nothing. And he died a dog, so we've got no prints."

"He'd probably been so many people, he didn't remember who he started out as," Katherine said softly.

CHAPTER 29

Katherine tossed her keys into the bowl next to the door as she entered her apartment, sensing Alexandra in her bedroom, her homework spread over the floor. The security system started beeping and Katherine turned it off and put aside her messenger bag as Alexandra came out into the living room.

"Hey," Alexandra spoke.

"Hey yourself," Katherine sighed, walking over and motioning. "Let me see."

"It's fine. It was barely even bleeding," Alexandra protested as Katherine took her daughter's head in her hands. "I cleaned it gently last night, and again this morning. Had a small headache at school today, that's it." She parted Alexandra's hair to get a better look at the wound, frowning seriously.

"It's a head wound, Alex, it's not a paper cut," Katherine muttered. She released Alexandra after a few long moments, taking a step back and folding her arms tightly. "So. You want to tell me what, exactly, you were thinking?"

Alexandra stared at her mother. "What do you mean?"

"What do I mean?" Katherine asked, incredulous.

"Two armed men attempt to kidnap someone and without any hesitation, you jump right into the fray."

"Of course I did," Alexandra told her. "What else should I have done? Stand there like an idiot and watch her get kidnapped?"

"Don't get smart with me." Alexandra's expression slowly started to shift to a glare. "There are a hundred ways this could have gone badly," Katherine said. "For Christ's sake, Alex, if you hadn't been close enough to disarm him when he'd drawn his gun, or if you'd been unsuccessful, he could have *shot* you!"

"But he didn't! And the girl is safe!"

"My point is not what did happen! My point is what could have happened!" Katherine shouted. "And this is not about her. This is about you!"

Alexandra clenched her fists at her sides, staring in disbelief at her mother. "So I saved someone's life today and you come home and yell at me?"

"Did you expect me to stop at Baskin Robbins to pick up a cake?" Katherine snapped. "We had this discussion when you were thirteen. I didn't think we needed to have it again."

Alexandra rolled her eyes. "Oh my god, seriously?" she asked. "This is nothing like what happened at the zoo!"

"What you don't seem to understand is that every time you put your life and your safety above someone else's is going to be exactly like all the other times you do it," Katherine said, pointing a finger at her daughter. "And if I have to say it every day for the rest of your life, I will: you come first. You will always come first. I did not raise you to be a superhero; I raised you to know how to protect yourself. And I am not going to stand here and let you risk your neck for someone else because you are convinced that you're invincible."

"I don't think I'm invincible!" Alexandra exclaimed. "I just know how to protect people! If Jessica had been the one that had tried to stop the kidnapping, yeah, that would've been stupid. But it's not for me. And I don't get why you don't see that!"

"Stupid is the wrong word. It's not stupid; it is reckless," Katherine snapped. "And I know you feel you're old enough and strong enough and smart enough to be out there saving people, but you're not, and I'm not about to stand here and let you get yourself killed."

"This is my life and these are my choices!" Alexandra shouted. "Why do you think you have the right to decide whether I help people or not?"

"Because I know where you'll end up!" Katherine bellowed, stepping close to her daughter, towering over her. Despite herself, tears sprung to her eyes as she stared down at Alexandra fiercely. "Cradling your best friend in your arms, drenched in her blood. In the hospital after being shot and tortured for the location of a little girl. And bawling at the side of your husband's corpse, wishing that–"

Katherine suddenly stopped and blinked, tears sliding down her face. She took in and let out a few slow breaths as Alexandra stared in shock, her anger evaporating and her tight shoulders slowly lowering.

The image of David's unmoving body, his eyes wide and staring terrified at nothing, suddenly formed in Katherine's mind, relentlessly forceful and unwilling to go no matter how much she tried to blink it away. And now suddenly, right next to it, was Alexandra's corpse.

Somewhere, something had gone wrong. It had been nine years since David had been murdered, which meant nine years of much more intense training for Alexandra to protect herself. And Katherine didn't regret that. She couldn't. But she'd seen this path before; it was her own. And when she thought about that fact, she couldn't help but think of every moment where she'd been close to a death. When one of a million things could have changed just slightly, and Katherine wouldn't have made it. She knew it was the exact same situation with Alexandra, and every part of her screamed to change her daughter's path before that happened.

But that's not how Alexandra was thinking. And why would it be? At sixteen, Katherine felt the same way. Desperate to be strong enough to protect herself, yes, but even more so was the overwhelming desire to save people. Not because she hadn't been able to save her mother and this was compensating for that. Katherine knew she couldn't have saved her mother. But that loss, that attack, had triggered something in her. The force propelling her toward being an FBI agent had always been to get to a point where she could control the world and the situations she ended up in. It was an attempt to eradicate feeling helpless. And this was a step backwards.

Katherine wiped her hands across her face and took a breath. "It's easy to try to save everyone," she whispered. "But sooner or later, you fail. Sooner or later, you don't save someone. Or worse, something goes wrong, and–"

"But you can't protect me from everything!" Alexandra

protested. "I always try to be safe, and I always try to be smart. But there are going to be people that I see in danger and it's just not in me to just let them get hurt. And it's not your decision if I do."

"Alex, you're going to want to help people for the rest of your life, because you're a good person," Katherine murmured. "And I know, especially as a psychic, you know their pain and fear almost like it's your own. But something that I will never stop feeling in my gut is that you are absolutely...without a doubt...more important than them. Do you understand that?"

"Yeah. But I'm not." Katherine stared at Alexandra. "I'm not more important than them, mom. They're just as important as I am. I mean–" Alexandra shook her head. "Isn't that why you work as a tracker anyway?" she asked. "To keep people safe? To help them?"

Katherine's heart skipped a beat. "What?"

"What if I want to be a tracker and–?"

"No!" Katherine exclaimed.

Alexandra blinked, stunned for a moment. "I'm sorry.... No?"

Katherine stared in wide-eyed fear at her daughter, and suddenly found herself unable to speak. Because she had no words. Protecting people in danger had abruptly escalated to a whole other level, and Katherine was paralyzed.

"You're telling me that you're *forbidding* me to be a tracker," Alexandra sneered.

"I'm telling you that...." Katherine fell silent for a few long moments before she shook her head. "I'm gonna make dinner."

Alexandra gave her mother a strange look. "What?"

"It's dinner time, I-I just.... Go to your room. Finish your homework."

Alexandra stared at Katherine before she gnashed her teeth and spun around, leaving the room and going down the hall. She slammed her bedroom door and Katherine flinched.

Suddenly feeling incredibly lost, Katherine slowly walked out of the living room and down the hallway. She knocked on Rebecca's door before opening it. "Hey," she spoke quietly.

Rebecca's gaze didn't move from her computer screen. "Hi. How was your day?" she asked formally.

Katherine stared at Rebecca for a long moment as she slowly smiled. A part of her had been concerned that the argument had disturbed Rebecca, but the teenager had simply tuned them out, vaguely annoyed. "Good, thanks. I caught a bad guy yesterday."

"That's good," Rebecca remarked. Her fingers typing away on the keyboard didn't break stride.

"Dinner will be in about half an hour," Katherine said.

"Okay. Thank you."

Katherine shut the door and leaned against the hallway wall. She spent a minute or so staring at the wall across from her, lost in her thoughts. Eventually she let out a sigh and shook her head, rubbing her face with both hands, before going back into the living room.

CHAPTER 30

Katherine's instinct after having an argument with Alexandra was to try to figure out how she could smooth things over, but at the moment she was at a complete loss. The only thing she could think to do was bury herself in some work for an hour or two until she got tired enough to sleep.

Grabbing her messenger bag from where she'd left it, Katherine's phone rang and she took it from her pocket. The number on her phone was unrecognized, and she paused briefly before answering it, identifying it as an LA area code.

"Yeah?"

"Hey. It's Michael Weston."

Katherine's face went slack. The alias was a joke between her and a friend, Austin Corlett. She'd compared him to the burned spy on the TV show Burn Notice and he'd found it amusing. And if he was using it on the phone, that meant he was off the grid.

Corlett was an LA local, a former Special Forces Ranger that currently freelanced for private security agencies and people who needed help. He was a Grizzly Adams type, though with a significantly less intense beard, and a small ponytail. The kind of guy who would give you a gregarious bear hug if you were a friend, or break your spine if you were an enemy. Corlett had numerous contacts, those who danced on that line between illegal and legal as well as those who definitely favored the illegal side, so Katherine occasionally called him for information on local trouble or visa versa.

"What's going on?"

"Call me back on a secure line?" he asked.

"No problem. I got the number on my caller ID. One second." Katherine hung up, getting a burner phone from a kitchen drawer, popping in the battery and turning it on. She brought up the number on the cell phone's screen, dialing it and waiting as it rang.

"Hey. Think I could get sanctuary? I'm nearby," said Corlett.

"From who?"

"More like from 'what'," he spoke. "That's why I'm calling you. I've got a family I'm supposed to keep safe and suddenly this thing is after us. And turns out it is a 'thing'. This is definitely a vampire. Female."

"How many am I sheltering?" Katherine asked, heading down the hall to her bedroom.

"Mom, dad, two kids. And me."

"Any injuries?"

"Dad has a few shallow gouges, but they're nothing lethal."

Katherine's expression became concerned, but she didn't say anything in response. She grabbed a duffle bag from her closet and started switching a few things out for other supplies on her shelves. "I've got a safe house I'll take you to," she told him.

"It makes me itchy not to be able to clean myself of a tail," Corlett muttered.

"For a guy that likes to be clean, you play in the mud a lot," Katherine pointed out.

"Point taken. I've got no right to complain."

"Let me call you back when I'm on my way."

"Got it. See you in a bit."

Katherine hung up and shot off a text message to Reese before she went into the old trunk sitting against the wall in her room next to her dresser, taking out a machete and a box of incendiary rounds. "What's going on?" Alexandra asked, walking into her mother's room. She glanced at the choice of rounds as Katherine put them in her jacket pocket. "Vampire?"

"Yeah, Corlett's got a problem," Katherine told her. She took a t-shirt and pair of sweatpants from her dresser and shoved them in the duffle as well. "Should go like clockwork, though," she spoke. "I'll make sure we're clean and then bring us to the safe house in Northridge. You can heat up a frozen pizza for dinner."

"I want to come with you."

Katherine blinked and froze, looking over to Alexandra, opening her mouth and shutting it. "What?" she finally said. "No. No, you can't come. What are you–? After the conversation we just had–"

"Shouting match," Alexandra corrected her.

Katherine glared at her daughter. "Please, enlighten me as to how you think you tagging along makes sense," she said.

191

"You said you want to be able to protect me," Alexandra told her. Her mother grabbed a water bottle from her closet and put it in her duffle bag, zippering it shut. "You'd be right there. So, better that I learn from experience now than get into trouble on my own."

Katherine shook her head as she took her badge and gun from her dresser drawer. "Alex." Her voice was terse and Alexandra's expression slowly grew disappointed at the solid end to the conversation her mother had just pronounced. "I'm sorry I have to head back out. You can make the chicken if you want."

"Fine."

Alexandra turned and left the room, and as Katherine slung her duffle over one shoulder and headed for the front door, Alexandra's bedroom door slammed shut again.

<hr />

Katherine merged onto the freeway, glancing at the GPS that was leading the way to her destination. The road in front of her was still clogged with the tail end of rush hour traffic, so she flipped on her flashers and siren as she increased her speed. "Okay. Talk to me," she spoke into the Bluetooth on her ear.

"When she found us at the last motel, she nearly got the younger brother, Paul," Corlett said. "I'd gone in to the lobby to get a room and she smashed in the car window, tried to grab the kid. And her fangs were out. Dad got some defensive wounds on his arm."

Katherine's expression tightened with concern at that information. "Younger brother?"

"Yeah. Seemed like the kid was the target, but when his dad got in the way, she didn't differentiate."

"Well, you can't lose her because she's tracking you by scent. Once she locks on prey, she'll pursue it until one of them is dead. It sounds like she's locked onto the kid."

"Shit."

"That's not the worst of it. I had a vision about a mother-son vampire duo," Katherine fibbed. "The son was just turned by his mother and he's hunting with her for the first time. This has got to be it. So you're only dealing with half the team so far."

"Double shit," he growled.

"What happened next?" she asked.

"Ah, I shot her, took her down, put three more bullets in her chest. And...then she started to get up. So I burned rubber out of there. Two blocks later I saw that dad had covered his boy with his own body, and she'd got him. I have a small first aid kit under the seat, so he patched himself up a bit."

"How far are you from Wilshire?"

"An hour, maybe. I'm in Long Beach. On the 405, heading north. I'm keeping them off grid from someone else, Colebrook. Now I've got this thing on my trail."

"All right," she muttered. "Listen, type this into your GPS. It's in Northridge. 1267 West Harlow Drive."

Katherine waited as Corlett plugged in the information. "All right. Perfect, should be an hour and twenty minutes. ETA 19:41.... It's taking us pretty much direct on the 405, though.... Yeah, there's an accident. I'll take an off-freeway route up almost to Santa Monica and then take the freeway from there."

"I'll probably still be there before you, but if not, the code for the key on the doorknob is 8224. Lock up tight until I get there."

CHAPTER 31

AFTER HANGING UP WITH KATHERINE, Austin
Corlett's attention went back to the road in front of
him. The four other occupants of the car remained silent
for a while until Marissa spoke up.

"Who is she?" she murmured.

"She's a friend," Corlett answered quietly, glancing over
to her. "FBI. I trust her." Marissa pursed his lips, nodding
slowly. Corlett adjusted the rearview mirror, checking
on Don and the boys, before angling it back out the rear
window.

It was about half an hour driving in silence before a
dark green Jeep appeared behind them that immediately
made Corlett uncomfortable.

Corlett started to check the rearview mirror every few
moments, wishing he'd taken the larger, more prominent
freeway instead, since they were quite isolated now. He
was already going a considerable amount over the speed
limit, and didn't want to risk getting pulled over. If he was
being pursued, though, it wouldn't be a matter of speed
that would get him out of there, so instead of going faster,
he slowed down.

The four civilians in the car didn't notice his change in demeanor, so when the Jeep got close they weren't paying attention, having crashed from the adrenaline rush of being attacked. But they immediately started paying attention again when the Jeep rear-ended them.

The boys yelled, grabbing onto their father, and Marissa let out a shriek, grabbing her armrest as their sedan swerved. "Damn it," Corlett growled. "Marissa, call Katherine on my phone. It's the last number on there. Tell her what's happening."

Marissa quickly picked up the phone and dialed, but let out a whimper. "There isn't any reception."

"Keep trying," Corlett barked at her, swearing to himself. A few seconds later, another car passed them in the other lane going the other direction, but failed to see that anything was wrong, apparently, because they kept going. It was another few seconds before the Jeep rear-ended them again, harder this time.

Corlett swore again as the car started to spin. He held tightly to the steering wheel, not overcorrecting in the least bit, and would have been able to straighten them out if the Jeep hadn't smashed into them again. "Hold on," he barked, as the car went hurtling over the edge of the road. The car skidded down the hill and Corlett tried to keep the wheels straight so it wouldn't flip, and was successful in that at least, as they went rushing through the brush.

After a few long moments, as they reached the bottom of the hill, Corlett eased onto the brakes and it slowly skidded to a heavy stop. About five seconds later, Corlett took in a long breath and looked at the other occupants in the car.

"Everyone okay?" he asked. There were murmurs and nods from each of them.

Corlett looked around and then up the hill they'd come down, which was the direction they'd ended up facing. He tried to start the car up again as Marissa picked up the phone from where it had fallen, but the engine refused to turn over. He took out his gun, checking the magazine and chambering a round, turning off all lights. "Okay, pull the back seat down and toss the luggage out the window, and get the kids into the trunk. If it comes for the car, it'll try to get to us through the windows."

"We're just going to hide?" Marissa whimpered. "You-You can't kill her! You already tried!"

"Backup's on the way," he told her as he pushed the button to open the back window. "Even if we don't get in touch, Katherine will figure out something is wrong and where we are. Get the boys in the trunk. Now. If you can fit in after them, Marissa, that's great. And keep calling Katherine. Don, you sit in front of the open window there. Here." He handed the man his backup weapon, which Don seemed tentative in taking, but did. "Just point and shoot, all right? But if you have to shoot, make it count." Don nodded as he put it aside and helped fold the seat down as Corlett got out of the car.

———◦✕◦———

Reese took his seat shotgun in Katherine's idling car and she barely waited for him to shut his door before pulling out of the gas station parking lot.

"Cripes," he muttered, grabbing a hold of the handle on his door as she steadied on the road.

"Sorry," Katherine said with a small smile. "I'm already ten minutes behind him."

Katherine's eyes flicked toward her cup holder as her cell phone rang and she pressed the button on her Bluetooth to answer it. "Yeah?" she answered. After a few seconds, she glanced at the phone and saw that it had dropped the call. Noticing that she had four bars, a heavy, anxious feeling settled in her stomach.

"Who is it?" Reese asked.

Katherine slowly shook her head. "It's Corlett. But the call cut out. Here, call him back." She handed the Bluetooth to Reese, who put it on his ear and redialed the last number on the phone. It went to voicemail, so he tried again.

Reese sat up a bit straighter when someone picked up. "Hey, who's this?"

"Th-This is Marissa," the voice on the other end of the phone quickly spoke. "Something happened."

<hr />

Corlett waited, crouched on the top of the sedan, gun in hand, doing regular visual sweeps of the area. He was a sitting duck if the vampire had a weapon, but he doubted that would be the case. And he had better odds with a good field of vision, especially since it was dark, and this gave him more access to the sounds of twigs breaking underfoot outside the car. Plus it was better to stop the vampire further from the civilians rather than attempting to push it back from inside the car.

Corlett suddenly froze, hearing a small sound to his left. His eyes had started to adjust to the darkness immediately and he'd taken the flashlight from his emergency kit, ready to shine in his adversary's eyes if need be. His stance was unwavering, his gun clenched tightly in one hand and his flashlight in the other. And suddenly, in a burst of motion, the vampire emerged from the brush, darting at him, and Corlett turned on the flashlight and aimed it at her eyes as he fired. He was able to get off two shots at the vampire's chest, and she shrieked as she tackled him from the top of the car, her fangs sinking into his shoulder.

Letting out a yelp of pain as they fell to the ground, Corlett gnashed his teeth and kept his grip on his gun as the woman withdrew her teeth from his wound and started to drink. He shoved the gun toward her head, but she grabbed both of his arms, pinning them to the ground, her fingers curling like claws, wrapped around his forearms in an iron-tight grip. Knowing that with every second that passed she healed from the gunshots and he lost more blood, Corlett bucked against her with all the strength he could manage. He failed to throw her off, though; she clung to him like a giant leech. His vision started to swim and the area around his collarbone started to grow cold.

Suddenly, Corlett heard another gunshot and the vampire flinched and released him, jerking backwards. He blinked rapidly, trying to steady the swirling world around him and groped for his gun, which had slipped from his hand. More shots echoed in his head and the vampire suddenly turned and bolted into the woods.

Gnashing his teeth and shoving a fistful of his shirt into his wound, Corlett pushed himself unsteadily to his feet, raising the gun in the direction of the vampire, but wasn't able to get it in his sights before she disappeared from view.

He lowered his gun to his side and stumbled toward the car, leaning against it.

"Are you okay?" Don asked breathlessly.

"Yeah, thanks," Corlett managed. "Grab the flashlight; turn it off." Don got out of the car and did as he was told. "Get back in the car."

"You can barely stand," Don stammered. His finger danced over the trigger of his gun, which was shaking his hand, as his eyes raked the trees around him.

"Doesn't matter," Corlett told him, shaking his head. "Having a smaller area to target gives you an advantage." Don eyed him warily before slowly doing as he was told. "Did Marissa get through?"

"Yeah, your friend's on her way. And Marissa's on the phone with 911 now too."

"All right." Corlett considered trying to get back up on the top of the car, but dismissed the idea as having more cons than pros. After a moment, he grabbed a roll of gauze from the first aid kit, shoving it against the bleeding punctures in his neck.

Five minutes passed, blood continuing to soak down his shirt. Ten minutes. Fifteen. And then his vision started to blur. And his leg muscles started to protest.

"…Don?"

"Yeah?"

"I'm gonna need you to stay in the car, okay?" Corlett managed.

"…I am."

"Good." And a few more seconds passed before Corlett couldn't hold himself up anymore, even with the help of the car, and he slid very ungracefully to his right, collapsing.

CHAPTER 32

"MY MAIN WORRY IS HER son," Katherine said. "Because if he isn't there and we can't find him, there's always the chance of him going after the civilians again, or Corlett, or us."

Reese nodded slowly. "But you said this is his first hunt, and vampire or not, he's a kid. He might get reckless and give us an opening. Or he might get smart and realize attacking sapiens is a good way to get dead."

"Possible, and that's what would be second best," she murmured. "He hasn't even hurt anyone yet. We could probably get him into a juvie center."

The two of them fell silent for about twenty minutes before Katherine sat up in her seat.

"You feel them?" Reese asked, noticing the change in demeanor.

Katherine hesitated before muttering, "Shit." Speeding up, Katherine skidded to a stop adjacent to an SUV, quickly throwing the car into park. "Secure the kid," she barked.

Katherine leapt from the car and bolted forward, heading down the hill, as the teenage boy in the car fumbled for the car door on his side. Reese was promptly out of the car as well, drawing his weapon as he darted around to the other side of the Jeep. The young vampire managed to unlock and open his door and took off.

"Stop!" Reese shouted, running after him. "I said stop! I'm armed with incendiary bullets!"

The vampire didn't break his stride or show any signs of slowing, so Reese came to an abrupt halt, aimed, and fired a single bullet.

The boy startled at the gunshot and cried out as the bullet ricocheted off the asphalt and he stumbled, tripping and falling to the ground. Reese ran forward as the boy stared at him, teary-eyed and angry. His fangs were out and he glowered at Reese.

"Face down, hands behind your head," Reese told him, his voice low and terse, his gun sighted on the boy's chest. "Or I will shoot you."

The boy stared at Reese for a few long moments, shaking with pain and anger, before slowly turning around and lying down on his stomach, doing as he was told. Reese walked forward and took out his handcuffs, holstering his gun and cuffing the boy's right wrist, then pulling it down behind him with the other.

Katherine attempted to keep her balance as she staggered unsteadily down the hill, the tall grass catching her legs briefly as she bolted through it, almost losing her footing several times. As she ran, she sensed the vampire running toward her son, having heard the gunshot and him shouting. After a few seconds though, Katherine felt the vampire change her mind, realizing that she was next. But it was too late; Katherine got within shooting distance and fired off half of her magazine at the vampire's back, lighting her up.

The vampire shrieked, thrashing against the flames that spread across her clothes and wrapped her body like a stick that had been soaked in gasoline. She screamed and struggled backwards for a few moments, but it was barely ten seconds before she collapsed to the ground. The fire destroyed her flesh and scorched her bones, and within twenty seconds she was just charred remains, smoldering on the ground.

Katherine rushed to the side of the middle-aged man on the ground beside a half-conscious Corlett. "Damn it," she growled. Her upper lip twitched but she only spared the vampire's victim a short glance before she went to Corlett's side instead, taking off her jacket and holding it against his wound. "Corlett? Corlett, come on. Wake up."

Katherine reached out mentally toward Reese, taking her phone from her pocket and dialing his cell number. "Yeah, hey, we're clear. Civilians are in the car. Three uninjured, one dead. Corlett's suffering severe blood loss. Call for backup. Get the first aid kit from my trunk."

"Got it."

"...Hello?" whimpered a female voice behind Katherine.

Katherine hung up her phone. "It's safe. We're FBI," Katherine told her.

Marissa stumbled from the car and let out a cry at her fallen husband. "Don!" she screamed, rushing to his side. "No! Don! Please!"

"He's gone," Katherine muttered. "I'm sorry."

"No, no, no, no, no," Marissa sobbed. She tried

desperately to put pressure on the wound from which blood had already stopped flowing. "Please, please, Don…."

Katherine stared at the woman in front of her as her rapid breathing slowed, the danger having passed. After a few moments, Katherine managed to tear her gaze away and tried to tune out the woman's sobs as she kept pressure on Corlett's wound, her arms shaking from adrenaline.

CHAPTER 33

KATHERINE LOOKED UP AS REESE walked back into the hospital waiting room, giving him a tired smile, as he put his phone back in his pocket. "Hey," she spoke.

"Hey," he murmured, taking a seat next to Katherine. "Jackson said good work. He'll coordinate with Corlett's boss. Did we get an update?"

"He's doing fine," she replied. "Getting some stitches and a liter or two of blood and he'll be good as new. And… the rest of the family left with one of Corlett's coworkers."

"Good. Ah, what's procedure on this?" Reese asked. "I mean Jackson said he'd take care of one side of it, but…."

Katherine shook her head. "A ton of paperwork. The usual. Procedure only gets you so far in this job, you know that, but…what you don't know is how much farther the job can actually go," she murmured. "There's no paperwork specifically for helping out a friend who's acting as a bodyguard-for-hire and runs up against a vampire. You just fill out what you're told. So, ah, give a lot of details in your case file. Um…I'll also need to do a 418, and Corlett's an asset, we've had a 245a-3 on him for a while, so I'll do a

209. Etcetera. When I forward everything to Jackson, he'll let me know if I missed something."

"All right. Thanks."

"Yeah."

The two lapsed into silence for a long while before Katherine suddenly spoke up. "Alex wanted to come. To be an extra set of hands or something."

Reese glanced over to her. "Sorry, what now?"

Katherine shook her head. "We had a bit of a...shouting match. She saved a girl from being kidnapped and could've gotten shot. Just had a knock to the head, luckily."

"What?" Reese asked, his eyes widening. "Jesus."

"Yeah. She...she's got a lot of training," Katherine explained. "She's been taking aikido since she was seven, jiu jitsu since she was eleven. She knows how to handle a gun. Very well. And...that's kind of just the foundation of what she knows."

"I don't...." Reese stared at her. "How? I-I mean, why?"

Katherine stared at her partner for a long moment, examining his expression. She hated talking about this. Not just because of the emotional wave that crashed over her when she needed to explain the smaller details, the ones that really brought it back. Not just because of the way people looked at her when she did. The way Reese was, or the way a civilian did, or a parasapien, each in their own horrified, pitying way. Or the way they treated her differently after they knew.

It was because it was a reminder of everything she couldn't control.

Katherine started with the basics, knowing that as an

agent he had a decent amount of history on her already. "Reese...you know my husband was murdered."

Reese blinked. "Um...yeah. Yeah, I knew that." He clasped his hands in his lap, his stance tightening like he knew the conversation had just taken a particular turn.

Katherine finally slid her gaze away from Reese and down to the floor. "...David wasn't the only target that day."

Reese swallowed hard, comprehension dawning on him. "The pùca went after Alex?"

"She...was fine," Katherine whispered, staring at nothing. "But...a few months later she got grabbed by something else. And...she wasn't so fine."

Reese's mouth opened to say something, but when he realized he wasn't saying anything, he closed it. Katherine could feel him wanting to say something, aching to really. The way you want to know the right thing to say when friends give you bad news about themselves. But there was nothing to say here.

"Alex needed to learn how to protect herself," she spoke, filling the silence. "Somehow though, that's turned into looking for trouble. And I was trying to convince her that...." Katherine fell silent, suddenly annoyed. "I don't know what I was trying to convince her of."

"...From your reaction there, I'm pretty sure you don't want to say out loud what you were trying to convince her of," Reese said slowly.

Katherine stared at her hands. "She posited the hypothetical of her becoming a tracker. And I just kind of...froze."

Reese examined Katherine's expression carefully. "Alex wants to be a tracker?"

"I don't know," she muttered, keeping her gaze firmly away from her partner's. "But what if she does? I'm not stupid. I know I can't stop her. But I can't just *let* her either."

"Why not?" Reese asked. "I mean, you're describing Alex following your choice of career path and it sounds like you're describing how she's decided to walk off a cliff."

Katherine rubbed her hands together anxiously. "Maybe she should have come tonight."

"What?" Reese asked, surprised into a shocked smile. "I don't...okay, am I missing something else here?"

"I knew we could take down both vampires, and this way I would've been there to look after Alex," Katherine whispered. "So she would've been able to be in a situation like this, but I could look after her. And she's...capable."

Reese stared at her. "Capable," he repeated. "Your sixteen-year-old daughter is...capable. Of what? Of getting her first kill younger than you did?" Katherine stiffened and she suddenly looked over to him. His face went slack. "I'm sorry, that was out of line," he muttered, averting his eyes.

Katherine tore her gaze away and blinked rapidly, feeling the burning threat of tears. "No, it wasn't," she said. "It was reasonable." Pursing her lips, Katherine looked down at the floor. "Not that she could, now. Mine was at fifteen." Reese looked back at her, incredulous, just staring. Again, no words.

Katherine took a small breath, her eyebrows twitching together. "You think I'm a good mother, Reese?"

"Christ," he sighed, rolling his eyes, "I didn't say—"

"It was a question," Katherine whispered, her voice cracking.

Caught off-guard, Reese hesitated. And then he slowly nodded. "Yeah," he murmured. "Yeah, Colebrook, I think you're a good mom. But honestly, I do think you did the right thing by not letting her tag along on our mission to kill two vampires and handle a crime scene that included a bodyguard that was bleeding out and a corpse," he said slowly.

Katherine nodded. "It's just that she's just like me," she breathed. "And that terrifies me, Reese. I want her to.... I want her to be completely able to protect herself from anything she runs into, and never have to. I don't want her to turn out like me."

"You turned out okay," Reese muttered. Katherine didn't respond. He rubbed the back of his neck, shifting in his seat. "You're still alive," he added.

Katherine let out a morose chuckle. "Yeah. Yeah, I guess so."

"Austin Corlett?" called out a voice. Katherine looked toward the voice and stood, prompting a doctor to walk over to her. "Hamid Rashidi," he said, holding out his hand.

Katherine shook off the remnants of the heavy conversation and put herself in the moment, shaking the doctor's hand. "Katherine Colebrook," she replied.

Hamid blinked. "Alexandra's mother?" he said, a shadow of a smile surfacing on his face. Katherine stared, confused.

"Usually you're the one that does that," Reese noted, glancing to his partner. Katherine pursed her lips at him in a small glare.

"I examined an Alexandra Colebrook yesterday afternoon for a bump on the head," Hamid explained. "Mom's name was Katherine. I'm assuming you're mom?"

Katherine suddenly smiled tiredly. "Yeah, hi," she said. "This is my partner, Reese Johansson."

"Good to meet you," he said, nodding once at Reese. "Mr. Corlett is in recovery right now. No complications; stitches were fairly straightforward."

"Good," Katherine said. She noticed that she'd had some tension in her shoulders when it dissipated.

"Mr. Johansson is your partner you said?" he asked. "You're law enforcement?"

"FBI," she replied.

"Well, now I get where Alex gets her capacity for getting bad guys," Hamid remarked.

Katherine smiled at him tightly. "Sometimes more than I'd prefer."

"I understand. Well…." He paused. "It was very nice meeting you."

Katherine's smile relaxed. "You too. Hopefully you won't be seeing us again anytime soon."

"Eh, I wouldn't mind that," he replied with a lingering smile. He gave a small wave to Reese before turning and heading back down the hall.

"A doctor," Reese remarked. "You could do worse."

Katherine rubbed her hands over her face, taking a long breath that turned into a yawn. "Knowing myself and Alex, probably wouldn't be a bad idea."

There was a knock at the door and Frank Calabrease stood

up from his sofa, putting the television on mute. He walked through his penthouse apartment to the front door and opened it, knowing that whomever it was had been vetted by the guard that stood at the elevator on his floor. Rick Lazos stood at the door and Calabrease nodded at him to enter.

"Hey," Calabrease spoke, shutting the door behind him. "Drink?"

"Nah, I'm just here to report on something," Lazos answered. "Something you aren't gonna like."

Calabrease eyed him for a moment, noticing the oddly tight expression on Lazos's face before letting out a breath and heading over to the liquor cart in the corner of his living room. He poured himself two fingers of scotch, heading over to the loveseat adjacent to his sofa and sitting back down. "All right. What's going on?"

"I got the police report and found the girl that threw a monkey wrench into the kidnapping," Lazos answered. "Turns out it's Katherine Colebrook's daughter. Not only that, but the Monaldos were in the market for a certain necklace, and hired The Ghost to get it. The job was supposed to go down next week. And The Ghost turned up dead in Laguna Beach. Guess who took an impromptu trip to Laguna last week?"

Calabrease stared at the man standing a few yards away from him before slowly downing his drink. After a brief pause, he abruptly stood up and threw the glass at the wall to his right, shattering the glass and prompting Lazos to flinch. Calabrease started to pace. "That family is gonna drive me to my fucking grave," he muttered. He abruptly halted and turned to Lazos. "That's all of them, right? Just the mom and the girl?"

Lazos nodded once. "There's a teenager that just moved in with them too, but she's just some computer geek retard. She's apparently a genius, but not much trouble. Not like they are. And you already know daddy died a while ago."

"I'm just grateful there's only two of them," Calabrease growled.

"Daddy wouldn't have been much trouble either, by the looks of him," Lazos replied. "But that's beside the point. What's our move here?"

Calabrease snorted. "Our move? By the looks of this kid, we take out the mom, she'll track us all down and slice our throats. And we take them both out, there are too many people out there on her side who would do the same thing. And it's not like they'd be easy to take out, especially if we needed to make it look like an accident; this is a tracker we're talking about. It's too much trouble. But the fact that I've got friggin'...*Wonder Woman* and her daughter *Bat Girl* running around my city is just...fucking unnerving."

Calabrease started to slowly pace. "We can't do business like this. I mean, they've only been here, what, a month? It's just bad luck with the kidnapping and Colebrook, she's good at her job, so they put her on the Ghost. But it's the future I'm worried about. It's that mole hunt. The fact that she waltzed in and out, leaving a bomb behind her. Usually FBI follows procedures and they can be bought, or at least threatened, if we have to. We can and we do work around them. But Colebrook and her kid are unpredictable." Lazos remained silent, hands clasped in front of him, as his boss stopped pacing.

The thing was, this was more than unnerving to Calabrease. What he wouldn't say out loud, but what Lazos was smart enough to know, was that he needed to handle this. Because if Katherine left another bomb behind, so to speak, he'd start to look weak. And that would leave him on the edge of a very steep cliff.

"You want to try to send her a warning?" Lazos finally asked. "Or a bribe?"

"Bribe won't work, and another warning will piss her off again, no matter how intimidating we make it," Calabrease muttered. He let out a breath and finally looked back to his employee. "Just…wait. I can't afford to make more of a mess out of this than it already is. I'm gonna figure out what our best option here is…and I'll let you know."

CHAPTER 34

KATHERINE GLANCED TO REESE AS he checked his email on his phone, sitting shotgun. She pulled onto the 405 and set her car on cruise control, since at this hour the freeway was barely populated.

About ten minutes later, Katherine blinked a few times, straightening in her seat. And without hesitation, she immediately, though not jarringly, slowed the car to a stop, pulling over to the shoulder and flicking on her flashers.

Reese looked up and around, then over at her as she put the car in park. "Colebrook?"

Dread. Impending danger. Vision blurs. She blinks, but it doesn't steady. Stars dance in her eyes like she'd glanced into the flash of a camera.

"What's wrong?" he asked. He stared at her, trying to decipher her facial expression, seeing dizziness and pain and sadness.

Katherine blinked away tears that were coming to her eyes at the almost tangible despair wrenching at her heart. And suddenly she cried out, gnashing her teeth and her hands flying to her forehead. Reese quickly got out, sparing a glance to the side mirror first to make sure he wasn't about to get hit by a passing car. He went around to the other side of the car, flinging opening her door. Katherine had shut her eyes tightly, clenching her fists against pain. Reese pursed his lips and remained silent. He reached out to put a hand on her shoulder, then drew back, deciding against it.

Then, Katherine's eyes abruptly flew open.

Reese stared at her uneasily. "That was a vision, right?" he asked.

Katherine's face crumpled and she blinked a few times as tears leapt to her eyes. She managed a nod and swallowed past a lump that started forming in her throat as her eyes refocused on the dashboard.

"Colebrook?" Reese asked.

"A man and a woman are dead," she said numbly. "Killed by a vampire. And their daughter's next." She motioned vaguely to the back seat. "Get my laptop," she told him, fumbling with the water bottle in her jacket and taking a long drink. Reese went around to the backseat, getting her computer. As he did so, Katherine got out and walked around the car, getting into the passenger's seat. Reese took that as a cue to take the driver's seat and he brought the laptop with him, sitting down and opening it. "There's an encrypted file named Cadejo, password gk1937. Open it, then give me the laptop and book it for UCSD."

"On it," Reese answered, starting to type even before Katherine had finished speaking.

Once he'd logged in, Katherine took the laptop from Reese and they put on their respective seatbelts before he pulled back onto the freeway. She glanced at the address in the file and pulled up a new text message to Sweeney.

Julie Calloway's parents were just murdered. Vision. Can you get to her place to stand guard until I arrive?

Katherine then called a seldom-dialed number in her contacts, waiting as it rang.

Reese spared a glance from the roads to Katherine's near-devastated expression. "Do you know the victims?" he whispered.

Katherine nodded. She let out a breath she didn't realize she'd been holding when someone picked up.

"Hello?" asked a sleepy voice.

"Julie?" Katherine asked urgently, trying to keep the panic out of her tone.

"Yeah, who is this?"

"It's Kathy. Kathy Colebrook."

There was a brief pause. "Kathy? What…? Why are you calling this late?"

Katherine heard the subdued sound of a text message alert and glanced at her phone briefly, seeing Sweeney's reply.

On my way.

Katherine brought the phone back to her ear. "Julie… do you trust me?"

Julie hesitated. "Of course," she whispered, her voice suddenly shaky.

Katherine blinked slowly. "My old partner is going to be on your doorstep soon. His name's Sweeney. He's deaf. As long as he says that I sent him, you can let him in."

"Why?"

"I'll get there in about two hours. You are not to leave your apartment under any circumstances, Julie, do you understand me?" Katherine asked. "You lock your doors and windows and you stay inside. And you don't let anyone else in unless I give you the okay."

"What's going on?" Julie asked.

"Do you understand me?"

"Yes! I understand! Now what is going on?" she cried.

Katherine hesitated. "Steven and Denise are dead," she murmured. "I had a vision. Someone killed them and it's coming after you next." Julie was silent. "Julie?" She didn't respond. "*Julie?*"

"No," she choked out. "No…no, they…oh God…."

"I need you to do everything I've said and I will keep you safe, all right?" Katherine told her, her voice firm but gentle.

"Oh God…." Julie sobbed.

"Julie," Katherine murmured. "I'm sorry about what happened. I'm so, so sorry. And I know you can't really comprehend functioning right now. But I'm not going to let anything happen to you. Double-check your locks. Close all your shades. Wait for Sweeney to get there. Everything's gonna be fine. I promise."

Julie took in and let out a shuddering breath. "Okay," she whispered. She took another breath. "Okay."

Katherine swallowed tightly as she forced herself to hang up the phone.

CHAPTER 35

"WHO IS SHE?"

Katherine glanced to Reese, bringing her out of a daze. "Ah…Julie Calloway. She was with me at my adoptive home for about a year as a foster before she was adopted."

It was a strange feeling to suddenly have one of her foster siblings in danger again. Most of them had come to Randall because the reason they were orphaned was violent. Randall had been, and still was, a wonderful father to all who came to his home. But then as Katherine had grown older, she'd taken on what she'd felt was a role Randall couldn't fulfill, and that she could with her increasing amount of self-defense training through the years: the responsibility of protecting them from any more harm befalling them. And tonight was no different.

Realizing that she hadn't yet filled Reese in on the details of the vision, Katherine did so. "Julie and her parents…oh my god, they were amazing," she murmured. "I mean I hadn't seen them in decades, but I remember them being…."

"I'm sorry," Reese said. His tone carried heavy sympathy

that made Katherine feel like she should be grieving for someone.

"This shouldn't have happened to Julie," she muttered, bringing up another phone number on her phone.

Reese glanced to her. "What do you mean?"

Katherine shook her head. "She went through a lot. She deserved better than this." She dialed the number and Reese fell silent.

The person Katherine had decided her next call needed to be was a middle-aged man named Alvin Seager that lived in Culver City. He played liaison between the vampire families of Southern California, both psychic and blood drinking. Sometimes it was a dirty business, and he wasn't Katherine's favorite person, but right now it was imperative that she speak with him. Even if it didn't involve the families, if a targeted double homicide involving multiple vampires happened, chances are he'd gotten wind of it.

Katherine waited as it rang, closing her eyes and propping herself up on her elbow against the armrest.

"Yeah?" came the muttered answer.

Katherine's eyes opened and she straightened, confused at the oddly sleepy-sounding voice. It was past midnight, a little late for a phone call, but early for the particular person she was calling, since he usually kept sunlight-averse vampire hours. "Seager?"

"…Colebrook?" he responded, presumably spotting her name on his cell's caller ID.

She hesitated. "I'm sorry, what time is it where you are?"

Seager paused. "You…called to ask me what time it is?"

"No, it just sounds like I woke you up."

"Oh. Yeah, no, I'm in LA. I'm just really popular. I've been awake all day in crisis mode," he grumbled. "I swear, family drama is the only thing that can create a disaster instantly.... Sorry, why are you calling?"

"I've got a girl whose parents were just killed by vampires," she told him. "And they're after her next."

"Well that doesn't make any sense," he muttered. "Why would vampires target humans in a specific family?"

"That's why I'm calling you," she told him. "Her parents are Steven and Denise Calloway. Her name's Julie. As far as I know, she's no one, but her parents are dead." Seager was silent. "Seager?" she prompted.

"Shit," he breathed. "The Calloways are dead?"

"What do you mean–?" Katherine asked, barely finishing the sentence before she realized his question. "This is your family drama? You're kidding me!"

"It's not...I mean it's kind of—."

"Seager, you've got five seconds to tell me what the hell is going on," she growled. Annoyingly, Seager fell silent again. "...Five...four...."

"Temper, temper. Speaking of family drama," Seager said quietly. Katherine gnashed her teeth. "Who is she to you?"

"You first," she snapped. "Why are they after her, and why kill her parents?"

Seager sighed. "Fine. Because the vampire that impregnated her is supposed to be marrying someone from another family."

Seager had packed so much information into one sentence that Katherine blinked a few times to try to process

220

it, running through it again twice as her heart progressively sank further into her chest.

You couldn't birth a vampire; you could only turn one. But she knew that vampires could get humans pregnant and visa versa with human babies just as easily as humans could impregnate each other. Interestingly, it was more likely for a vampire to have only a mother than only a father, since two vampires couldn't have a human baby and it was common for a female vampire to find someone to impregnate her and then never tell him, to be able to continue her line without any fuss.

The vampire families themselves were practically a mafia, playing their games in a delicate balance, controlling certain parts of the city with occasional territorial squabbles, and playing politics like chess masters. Not surprising since they had centuries to do it through, if they were good at staying alive, which most were if they were still around.

And this was the soap opera that Julie had been thrust into the middle of.

"Julie's pregnant?" Katherine finally managed. Out of the corner of her eye, she caught Reese shoot her a concerned glance.

"Yeah," Seager said. "There've been some issues between the families and Javier Calguri was supposed to marry Tanika Levitre. He decided he didn't want to and took off, like some rebellious teenage boy. After a month, they found him in San Diego and dragged him back home, only for him to get a call a few weeks later from Julie telling him that she was pregnant. He wasn't going to tell anyone, he was just going to go back to her, but someone heard the phone conversation."

"Damn it," Katherine muttered. "But why go after her parents? Why not try to find Julie?"

"Well she's at college in a dorm, she's not listed, but her cell phone is still paid for in a family plan by her parents. So I guess when they couldn't figure out where she was, they went to the source."

Katherine closed her eyes, starting to massage her forehead. "You know, it's really creepy that you knew that."

"Kinda my job."

"Right. So someone in the family gets Julie's address at school, and once she's dead, who cares who she was?" she muttered. "Just some human, right?"

"Actually..." Seager began. He hesitated. "See, that doesn't track. If this was really Roslyn pulling the strings, she wouldn't have been this sloppy."

Katherine knew that Seager was referring to a mother in the Calguri family. As the mother of the boy who'd caused the trouble, she would be responsible for cleaning up his mess. And he was right; this wasn't her work. Part of Roslyn's job, or at least it would be if she wanted to do it well, was play nice with sapien law enforcement. That wouldn't involve murders like this, quite obviously, at least not if she wanted to keep her family members from being executed. Things would have played out differently if this particular vampire had been in charge.

"What was Roslyn planning on doing?" Katherine asked.

"She was planning on brushing the whole thing under the rug. Like a married politician that had an affair and got the mistress pregnant. So it makes more sense that Roslyn isn't the one pulling the strings. That this got out of her control and…." Seager stopped and groaned. "Ah, friggit."

"Don't tell me. The Levitre he's supposed to marry has a temper," she muttered.

"A bit. I met Tanika once. Not a pleasant girl. So, quid pro quo, Clarice," he spoke. "Who's Julie to you?"

Katherine hesitated. "We grew up together."

Seager paused. "Wait, you mean from…oh." He let out a breath. "Ah, okay."

"So," Katherine spoke, clenching her left fist on top of her armrest, cracking her knuckles. "This thing, one of their own, just killed two humans like it was nothing. What's their next move?"

"You do understand they're trying to create an alliance between the families, not a blood feud, right?" he asked tentatively.

"I don't care, Seager," she growled. "Tanika just slaughtered two humans. This is out of control now. You cannot fix this."

There was a long silence on the other end of the line. Katherine knew it was the last sentence that had done it, which was why she'd said it. It was Seager's job to fix things and if he couldn't, he needed to find the second-best thing to fixing it, making him more open to suggestion and giving Katherine an advantage.

Katherine held her forehead in her hand. "Listen. Get Emalia Levitre on the phone," she said, prompting an uneasy look from Reese, who recognized the name. "Tell her that she needs to get Tanika to turn herself in for the murder of Denise and Steven. Julie will raise the baby on her own; she'll never make contact with Javier again. I'll put her in another state if that'll make Emalia happy. And Emalia can find someone else to get hitched to Javier."

Seager paused. "I'm not sure that turning in her niece for murder will be appealing. What if she doesn't go for that?"

Katherine's jaw tightened. "Then I will bring the full force of every one of my law enforcement contacts down on her *head*," she snapped.

"All righty then," Seager responded. "In that case, your idea sounds just peachy."

"Good. I'll wait on your call." She hung up, putting aside her phone and pinched the bridge of her nose, trying to stem the beginnings of a headache. "I hate politics."

"We're trackers. When did we get into politics?" Reese muttered.

Katherine leaned back in her seat. "Comes with the territory with the vampire families. Slap me upside the head and remind me of this shit storm if I ever decide to so much as speak to one of them ever again."

"Duly noted. But I don't get it. If we know who killed Julie's parents, why not pursue that first?" Reese asked. "We have the lead, so it'll be fairly easy to prove."

"This is more delicate than that," Katherine said with a grimace. "We could prove Tanika killed them. We could track her down, arrest her or, more likely, kill her. Then what?" She looked to Reese. "We still have Julie pregnant with a vampire child, and now the foundation for a civil dialogue on the subject has pretty much been obliterated." She sighed and looked back out the window. "No. We try talking first. Incendiary bullets will be saved for later."

Reese glanced at his watch. "Never a dull moment."

CHAPTER 36

KATHERINE CALLED JULIE NEXT, SPEAKING to her about her pregnancy and whom exactly it was that she'd slept with, which was a complete surprise to her. Though she'd known he was a vampire, Julie hadn't known about his family. Katherine then received a text from Sweeney when he arrived at Julie's house, who assured her that Julie was safe and sound and that he would defend her with his life if necessary.

Oddly enough, she then got a call from Rebecca. "Hey, you okay?" Katherine asked. "It's late."

"Hello," Rebecca spoke. "I'm fine. I just got your email telling me and Alex that you won't be home soon, so I knew you were still awake. How are you?"

"Don't ask. Why are you calling?" Katherine asked, rubbing the back of her neck.

"You sound grumpy," Rebecca told her. "I was asking how you are because that's polite, but that was grumpy. So I guess you're grumpy." Katherine's mouth opened to apologize, but Rebecca just barreled on. "I'm calling because I know something important. You told me to spy on Frank Calabrease, and I've been doing that."

Katherine blinked, surprised. Her surprise then turned to concern. "And you found something?"

"I did," Rebecca answered. "They were talking in code in emails. They talked about the jewel thief you killed. That made them very angry. And the kidnapping that Alex stopped was something they were doing too. It was supposed to be leverage to keep one of Calabrease's employees from going to prison."

Gnashing her teeth, Katherine shut her eyes. She let out a long breath. "Brilliant," she muttered. "And?"

"That's it. He's very angry," Rebecca told her.

"But he's not planning to make a move against me?" Katherine confirmed.

"I don't know," she responded. "He didn't say anything in his emails and I can't know people's feelings unless I'm near them. And you said I'm not supposed to leave the apartment if I'm not with someone else, so I can't go find him to find out."

"No, definitely not," Katherine told her, her eyes widening. "I mean, he didn't talk about that in his emails?"

"No, he's just angry."

Katherine fell silent. "But he wants to," she finally said. "He wants to make a move. It's just that he knows how much trouble it would be if he did."

"If that's true, that makes sense. You're a very strong person."

Katherine smiled. "Look, ah…good job. And…if anything else comes up, let me know."

"I will." Rebecca hung up without another word.

Katherine slid her phone back in her pocket as Reese spoke up. "Everything okay?" he asked.

Katherine shook her head. "Same old," she muttered. "I'm being stalked by an angry mobster."

Reese snorted. "Just another day in paradise," he said. "How'd you piss him off now?"

"Well, apparently that pùca burglar that I killed was on his payroll, and that kidnapping that Alex made implode was one of his jobs too."

Reese whistled, shifting his grip on the steering wheel. "Two in as many weeks. You guys are hitting him hard."

"Christ, I'm just doing my job. Isn't it guys like him that say stuff like, 'It's just business'?" She shook her head. "Well, he's not making a move yet. I'm just having Rebecca keep an eye on things," she said.

"As long as you're being careful," Reese responded. "Don't go egging his house or putting Saran wrap over his toilet seat."

"I'm much more creative in my aggravating childish pranks," Katherine assured him, leaning back against her headrest.

"I'll do some research on Calabrease also," Reese spoke. "From the FBI angle. Complement Rebecca's work."

"That'd be great, thank you," she murmured.

Katherine closed her eyes, letting the hum of the engine and the wheels on the road soothe her toward sleep, but a few minutes later she got a call back from Seager that brought her back to full consciousness. She cleared her throat before answering. "Yeah?" she spoke.

"Hi. Ah, Emalia wants to speak with you."

Katherine narrowed her eyes. "All right. Have her call me."

"No, in person."

Her eyes narrowed further. "Why? To tell me in no uncertain terms to screw myself, or to negotiate?"

"If Emalia wanted to tell you to go screw yourself, she'd just tell me to relay the message," Seager responded.

"Fine," Katherine muttered after a brief pause. "We'll head over there now."

"Good luck."

Hanging up, she shifted her gaze out the window. "Get off the highway and make for Beverly Hills. We're meeting with Emalia."

Reese paused for a long moment. "Should I slap you upside the head now or wait until I can get more momentum for a real–?"

"Shut up."

CHAPTER 37

"SO WHAT EXACTLY SHOULD I expect in there?" Reese asked, pulling Katherine out of her laptop screen, where she had been researching the latest on the family they were going to visit. She realized they'd reached their destination in Brentwood. "Aside from the normal vampire shit?"

"Ah...you ever deal with a mafia family?" she asked, cocking an eyebrow.

"...I've seen Goodfellas."

Katherine snorted. As they pulled up in front of what could not really be called a house and was more likely referred to by the occupants as a manor, Katherine shifted in her seat uncomfortably.

Need. Need her. Need her life to fill me as I fill her, take all I can without killing. Want more. Can't take more–.

Katherine pulled in her feelers, simply not wanting to be exposed to who and what she knew was inside. It wasn't anyone who was there against their will, of course, but the parasitic relationship between a vampire and the person it fed upon was a disturbing feeling.

"Well...these families are somewhere between Mafiosi

and politicians. They've even got their own *Growing Up Gotti*. My daughter and I watched half an episode once. Thought her eyes were going to roll right out of her head."

Reese chuckled. "Yeah, I've heard about those shows. Don't see the attraction. Ah, what about persuasion? I mean, I know that's not Emalia's family, but if she wanted to call someone over–"

"Emalia wouldn't try anything. We're there on a peacekeeping mission. Not to mention, she has my name, so she knows it would only piss me off."

Reese nodded slowly. "What if...? What if something did happen?" he asked, giving her a sideways glance. "It's water off a duck's back for you, but–"

"I'd knock you out before you could do any damage," Katherine replied easily.

Reese blinked. "Oh. Uh...good. Great."

Katherine took in the manor as Reese paused briefly at the end of the driveway. Several small trees with tiny pink buds spotted the lawn and Katherine spotted a sleek manmade stream to the right that continued around the house under a wooden bridge, only able to see a small portion of it before the large stone barriers around the property cut off her view. The front walkway was lined with pillars that slid gracefully up into arches under the porches on the second floor, and a golden glow from dozens of from porch lights bathed the whole house. At the beautiful sight, Katherine mused on the possibility that the vampires who lived there tried to compensate for the lack of sunlight in their lives with artificial light.

The sapien guard at the front gate looked out the

window of his booth at the two FBI agents, narrowing his eyes suspiciously as their car pulled up.

"Reese and Katherine. We're here to speak to Emalia," Katherine told the guard, leaning toward him so he could see her.

After a brief staring contest, the guard turned to his phone, dialing the house and explaining who was at the gate. A few seconds later he buzzed them in and the gate opened, prompting Reese to slowly pull the car up the long driveway.

They parked in front of the house, to the side of the circular end of the driveway, and Katherine surveyed her surroundings as she got out of the car. She had to admit that even at night the grounds were gorgeous, the flowers, bushes and trees well kempt and beautiful.

A young man came slowly down the front steps, eyeing them. His gaze flicked briefly to the bulges under Katherine and Reese's jackets that revealed their holstered service weapons. He looked just a bit younger than Reese, sporting an outfit that Katherine thought would fit in at a country club; a white and blue striped shirt, the collar popped up, and tan slacks with a crease straight down the front. "My name's Ben," he said quietly. "I was told to show you to the parlor."

Katherine simply nodded once, following him up the steps and into the large foyer, Reese by her side. Katherine took in her surroundings and her eyes flicked to her right as they caught movement.

"Who might they be, Ben?" the young man making his way down the stairs asked curiously.

Katherine felt Ben tense. "Guests of Emalia's," he answered the other vampire. "Not your concern, Gerard."

Gerard strolled over toward Katherine, his eyes raking over her. Unlike Ben, Gerard's slick black hair, loose denim jacket and tight pants made him look like the kind of guy who would fit in at a club in downtown LA. The kind who wouldn't blink at handing a bouncer a hundred through a handshake. And Gerard wasn't a member of the family; he was just visiting for the evening with one of Ben's brothers. He was a psychic vampire.

"She feels special," Gerard murmured.

"Just regular special, though, not restaurant menu special, right?" she muttered, glaring at him.

Gerard smiled. "Feisty one, hm?" he asked softly. "Would you consider forgoing your meeting with Emalia to come back to my room with me? I assure you I could make you purr like a kitten and squeal like a little pig. And it will be the most intense pleasure you've ever experienced."

Ben shifted his weight, looking from Katherine's stern gaze to the vampire. "Gerard," he muttered. Reese clenched his fists, but said nothing.

"I would consider that rape. How do you think Emalia would feel about you raping one of her guests?" Katherine asked, cocking her head just slightly. "One of her guests that happens to be a tracker?"

The smile slipped from the vampire's face at that and he pursed his lips, glaring at her, and slid his eyes to Ben. "What the hell is a tracker doing here?" he growled.

"I told you, she has a meeting with Emalia," Ben told him. "If I were you I would take this opportunity to make yourself scarce." Gerard hesitated before turning and wordlessly heading back the way he'd come.

Katherine looked to Ben. "Where is she?"

Ben nodded once toward the living room and opened the sliding doors, letting the two trackers in before he left and closed the doors again for privacy.

Katherine pursed her lips at the woman seated on the sofa, or lounged rather, since no one could really just sit with the beauty this woman displayed. Her long, sleek black hair accentuated the curves of her body and Katherine could imagine hundreds of thousands of men, and probably the occasional woman, getting lost in her eyes. Her beauty was an asset and she knew how to use it, which was with no doubt a contributing factor to what Katherine sensed had been a very long life so far.

Knowing that speaking audaciously was the surest way to make the situation pointlessly more complicated, Katherine forced herself to keep her mouth shut, although what she ached to do was explain to the vampire in no uncertain terms who the impregnated girl was and what she meant to her.

"Gerard does have reason to be confused," Emalia murmured, staring at Katherine. "It's a rare occasion that we invite someone like you into our home." Katherine didn't reply, simply staring Emalia down. "Would you like a drink?"

"I do believe I'm here on business," Katherine told her. "Not to drink."

The pleasant, comfortable look on Emalia's face vanished promptly at that statement and she pursed her perfect lips. "I suppose you're right. Please do explain to me what your idea is? Seager told me, but I'd like to hear it from you."

"I'm unsure why it requires explanation," Katherine answered quietly. "It seems fairly straightforward. You want Julie dead because she's carrying Javier's child. What is it going to take to let her disappear into a new life?"

Emalia's gaze slid to Reese, who was standing motionlessly beside Katherine, before she slowly stood up. "I don't want anyone dead," Emalia said. "I'd just like this all to go away."

"Then we have something in common," Katherine responded. "My proposal is that you convince Tanika to turn herself in for the murder of Julie's parents. I'll move Julie to another state and she'll raise the child on her own. You can find someone else to make nice with the Calguri family bachelor."

"Turn in Tanika," Emalia muttered, her eyes narrowing in a piercing glare. "Kill her, essentially."

"She's already as good as dead and you know it," Katherine growled.

Emalia sighed softly through her nose, some of the tense anger melting from her shoulders as she considered a new train of thought. "Not to mention I don't exactly have many young women eager to get married. This is such a mess she's made," she murmured absently.

Emalia strode over to the small bar in the corner, putting some ice in a glass. "There is an actual problem to this whole debacle. Since it is quite well known by this point that Javier did run off and knock up little Julie, she's carrying a child that will grow up to be Javier's son or daughter. That makes it family. And denying Javier access to his child is not something that would facilitate cooperation on his part. He's already not ecstatic about the idea of the arranged marriage."

Katherine clenched her right fist, then hoped the vampire hadn't picked up the crack of her knuckles. "Not my fault," she noted. "And not Julie's either. She didn't even know who Javier was."

Emalia rolled her eyes languidly. "Right. But that's beside the point. It's out of my hands. The Calguri family needs this to end well, and ignoring it might be appealing, but they will want Julie to be brought into the family. They'll want Javier to marry her and raise the child, possibly turn Julie, and definitely turn the child. Otherwise, this becomes an embarrassment to the whole family. So your plan isn't exactly ideal."

"But you could convince them to leave her be," Katherine told her softly. "You could manage this territorial disaster without her involved. Make it all go away, like you said."

Emalia gazed at Katherine for an uncomfortably long moment. "Why on Earth would I do that?" she murmured.

"Because you'd like to know which one of the vampires on this property is blackmailing you," Katherine answered simply.

Reese blinked in surprise. Katherine felt irritation flare up in the vampire and Emalia's eyes widened just noticeably, pausing as she considered the statement. "Have you ever been told that could get you into trouble?" she whispered.

"Countless times," Katherine replied.

After another long moment, Emalia walked over, her stance utterly relaxed and her expression curious, until she was standing about five feet from Katherine. "I might be interested in such an accord."

———— ✦◈✦ ————

Katherine pulled up outside Reese's apartment, stopping her car parallel to another that was parked curbside and flicking on her flashers. They'd driven the whole way back in silence, and Katherine had been glad for it, but she had to break the silence at that point. "This wasn't a case," she finally spoke.

Once they had solidified a deal with Emalia, and Katherine had given the description of the traitor, whom Emalia quickly identified, the two trackers left. Katherine called Julie, assuring her that she was safe, though she had to leave the state and she'd be set up with a new identity. Tanika walked into a police station an hour later accompanied by her father, confessing to her crimes, concluding the investigation into the murders.

Katherine's interaction with Emalia hadn't exactly been pleasant and she didn't look forward to ever working with the vampire again, but as with any other part of her job, she was glad for the experience, if only for the fact that she now had a foundation to build on if she ever needed to. The thing was, she needed to clear something up with Reese that, after a cursory brush over the current thoughts at the front of his mind, he hadn't been thinking about.

Reese narrowed his eyes. "What do you mean...this wasn't a case?" he asked.

Katherine hesitated. "Well. What happened?"

Staring at her for a moment, Reese gave her a strange look. "Ah...you had a vision," he said slowly. "So you knew your friend was in danger. Figured out the vampire murder conspiracy thing. Saved the day."

"I got Julie out," Katherine murmured. She met his gaze straight on. "The murderer turned herself in. I'm going to get Julie a new ID to keep her off the radar, and the family is going to look the other way. They're going to forget there's a bastard child out there. This whole thing never happened."

Reese stared back, the gears turning in his head. "And if it's a case, Julie gets dragged in. She'll need to give a statement. Go on record that she's pregnant with Javier's kid." Katherine didn't blink. Reese nodded once. "Okay."

"Okay?"

"You did a favor for a friend," he murmured. "Actually, you dug around in the minds of a vampire mafia family, everyone in that house, and found dangerous secrets you could use as leverage to keep her safe. I'm not gonna jeopardize that just because some suit up the ladder somewhere would want me to file paperwork on this."

Katherine nodded slowly, averting her gaze. "All right."

"All right." Reese opened his door to get out, then stopped. "I'm not going to slap you upside the head, by the way," he noted, prompting Katherine to turn back toward him. "I'll take a rain check on that."

"You know what I meant when I said that," Katherine told Reese.

"Yeah, but I hate playing politics too. So next time, I will call in that marker," he said, pointing a finger at her. "And if you use your shining to dodge it, I'll take a warding potion and creep up behind you at your cubicle."

Katherine rolled her eyes. "Get out of my car, Reese."

Reese grinned. "Later." He left, shutting the door behind him, and Katherine pulled out back onto the street as he headed up the stairs to his apartment.

CHAPTER 38

REBECCA ENJOYED BEING IN HER room. Just her and her computers, staying in one place and still going all over the world, losing herself in the internet, exploring, going places she knew she wasn't allowed. It made her feel special to know she was smart enough, good enough, to do that, and to know she was helping to rid the world of criminals made her feel good as well.

Plus Katherine's expression turned funny when she told her how long she'd been online, often losing track of time. This was usually right before she was reminded to take a shower, even though she kept to her schedule and showered regularly, of course. Katherine said that Rebecca was the easiest adoptive daughter to have, actually, because half the time it seemed like she wasn't even there.

But just because she was in her room, it didn't necessarily mean she was safe.

When the power went out, Rebecca actually jumped, since all of her computer screens shut off at the same time. "No," she muttered in annoyance. "That is not supposed to happen!" Rebecca's mind instinctively looked for Alexandra and, not finding her, she looked to the clock and realized that it was the middle of the day, so she was still at school.

It then became apparent to her that the electricity going out wasn't a chance occurrence. When she'd reached out, Rebecca found that there was a man that had made the blackout happen. And it was because he'd needed to get into the apartment without the alarm alerting the police.

Reese exited the elevator on the tenth floor of the FBI's Los Angeles field office, heading down the hall to Katherine's cubicle, where she was sitting at her desk. He handed her one of two cups of coffee he was holding. "I resent becoming a cliché," he remarked.

Katherine glanced to him with an amused smile as she took the coffee from him and put it down on her desk. "You've gotten coffee for us multiple times. What makes now any different?"

"You had me go to the cafeteria for it, because it's better than the break room coffee," he told her. "And I did. Without protest."

"You're protesting now," she noted before taking a sip of her coffee.

"This is post-retrieval," he corrected her. He pulled up a chair to her desk as her cell phone rang. "It's not protest. It's an inquiry. How's your case file coming?"

"Hold on," Katherine told Reese, taking her phone from her pocket. "Rebecca?"

"Katherine, there's a man in the apartment and he's here to kidnap me," Rebecca said loudly. "I'm scared."

"What?" she breathed. A pang shot through Katherine's

chest as she glanced at her watch, realizing that it was two in the afternoon and that Alexandra was still at school. If the security system had been triggered, help was on the way, but if they got past the locks, there wasn't another line of defense for a human assailant. Help would arrive too late. "Rebecca, lock your door and go out the window! Climb down the fire escape," she said, getting to her feet and turning away from Reese.

Reese promptly stood up as well, stepping to Katherine's side, tense in wide-eyed concern.

"I already locked my door. I'll go out my window," the teenage girl told her. The small clatter of the window unlocking and sliding open sounded through the phone. "Like Spiderman."

Then Katherine heard the smash of a door and Rebecca let out a frantic yelp. "Rebecca!" she yelled. Her chest tightened anxiously, hearing the hysterical struggles and cries of the girl, knowing that Rebecca was being restrained when she could barely stand the contact of shaking someone's hand. Reese gnashed his teeth, looking around to the other nearby agents who were now staring worriedly.

"You son of a bitch, *let her go*!" Katherine shouted. Her heart raced, desperate for the intruder to pick up the phone.

Katherine's breath caught in her throat as the girl's protests faded to whimpers and then the call cut off. She moved the phone to stare at it as all the air in her lungs left in a shaky breath as she turned to face Reese. "Rebecca's been kidnapped," she managed. She moved forward and grabbed her jacket from the back of her desk chair and her badge and gun from her desk drawer. Reese did the same, noticing the agents that had been staring started to reluctantly go back to work, assuming the situation was under control, and Reese bolted after Katherine.

Katherine punched the elevator button hard multiple times as she dialed another number on her cell phone.

"Yeah?" came the answer.

"Corlett, you still in town?" Katherine snapped.

"Yeah, I'm at a motel. Like ten minutes from your place. You got trouble?" he asked.

"Rebecca was taken," she told him. "I need you to meet me at Reese's apartment. I'll text you the address."

"Got it."

Katherine ended the call and shoved her phone back in her pocket. "No way the police would get there in time," she told Reese. "We get to your apartment and get on this ASAP. I want to know everything about these guys before we get a ransom call."

To Katherine's utter gratefulness, the elevator somehow descended all ten floors without stopping for any other passengers, to whom she would've barked, "Sorry, emergency," before promptly hitting the *close door* button. The two of them exited the elevator and speed-walked through the lobby.

"Call in HRT?" Reese asked.

"No, we've got to figure out what this is first," she growled, her fists clenching at her sides.

It was five minutes into the drive to Reese's apartment, her siren and flashers going as she sped down the street, Katherine received a text message, prompting her to pull over before opening it. She took in and let out a shaky breath at the image, staring at Rebecca's tearstained face, her eyes closed as she slept, most definitely having been drugged. She was bound hand and foot, a piece of tape over her mouth, lying in the trunk of a car.

Katherine gnashed her teeth, her blood boiling.

"Colebrook?" Reese asked quietly. She didn't reply. She didn't need to. The fury was etched across her face like a neon sign.

Suddenly her phone rang. Forcing herself to take several slow, shallow breaths, she answered the call.

"This is Katherine Colebrook, I'm assuming?" asked the quiet male voice on the other end of the line.

"I'm going to cut your heart out of your chest…and feed it to you as you die," Katherine growled, "if you don't let that girl go…right now." Reese's gaze flicked briefly to Katherine's face as she stared straight ahead at nothing, her expression tight and cold.

"He said you'd be feisty," the man murmured. "Look, this is just a job for me. You do what he wants, Rebecca gets to go home safe and sound."

The fingernails on Katherine's left hand dug into her palm. "Do what who wants?" Katherine muttered.

"He prefers to remain anonymous," he answered. "It's very straightforward. Go to 3294 East 15th Street. Bring your service weapon and the registration paperwork. You'll stay there for a bit, under lock and key, and then you'll leave, and Rebecca will be dropped off somewhere for you to pick her up."

"Let me talk to her."

"No. You know how this works. You already got proof of life. You do what he wants, she'll be fine. You have an hour to get there, or I'll get a call and Rebecca gets a bullet in her head."

Katherine's eyes widened. "An hour?" she snapped.

"3294 East 15th Street." The click of the man hanging up echoed in her ear.

Reese and Katherine walked into Reese's apartment and Corlett followed, closing and locking the door behind him. Heading over to his office, Katherine handed him her phone and Reese pressed a few buttons on it. He walked quickly over to his computer, knowing that he needed to get everything he could from the phone about the man Katherine had just spoken with.

Reese plugged the phone into a cord that led to his computer, opening a few windows, his fingers flying over the keys. After a few moments, he slowly nodded.

"It's a burner," he muttered. "It's not on anymore; it's a good bet he trashed it. But I can find where he sent the video from...." Reese paused, his eyes narrowing and twitching in concentration. Time passed achingly slowly as Katherine paced behind his chair, her hands clenching and unclenching into fists.

"Anything?" Katherine snapped.

"Just...." Reese's voice trailed off. "There. Yeah, it was in east LA."

Katherine let out a harsh breath. "That's all I needed to hear. Find out exactly where," she told him. "And give me a few minutes."

Katherine went to Reese's bedroom, going into the small, refrigerated safe in his closet. She unlocked it and took out a vial of blood: Rebecca's. She then shut the safe and went out into the living room, taking out a plastic bag from her jacket that contained the materials she'd grabbed from the trunk of her car. After she combined the ingredients in a small wooden bowl, she poured half the vial of blood over them and then added some gunpowder. She then lit them on fire and, in the middle of the bowl, she laid down a crystal on the end of a thin wire about a foot long, closing her eyes and concentrating.

As she opened her mind, the hairs on the back of Katherine's neck prickled and she shifted her shoulders at the goose bumps appearing along her arms. Taking in and letting out a deep breath and focusing deeply, she allowed herself to be used as a conduit for the energy needed to perform the spell. After about five minutes, she felt it *snap* as it finished and she opened her eyes, waiting until it glowed and then picked up the end of the wire, slowly getting to her feet.

Katherine remained completely still as she anxiously waited for the crystal to settle on a direction. Finally it stopped. And she let out a long breath. "All right," she murmured. She went back out to the living room, where Reese turned to face her.

"Twelfth and Lincoln," Reese told Katherine, prompting her to nod and let out a long breath. "What else do you need?"

"What's at 3294 East 15th Street?" Katherine asked.

Reese blinked. "Wh...? Why?"

"What do you mean, why?" Katherine snapped, narrowing her eyes. "I need to know–"

"I-I mean, I already know," Reese stammered. "Because you told me to keep track of Calabrease. It's a brownstone where one of his men lives."

Katherine's face slowly went slack and she gritted her teeth for a moment before speaking. "It's where they want me to go with one of my weapons, and the paperwork that proves its mine," she growled.

Reese's upper lip curled. "They want to frame you for something."

"Not gonna happen," Katherine said. "Look, Corlett, you need to take this and find Rebecca. She should be close...." Katherine's voice trailed off as she stared at the crystal.

Reese looked from the crystal to Katherine's gaze and back again. "What?"

Katherine's lips parted as she stared at it. "Wait," she muttered. She swallowed tightly. "It's moving."

"She's still in motion?" Reese asked. "How fast? On a plane?"

Katherine paused, painstakingly probing the motion of the crystal with her eyes and feelers, before slowly shaking her head. "No. Angle's not right. It's gotta be a car." She shook her head. "I don't see how they could know she's psychic and knew we could scry, so they're just smart. Timestamp on the first call was 13:58. I'll call and get someone back at headquarters to get the plate off the car that took her from my place from cameras and put out an APB just in case. But if they're smart enough to keep her moving then they're too smart to be that careless."

Corlett glanced at his watch. "I've gotta really book it if I need to make it there in...thirty-nine minutes. Wherever *there* is."

"Wait, wait, we're saying Calabrease kidnapped Rebecca to get his hands on one of your guns for a frame-up," Reese said quickly. "That's total bullshit. We tell the FBI what happened, that we gave up the gun as ransom--."

"Whatever happens, this ruins me, Reese," she growled. "Because I'm not doing anything besides getting Rebecca back. The plan is to keep them from doing the job they're framing me for at all, but there are a thousand and one ways this could go sideways. I'm not calling in to Jackson that I know who's behind it. I'm not negotiating, or buying for time. It's likely I'm handing over my service weapon to be used in the commission of a murder. But I'm doing it. Do you understand?"

The last statement held a lot more than those three simple words. Reese stared at her for a moment before giving her a curt nod. "Yeah."

"And you're on board?"

"No question."

Katherine let out a breath. "I'm gonna try to give you as much time as possible. I'll wait in my car and won't go in until a few minutes before my deadline," Katherine said, turning to Corlett, "but hopefully whoever has Rebecca isn't heading in one direction or you'll never catch him in time. Reese, you know the city better, and you have more resources if anything gets hairy, so you need to stick with me," she continued. "You need to assume that if someone comes out of the apartment that they've taken my gun, and I need you to follow them. As soon as you get a call from Corlett that he has Rebecca, you take them down and get my weapon back."

"Corlett, I don't know how much you know about scrying, but this crystal is the epitome of multitasking," Katherine said, turning back to him. "You can't let the crystal touch *anything* else until you're done using it or it'll get confused. And you'll need my brain or another psychic or witch to get it back on track. And it's not a GPS, it won't give you the fastest route; it'll just point you in her direction. After you get her back, once you've called Reese, you call me. And she's autistic and she hates physical contact. And she's psychic, like me."

"Got it," he said with a stiff nod. He carefully took taking the end of the wire from her, holding it at arms length.

Katherine let out a harsh breath. "All right, let's move," she muttered.

CHAPTER 39

KATHERINE BANGED THREE TIMES ON the front door of the downtown brownstone to which she'd followed her GPS, waiting for one of the two men she felt inside to come answer it. Her expression was nothing short of glaring bullets at the man who opened the door, but he didn't react. He just motioned her inside, shutting the door behind her.

"You touch me, I will rip your arm off," Katherine said, her voice quiet and deadly, when he went to frisk her.

The man slowly walked around to face her. "Our house. Our rules," he said.

"You've got the power here," she told him. "And while putting a bullet in your head is something I very much want to do, I haven't held back for the past ten seconds just to blow it now." Katherine handed him the paper bag she was holding and he paused, pursing his lips, before taking it from her and motioning toward the living room.

Katherine walked in and sat down at the coffee table as the other man in the room took her gun and the paperwork that identified it from the paper bag with gloved hands. Katherine leaned forward on her knees and clasped her hands so she wouldn't fidget, wishing desperately that her abilities extended to detecting where Corlett currently was.

The primary thought on Corlett's mind was that he was glad he occasionally talked on a cell phone, drank coffee, and avoided asshole drivers all at the same time while in his car, because it made for great practice for what he was doing now. After fifteen minutes of driving, his arm started to ache so much that he had to rest his elbow on the top of the front passenger seat, which made for awkward driving it and of itself.

It was an acquired skill, though, and after about half an hour Corlett started to get the hang of the crystal. He had spent many days playing bodyguard to clients in Los Angeles, so he knew the layout pretty well. He was able to make good judgment calls, using his GPS to help him out, as he tried to figure out what route the man holding Rebecca hostage was taking. And there was a certain kind of vehicle the kidnapper was likely to be driving. Something that would blend in. Something that would be easy to make modifications to, to hold a hostage.

As the one-hour mark passed since Katherine had gotten the phone call, Corlett gnashed his teeth in frustration. From the route the driver was taking, Corlett established that he wasn't just driving away from Los Angeles, which he was grateful for. And he had assumed that the kidnapper wouldn't go faster than the speed limit, not wanting to take the chance of getting pulled over, so Corlett was able to go ten miles over the limit safely and be confident he was gaining on his prey at least slightly. It wasn't just circles in a parking lot, though; the guy was mixing it up on the freeways. But finally, Corlett felt a cautious bit of optimism when he found himself realizing there was a pattern emerging.

Eventually the crystal started to turn slower, which meant Corlett was gaining on the vehicle he was pursuing, causing him to have a smaller angle against where the kidnapper was. Finally, his eyes widened when it made a smooth turn to its right as he gained on and passed a blue sedan. Swallowing hard, Corlett played out his strategy slowly, not wanting to call attention to himself. He kept the sedan in his sights as he got ahead of it by about two car lengths and then moved over two lanes so he was on the other side of it. Slowing down, he let the sedan overtake him and he slid into the spot one car length behind it, one lane over. And as he smiled as, making the semi-circle around the car, the crystal turned to keep pointing at it.

At that, Corlett let out a sharp breath of victory, finally letting the crystal drop to the seat beside him, shaking out the pins and needles in his arm and letting it rest for a moment as he took stock of the situation. He quickly went through the options he'd listed in his head driving around for an hour, settling on one. Rebecca had to be in the trunk, so rear-ending the guy was out of the question. Speeding up and making sure his seatbelt was taut, Corlett slid right in front of the kidnapper's car. And he quickly, abruptly, slammed on the brakes and let up.

The car behind him smashed into him, the driver flying forward and into the airbag that deployed. The momentum almost halted the blue sedan, and Corlett carefully pumped his brakes again, slowly bringing the car behind him to a full stop, his muscles tight as he focused on not sending it into a spin. He checked his rearview mirror and relaxed when he saw the cars behind them slow down and switch lanes to avoid smashing into the trunk.

With other cars whizzing by them, some slowing down when they saw what had happened, Corlett wasted no time getting out of his car and going over to the blue sedan. The driver behind the wheel was nearly unconscious from his impact with the airbag, but alive and well. Corlett attempted to open the door, but finding it locked, he took the gun from the back of his waistband and swung it by the barrel, smashing the butt against the glass multiple times.

Clearing away enough glass to reach in, Corlett put his gun away and unlocked and opened the door, taking zip ties from his pockets and putting each of the man's wrists against the steering wheel, tightly securing them in place. He pulled the emergency brake as a small, quick backup to keep the car from moving, and then found and pressed the button for the trunk release, going around to the back and opening it.

Until he laid eyes on Rebecca, there was an niggle of doubt in the back of Corlett's mind about his target, that somehow he could have messed up. That this was just some poor guy on his way home from work, heading to pick up dinner for his wife and kids. But no, throwing the trunk open, the tightness in his chest loosened when he saw the semi-conscious, restrained young woman from the photo.

Corlett checked her pulse, which was sluggish but thankfully there, before he took his folding knife from his pocket and leaned down, cutting her restraints and taking the tape from her mouth. He carefully picked her up under her arms and legs, seeing that the traffic had slowed to a crawl as the rubberneckers stared and the good Samaritans started to come out of the woodwork.

"Oh my god!" cried a man that had gotten out of his car and rushed over. "She was in the trunk?"

"She's been drugged," Corlett told him. He shifted Rebecca in his arms as she started to stir. "I'm going try to get her conscious. Everyone's calling 911 and I've got the situation under control, so the best thing you can do is keep traffic moving so the ambulance and police can get here."

The man nodded jerkily, turning to head back to his car. "Okay."

Corlett carefully walked across the freeway to the edge of the shoulder, carefully laying Rebecca down. She was conscious but definitely still dazed, still keeping her eyes closed against the sunlight, twitching and attempting to regain full control of her muscles. She looked agitated and desperate to get away, but she relaxed once he put her down again. He took his cell phone from his pocket, dialing Reese's number. "I got her. She's okay."

"Got it."

Corlett hung up the phone, putting it back in his pocket, moving into her line of vision and shielding her eyes from the sun. "Rebecca?" he spoke. "Can you hear me?" Rebecca attempted to open her eyes and took in a long breath. "Rebecca, you're safe," he told her. "Look at me, you're safe now," he said. "I'm a friend of Katherine's. You're okay."

Rebecca stared at him and she swallowed against her dry throat. "My body is tired," she muttered. "I got kidnapped and he injected me with something."

Corlett smiled tightly, dialing a number. "I know. But do you feel okay other than being tired?"

"Yeah," she said. "Yeah, I feel okay."

———⋆⊰⊱⋆———

Katherine blinked as her phone started ringing, reaching into her pocket and taking it out under the heavy glare of the man that was sitting in the room with her. She glanced at the caller ID. "It's my daughter," she told him before picking it up. "Hey."

"Hey," spoke Corlett. "I got her. She's unhurt."

"All right," Katherine murmured. Corlett hung up and she kept talking. "I've got a lot of work, so I might be home a bit late. You can order pizza. Use the cash in the cookie jar. That sound good...? Okay. Love you, sweetie," Katherine said with a smile before hanging up the phone, staring at it in her hands.

The man on the other side of the room pursed his lips and looked back to his magazine, apparently satisfied with Katherine's phone call. So he wasn't prepared for her to stand up and walk over to him, but he did tense and narrow his eyes at her. "Hey–"

Katherine smashed her fist into his nose and he cried out, raising his hands to cover his nose and shield himself. She grasped his hair, pulling his head up and slamming it into the table, causing him to let out a moan, and snapped her leg forward, kicking him harshly in his stomach and throwing him backwards and out of the chair, crumpling to the ground. He choked out a gasp and curl inward, taken off-guard by the ferocity and strength of Katherine's attack as she kicked him again and again in the stomach, aiming for the organs that were easy targets.

Taking in and letting out quick, angry breaths, Katherine frisked him, taking the cell phone and gun from his jacket. She then took the duct tape that was on the table the man had been sitting at, presumably to be used in case she had caused trouble, and bound his wrists and ankles. She didn't gag him, knowing that since his nose was broken that would suffocate him, but dragged him by his jacket to the nearby closet, shoving him inside.

The man stared up at her, shaking his head. "That girl is *dead*," he rasped.

Katherine slowly leaned down in front of him, prompting him to tilt his head back away from her. "That wasn't my daughter on the phone," she whispered at him, "you goddamn *moron*." His eyes widened. "You're lucky it's more paperwork for me if you're dead."

At that, she slammed the closet door shut, putting the chair from the living room in front of it horizontally, barely leaving space between it and the hallway wall, so it couldn't open. She grabbed the registration paperwork for her gun and bolted out the front door.

CHAPTER 40

"I GOT HER. SHE'S OKAY."

"Got it." Reese hung up his cell phone, keeping pace behind the car driving down the streets of the near-Stepford San Fernando Valley suburbs. He hadn't had a ton of experience with pùcas or vampires yet, but tailing someone was something he'd had extensive practice at.

It was about ten minutes later that the black Jeep he was following turned onto a side street and parked. Reese passed the house it had stopped at, parking in the empty driveway of its neighbor. Getting out of the car with his cell phone up to his ear and pretending to be completely engrossed in the phone call, Reese fully ignored the two men that were getting out of the Jeep. He went to the mailbox at the end of the driveway, removing the contents casually.

"No, I told her I'll up pick it up tomorrow," Reese said. He sighed, flipping the metal mailbox shut with a harsh clang and shifting on his feet. "I'm not signing those goddamn papers until I get a call from my lawyer."

Out of the corner of his eye, Reese saw the two men walk around the side of the house and toward the backyard. Reese immediately shoved the mail back in the box and put his phone back in his pocket, speed walking up to the front door and ringing the doorbell, taking out his badge and holding it up. After a few seconds, the peephole darkened briefly, and the door opened, revealing a middle-aged man.

"Can I–?"

Reese moved forward, motioning for the man to go backwards into his house. "Stay quiet," he said, closing the door behind him. "I'm FBI. There are two guys that are about to break into your house from the back. I'm pretty sure they're here to kill you. How many people are there here?"

He shrunk back, his mouth agape. "M-Uh, just, it's just me and my two daughters," he whispered. "They're upstairs in their room."

"Go upstairs, get them into the bathroom into the tub, lock the door, and call 911," Reese told him, drawing his weapon. The man hesitated, frozen, and Reese glared at him, motioning with his gun. "Go!" he hissed.

The man spun around and bolted up the stairs, stumbling as he went. Reese knew that a targeted murder like this didn't just happen randomly, and rarely without the victim knowing why, or at least being able to guess at a motive. And it was likely that motive had immediately come to the front of the man's mind. A good thing, since it gave him a good reason to promptly put his trust in Reese, to stay out of the way, and to keep quiet without the need for an extensive, convincing explanation. Which they did not have time for.

Reese crept down the hallway, aiming his gun at the other end, his ears pricked to hear the slightest sound. After a few moments, he heard the back door open and he slid to the side, into a small alcove that led to a bathroom, waiting, knowing that once the men cleared the area that they would pass him to go upstairs. Footsteps creaked on the floor softly as the men slowly proceeded down the hallway, and as soon as the first man came into view, Reese fired off a shot at him and slid out from his hiding spot.

The bullet exploded through the first man's skull and he crumpled to the ground, and the second man, taken aback and acting on instinct, aimed and fired at Reese. But Reese was already moving and the man missed, twitching as Reese hit him three times in the chest, and his gun dropped from his hand as he collapsed to the ground.

Reese immediately kicked the both guns down the hall, swallowing hard, taking in and letting out a few breaths. The man he'd shot in the chest would be a goner within a minute, but he was still conscious, his eyelids fluttering as he went into shock and slowly lost consciousness. Reese shakily holstered his gun and went over to the two weapons the men had brought with them, kneeling down to get a good look to confirm one was Katherine's, before taking out his cell phone and dialing his boss's number.

"It's Reese," he spoke tightly. "I just killed two intruders at a civilian's house. Sapien."

"The hell's going on?" Jackson exclaimed.

Calabrease sat on his sofa, going through paperwork on the coffee table in front of him for one of his legitimate businesses. He didn't hear Katherine enter through the window, having gone up to the roof of his building and climbed down to his penthouse apartment balcony. He didn't hear her come up behind him, her gun in her hand. But then she spoke, prompting Calabrease to startle and jump to his feet, spinning around toward her voice.

"I warned you not to come after me and mine," Katherine murmured. She slowly walked around to the other side of the coffee table.

As Calabrease saw her and realized who she was, he stared at her in wide-eyed shock, speechless for a few moments. "You–?"

"She's at FBI headquarters, safe and sound," she said. Katherine shook her head slowly. "You should've left me alone."

Calabrease's eyes darted to right left before looking back to her firearm. "I could have my men in here in five seconds," he whispered.

"You don't want that," she replied. She reached into the small backpack slung over her shoulder with her free hand and took out a thick folder, dropping it on the coffee table in front of him. "This is a private conversation."

Eyeing her uneasily, Calabrease slowly sat down and opened the folder, flipping through the contents. His expression went slack and he started going through the documents and photos more quickly, hastily, before he suddenly stopped, looking up to her. "Where the hell did you get all this?" he breathed.

"Friends," Katherine murmured. "I have lots of them. I remember making that very clear to you."

"This is useless to the feds," he barked. "You didn't have a warrant."

"If they got it from me," she told him. "But I wouldn't give it to them. Some anonymous whistleblower would.

Hackers these days are such do-gooders." Calabrease swallowed hard, gnashing his teeth.

"I doubt the men you hired for this will flip, so you're off the hook. As much as I want to strangle you with my bare hands," she whispered. "But this is over. If any of your men ever see me or Rebecca or my daughter, they will turn around and head in the other direction. If we cross paths, which I'm quite sure we will again considering I scrape scum like you off the streets on a daily basis, you will back down. I don't care how much money you lose or how much your reputation is at stake or how much you have to make me out to be the friggin' *anti-Christ* to make your men understand who I am," she growled. "And if you ever forget, I will be more than glad to remind you of exactly what I'm capable of. Because I'd much rather handle the devil I know running the businesses you control, but if you become more trouble than you're worth, I will *burn your world to the ground*. I will destroy...every single part of your pitiful existence and make you wish I'd put a bullet in your head. Understand?" she whispered.

Calabrease swallowed, his hands curled into fists, sweat starting to bead on his head. There was a long, heavy moment where he just stared at her. Then, breathing deeply, he nodded stiffly. "Understood," he muttered.

"Good." Katherine casually tucked the gun back in her holster, heading over to his liquor cart. She looked over the selection, leaning on the cart and grasping the sides tightly, before she forced herself to take in and let out a deep breath. She then picked a bottle of whiskey from the cart, pouring a couple of fingers worth into a glass, downing it in one gulp and winced, letting out a breath. "Wow. That is good stuff," she muttered. "Really needed that. I had a shit storm of a day." She put the glass down and motioned to the papers on the table in front of Calabrease, who currently had a death-glare locked on her. "You can keep those. There are plenty of copies. But you should probably show me out. If your security plugs me with holes, this whole conversation will have been a real waste."

CHAPTER 41

THE FRONT DOOR BEEPED JUST once at Alexandra's entrance and Katherine glanced in the direction of the front door from her seat at the kitchen table in front of her laptop. The beep signified to those entering that the front door had opened but the alarm was not armed, which meant Katherine was home. The rule of thumb was that if Katherine wasn't there, or if she was there but sleeping, that the alarm was turned on. Even if the power went out in the whole building, the alarm company would be alerted, but that meant nothing to an abduction that took less than three minutes. Katherine was going to place a call to a private security company first thing in the morning to figure out how to fill that hole.

Alexandra left her backpack in the hall and walked into the kitchen, her gaze concerned, and Katherine knew she felt that something was wrong. Rebecca was in her room as usual, but her mind was locked down like a vault, which was unusual. "Hey," Alexandra whispered. She hesitated. "What happened?"

"Hey honey," Katherine replied quietly. "Ah...Rebecca was kidnapped." Alexandra blinked and her mouth opened, but nothing came out. "Calabrease. He's no longer a problem."

Alexandra fell into a kitchen chair, staring at her mother, who was in turn staring at her paperwork, a pen in her hand. "Was she hurt?"

Katherine shook her head. "No. Just drugged."

"...Are you okay?"

That brought Katherine's gaze up to her daughter's. "What?"

Alexandra swallowed, clasping her hands in her lap. "You kinda do this thing where you worry about other people so much that I worry about you...worrying."

The simple statement prompted Katherine to find herself suddenly holding back tears. And speechless. "Ah...." Katherine pursed her lips and nodded. "I do worry."

"You do," Alexandra stated.

Katherine considered the fact that she and her daughter had only passed in the kitchen in the early morning a couple times since their argument. That was the thing about being an FBI agent; the busy work schedule made relationships tough. And it was worst on the most important ones. Katherine easily saw Sweeney twice as much as her own husband during those seven years they were married. If they didn't count the time she and David were sleeping in the same bed, David had once jokingly pointed out.

It had always been that way though, and it felt easier to manage the longer they'd done it. Or at least it was easier to be conscious of how much time they might miss and to focus on the important things. But then there were the times now where suddenly it had been days and Katherine hadn't spoken with her daughter. *Really* spoken with her.

"You think we need to also start saying goodbye to Rebecca with, 'Stay safe'?" Alexandra asked.

Katherine's eyebrows went up and she suddenly let out a small bark of laughter that threatened to allow the dam to break and let her start crying. "We can, ah…we'll try that. Can't hurt."

Alexandra smiled. "Are we good?"

"Of course," Katherine murmured with a smile. "We'll always be good, honey."

Alexandra fell silent for a moment. "Rebecca okay to talk?" she finally asked.

Katherine nodded. "Door's open."

Alexandra blinked in surprise at that and she went down the hall to Rebecca's room, peeking in. Rebecca was in bed, on her laptop, snapping her fingers rhythmically as she watched a television show.

"Hey. You okay?" Alexandra asked, walking over and sitting on her bed. "Mom told me what happened."

"I'm sore," Rebecca stated. "The man drove around with me in the trunk and I was unconscious mostly, but the momentum threw me around. It was uncomfortable."

Alexandra smiled. "Yeah, duly noted, trunk travel: uncomfortable." She hesitated. "I'm really glad you're safe," she said.

Rebecca nodded, her eyes narrowing. "Me too. I feel safe here. Your mom worries about me and she protects me. I know she feels guilty that I was taken. I told her not to. I know that monsters can't get me here, in the apartment. But sapiens can be monsters too. That's what that man was."

Swallowing hard, Alexandra slowly nodded again. "Yeah. Yeah, they can," she muttered.

Katherine appeared in the doorway and Alexandra looked over to her. "Hey, I'm going to be doing pizza tonight. Not really in the mood to cook. That sound good?"

"When isn't pizza good by me?" Alexandra asked, cocking an eyebrow.

Katherine smiled back at her daughter before turning her attention to her cell phone as it rang. She picked it up, ducking back into the hallway. "Colebrook."

"Hey, it's me," spoke Jackson. "Crappy timing, I know, but I've got bad news. Tech has been chasing down the phone number you got from the phone of the vampire that tried to grab Rebecca, but it didn't turn up anything."

"What do you mean?" she asked. "Was it a burner?"

"That'd have been my first guess, but no. FBI had tech chase down the number's source, and it was bounced all over," he told her. "This wasn't some punk vampire who wanted a patsy if the police came looking. This was someone who knew how to stay hidden."

Katherine worked her jaw. "Shit."

"Yeah, shit is right. Hopefully they were after Rebecca because she was psychic and she posed an easy target, which means they won't try again. But if they were after her in particular, I'm glad she's with you now."

Katherine stared at the ground. "Not as if she's in Fort Knox," she muttered.

Jackson paused heavily for a moment. "It's about as close as she can get, considering the circumstances. I know what you went through today getting her back, but you probably already know everything I'd say right now if you had the patience to listen to me, right?"

Katherine smirked. "Yeah, ah...Alex actually beat you to it."

"Huh. I like that kid more and more every day." Katherine's smile widened. "You stay safe, all right?" Jackson asked.

That prompted her smile to fade, the opposite of its usual reaction. Looking down the hall in the direction of Rebecca's room, Katherine felt something heavy in her chest and she slowly nodded. "Always."

———— ⬩✦⬩ ————

Alexandra blinked a few times as she woke up, looking around her dark room, an uncomfortable anxiousness weighing on her chest. Her eyes then widened in surprise as she pinpointed the cause of the feeling and turned on her lamp, quickly going over to Rebecca's room.

"Rebecca," she said, turning on the lamp on the bedside table. Rebecca grimaced at the sudden brightness. "Rebecca?" Alexandra asked loudly.

Rebecca jerked awake, blinking rapidly as her eyes flicked over Alexandra and she sat up abruptly, moving backwards until she hit her headboard. She let out a long yell, putting her fists against the front of her face in a shield against the world.

"It's okay," Alexandra told her. "You're safe."

Rebecca nodded jerkily. "I had a nightmare," she said, rocking back and forth.

"I know," Alexandra murmured, nodding. She sat down on Rebecca's bed, clasping her hands tightly. "You were dreaming about being kidnapped?"

"No," Rebecca said quietly.

Alexandra's eyes narrowed. "What were you dreaming about?" she asked. Rebecca continued to rock in place, not saying another word. Alexandra let out a breath. "I can... stay here until you fall back to sleep, if you want," she said.

Rebecca still didn't reply. She continued to rock back and forth for about a minute, humming a tune that Alexandra didn't recognize. Eventually she slowed to a stop and wordlessly lay down and slid back under her covers, trying to relax as she put her head on her pillow and closed her eyes. And Alexandra turned off the lamp, staring at the back of Rebecca's head until she fell asleep.

———◦✕◦———

Katherine kept her feelers out toward Alexandra as she headed back to her room.

Even though Rebecca was home now, she was safe, Katherine knew the harsh, cold reality in her gut, the haunting thought that plagued her constantly; she couldn't protect the ones she loved. Not to the degree that she ached to do so. Even if she moved to the Yukon, never leaving the house and forcing Alexandra and Rebecca to do the same, even if she took all the precautions in the world against the dangers she faced every day, she couldn't protect them from everything.

And even worse, until Rebecca told her about her past, about the things that still haunted her and from which Ronald had protected her, Katherine couldn't keep her safe from them either.

Katherine flicked on the lamp on her bedside table, sliding out of bed and going into the kitchen. Taking a beer from the fridge, she put a handful of the long t-shirt she was wearing over the top and twisted. Tossing the cap onto the counter, she took a long drink from it before leaning against the counter, letting out a long, tired breath.

"I doubt him telling me would've changed anything," Katherine said, *taking a beer from the fridge, "but he should have told me anyway. I'm the psychic, I know, but I can't know everything. And information is power. I can't be powerless, especially on the job."*

"You're acting like he left out a crucial piece of information that got somebody killed," David told her. *"It's an overreaction, and that's why Sweeney's angry."*

"It was not an overreaction," she responded, *opening her beer.*

"Kathy, he can't always know what's going to be valuable and what's not, and there's only a certain amount of information a person can convey before it becomes absurd," he said as she *took a drink from the bottle.*

Katherine glared at him. *"Don't patronize me——."*

"I'm not patronizing you——."

"You don't know what information can mean," she snapped at David. *"And I need to be able to count on my partner to give me what I need to do my job, and keep people safe. That girl could've died. I mean, what if it had been Alex?"* Katherine suddenly realized her eyes were tearing and she swallowed hard, putting the beer on the counter. *"Son of a bitch."*

"Kathy," David murmured. He moved closer to her and put his hands on her shoulders as she blinked back the tears. *"You cannot safety-proof the world——."*

"I am not trying to——."

"Hey," he interrupted, *squeezing her shoulders gently. "Let me talk."* Katherine pursed her lips, but remained silent. *"You*

cannot safety proof the world, although you do a pretty damn good job of trying," he told her, "and you cannot revolve the world around the possibility of something bad happening." The words 'of course I can' jumped to Katherine's lips, but she held them back. "You averted a crisis today. But bad things are going to happen and if you try to stop all of them or blame yourself when you can't, you're going to drive yourself crazy."

David let his hands drop from her shoulders as Katherine dragged her fingers through her hair again. "I hate it when I can't see an enemy coming, David," she whispered, sliding her eyes up to his. "It scares me so much. And being reminded that there are some things that I'm just never going to be able to see coming…it really rattles me."

David wordlessly took Katherine into his arms, letting her rest her head on his shoulder.

After staring at the beer in her hand for a long moment, Katherine took another long swig of it as she headed back to bed.

CHAPTER 42

ᴺELSON EDDINGER LOOSENED HIS TIE as he walked over to his wine cart. He poured himself a glass of scotch, taking a long drink.

"Long day?"

Nelson turned to see his wife Claire walk into the sitting room. Her long brown hair was damp and she was in a bathrobe, looking drowsy and ready for bed. He let out a small laugh. "Just a bit. Something big didn't go my way at work recently. Just sorting out the details now."

"Oh, I'm sorry," Claire murmured. She wandered over to him and he put his arms around her, careful not to spill his drink, as she slid her hand into his graying black hair. "Coming to bed soon?"

"In a minute. Allen already asleep?" he asked.

Claire averted her gaze with a grin before looking back to her husband. "Allen is still out with friends."

Nelson's eyes widened and he glanced at the grandfather clock against the wall. "It's almost 11:30!"

"His new curfew is midnight; you know that," Claire told him. She drew back. "He'll be home soon. Come to bed."

"Just have to make a call," Nelson said with a sigh.

"At this hour?"

He shrugged. "No rest for the wicked."

Claire gave him a wry smile and headed out into the hallway.

Nelson stared after his wife for a moment before finishing his drink and taking out his phone. He dialed the number listed under *Fluorine* and it rang twice before it was answered. "What's the verdict?"

"The agent adopted her."

Nelson blinked. "She what?"

"I'm not joking. I think we need to call this one a bust. The FBI is knee-deep in it."

Nelson let out a low growl of annoyance. "Unbelievable. Rebecca would've been perfect. No strings once the brother was gone. Brilliant young woman...."

"No argument here. There's something else, though," the man spoke. "I got the agent's name, and I recognized it. We ran across her before, almost ten years ago, just when the program was starting."

"Ran across her how?"

"It's Katherine Colebrook."

Nelson's eyes widened. He slowly sunk into in the loveseat beside him. "Colebrook? How did she even get involved?"

"She and her daughter are actually based in LA now, but she's got this asset in San Diego that works at a mental ward. Picked out the teenager as a psychic and gave Colebrook a call."

Letting out a breath, Nelson nodded. "All right. Well... just bad luck, I guess. Keep the file going on Colebrook.

The last thing we need is a psychic agent catching a whiff of Health Enterprise, so make sure she doesn't have any connections to potential candidates. Or if she does, make sure it's a completely clean break."

"No problem. Speaking of, I might have another candidate for us already."

"That would make me extremely happy," Nelson said. "Keep me posted."

ABOUT THE AUTHOR

 Karen Avizur was born in Montreal, and grew up in Long Island, New York, with stops in Connecticut and West Virginia along the way.

After graduating film school, Karen moved to Los Angeles, where she worked as a film editor for several years while also pursuing her writing. "I was taught that a film editor is really the final-draft screenwriter. It's true," she notes. "I'd written much of *Trackers* as separate short stories over the years, but being an editor helped me see how to weave those stories together into novel form."

Karen now lives in Florida with Ginger (her dog), and still keeps a hand in editing for special clients. "These two creative paths continue to reinforce one another," she says. "I hope that readers will find the *Trackers* novels to have the pace, style, and visual storytelling excitement of a good movie thriller."

Made in the USA
Las Vegas, NV
31 March 2021

20527960R00163